Sabine Baring-Gould

In exitu Israel

Vol. I

Sabine Baring-Gould

In exitu Israel
Vol. I

ISBN/EAN: 9783744641333

Printed in Europe, USA, Canada, Australia, Japan

Cover: Foto ©Andreas Hilbeck / pixelio.de

More available books at **www.hansebooks.com**

IN EXITU ISRAEL

AN HISTORICAL NOVEL

BY

S. BARING-GOULD, M.A.

Author of 'Curious Myths of the Middle Ages,'
'Origin and Development of Religious Belief,' 'The Silver Store,' &c., &c.

VOL. I

London

MACMILLAN AND CO.

1870

DEDICATED

TO

THE MEMORY OF THE LATE

COUNT CHARLES DE MONTALEMBERT

BY

ONE WHO, FROM A DISTANCE, HAS LOVED AND ADMIRED HIS LIFE,
HIS PRINCIPLES, AND HIS WRITINGS.

PREFACE.

THERE is a side to the History of the French Revolution which is too generally overlooked—its ecclesiastical side.

Under the *ancien régime*, the disadvantages of an Establishment produced a strong party of liberal Catholics prepared for a radical change in the relations between Church and State.

It was this party which organised that remarkable Constitutional Church, at once Republican and Catholic, which sustained Religion through the Reign of Terror, and which Pope Pius VII and Napoleon I combined to overthrow.

My object in writing this story is to illustrate the currents of feeling in the State and Church of France in 1789, currents not altogether unlike those now circulating in our own. It was my good fortune, during a recent visit to Normandy, to collect materials for a history of a representative character of that eventful period,—one Thomas Lindet, parish priest of Bernay. In writing his story, I do not present him to the reader as a model. He had great faults; but one can forgive much on account of his enthusiastic love of justice, and faith in his cause.

That my story may be taken to convey a moral, is possible. But let me disclaim any intention of preaching a lesson to the aristocracy; I believe that they do not need it. In France, the crown supported the nobility; in England, the nobility support the crown. The French aristocracy was a privileged class, exempt from the burden of taxation. In England, the heaviest burden falls on the holders of landed property. With us, the privileged class is that of the manufacturer and trader. The French nobility never made common cause with the people against the encroachments of the royal prerogative. The English barons wrung Magna Charta from reluctant John. Henry VIII would never have been able to consolidate the power in his despotic hands, had not the civil wars of the Roses broken the strength of the aristocracy.

Since then the nobility have made the cause of right and liberty their own, and a limited monarchy is the result.

The moral, if moral there must be, is this: In times when the relations between Church and State are precarious, coercive measures are certain to force on a rupture.

Of late, repression has been employed freely on a portion of the community, and this has suddenly created a liberation party which three years ago scarcely existed within the Church and the ranks of the clergy.

The English curate is as much at the mercy of the bishop as was, and is still, the French curé; and this he has been made painfully aware of.

In the Wesleyan revival, a body of earnest men who moved for a relaxation of the icy bonds of Establishmentarianism were thrust forth into schism. The first Tractarians were driven to Rome by the hardness of their spiritual rulers. At present, a party, peculiarly narrow, and rapidly dying, by means of a packed Privy Council, are engaged in hunting out and repressing the most active section of the Church.

Worship is the language of conviction. To a large and rapidly increasing body of Anglicans, Christ is not, as He is to Protestants, a mere historical personage, the founder of Christianity, but is the centre of a religious system, the ever-present object of adoration for His people. A passionate love of Christ has floreated into splendour of worship. To curtail liberty of worship is to touch the rights of conscience; and to interfere with them has ever led to disastrous consequences—such is the verdict of History.

A feverish eagerness to dissever Church and State has broken out among clergy and laity, and a schism would be the result, were the chain uniting Church and State indissoluble; but, as events of late years have made it clear, that with a little concerted energy the old rust-eaten links can be snapped, there will be no schism, but an united effort will be made by a body of resolute spirits within the Church to tear asunder crown and mitre. The disestablishment of the English Church will present a feature absent from that of the Irish Church. In the latter case, there was an unanimous opposition to the measure by all

within it; but, in the event of the severance of
the union in England, it will take place amid
the joyous acclamations of no inconsiderable
section of its best and truest sons.

If, from the following pages, it appears that
my sympathies are with the National Assembly,
and those who upset the *ancien régime*, it does
not follow that they are with the Revolution in
its excesses. The true principles of the Revolution are embodied in the famous Declaration
of the Rights of Man. 'Write at the head of
that Declaration the name of God,' said Grégoire;
'or you establish rights without duties, which is
but another thing for proclaiming Force to be
supreme.' The Assembly refused. Grégoire
was right.

Robespierre, Danton, and his clique made force
supreme—as supreme as in the days of the
Monarchy, and trampled on the rights, to protect
which they had been raised into power.

A Republic is one thing: the despotism of
an Autocracy or of a Democracy is another
thing.

I propose following up this historical romance
by a life of the Abbé Grégoire, which will illus-

trate the position of the Constitutional Church, of which he was the soul.

I have chosen the form of fiction for this sketch, as it best enables me to exhibit the state of feeling in France in 1788, 1789. That is no fiction ; the incidents related and the characters introduced are, for the most part, true to History.

S. B-G.

DALTON, THIRSK,
March 25th, 1870.

IN EXITU ISRAEL.

CHAPTER I.

The forests that at the present day cover such a considerable portion of the department of Eure, and which supply the great manufacturing cities on the Seine with fuel, were of much greater extent in the eighteenth century. The fragments of forest which now extend from Montfort to Breteuil were then united, and stretched in one almost unbroken green zone from the Seine to the Arve, following the course of the little river Rille. A spur struck off at Serquigny, and traced the confluent Charentonne upwards as far as Broglie.

The little town of Bernay is no longer hemmed in by woods. The heights and the valley of the Charentonne are still well timbered, and green with copse and grove; the landscape is park-like; here and there a fine old oak with rugged bark and expanded arms proclaims itself a relic of the *ancien régime;* but the upstart poplars whitening in the wind along the river course spire above these venerable trees. The roads lie between wheat and potato fields, and the names of hamlets, such

as Bosc, Le Taillis, Le Buisson, Bocage, La Couture, &c., alone
proclaim that once they lay embedded in forest foliage.

On the eve of the Great French Revolution, Bernay was a
manufacturing town, that had gradually sprung up during the
middle ages, around the walls of the great Benedictine Abbey
which the Duchess Judith of Brittany had founded in 1013,
and endowed with nearly all the surrounding forest. The town
was unhealthy. It lay in a hollow, and the monks had
dammed up the little stream Cogney, which there met the
Charentonne, to turn their mill-wheel, and had converted a
portion of the valley into a marsh, in which the frogs croaked
loudly and incessantly.

When the abbot was resident, the townsfolk were required to
beat the rushes and silence the noisy reptiles every summer
night; but now that the Superior resided at Dax, this require-
ment was not pressed.

After a heavy downfall of rain, the rivulet was wont to swell
into a torrent, overflow the dam, and flood the streets of
Bernay, carrying with it such an amount of peat that every
house into which the water penetrated was left, after its retreat,
plastered with black soil, and, in spring, smeared with frog-
spawn.

The mill was privileged. No other was permitted in the
neighbourhood. When M. Chauvin erected a windmill on the
hill of Bouffey, the monks brought an action against him, and

made him dismantle it. All the corn that grew within five miles was ground at the Abbey mill, and every tenth bag was taken by the Fathers in payment for grinding the corn indifferently and at their leisure. At certain seasons, more wheat was brought to the mill than the mill could grind, because the water had run short, or the stones were out of repair, consequently many thousands of hungry people had to wait in patience till the Cogney filled, or till the mill-stones had been re-picked, whilst the gutted windmill of M. Chauvin stood in compulsory inaction.

The great and little tithes of Bernay went to the Abbey; and out of them the monks defrayed the expense of a curate for the parish church of S. Cross. This church had been built by the town in 1372, by permission of the Abbey, on condition that the parish should bear the charge of its erection, and the abbot should appoint the curate; that the parish should be responsible for the repair of the fabric and the conduct of divine service, and that the Abbey should pay to the incumbent the *portion congrue* of the tithes. The incumbent of Bernay was, throughout the middle ages and down to the suppression of the monastery, a salaried curate only, without independent position, and receiving from the Abbey a sum which amounts in modern English money to about fifty pounds, and out of this he was required to pay at least two curates or *vicaires.* This sorry pittance would have been miserable enough, had the curé been provided with a parsonage-house rent free; but with this the Abbey did not furnish him, and he was obliged to lodge where he could, and live as best he could on the crumbs that fell from the abbot's table.

The parishioners of Bernay had made several attempts to free their church from its dependence, but in vain. The monks refused to cede their rights, and every lawsuit in which the town engaged with them terminated disastrously for the citizens. The people of Bernay were severely taxed. Beside the intolerable burdens imposed on them by the State, they paid tithes on all they possessed to the monks, who assessed them as they thought proper, and against whose assessment there was no appeal, as the abbot of Bernay exercised legal jurisdiction in the place, and every question affecting ecclesiastical dues was heard in his own court. The corn was tithed in the field, and tithed again at the mill. The Abbey had rights of *corvée*, that is, of claiming so many days' work from every man in the place, and on its farms, free of expense. The townsfolk, who were above the rank of day labourers, escaped the humiliation only by paying men out of their own pockets, to take their places and work for the Fathers.

It was hard for the citizens, after having been thus taxed by the Church, to have to expend additional money to provide themselves with religious privileges. Bernay might have been a far more prosperous town but for the Abbey, which, like a huge tumour, ate up the strength and resources of the place, and gave nothing in return.

The Abbey was also *en commende;* in other words, it was a donative of the Crown. Whom he would, the king made superior of the monks of S. Benedict at Bernay,—superior only in name, and for the purpose of drawing its revenues, for he was not a monk, nor indeed was he in other than minor orders. Louis XV, whose eye for beauty was satisfied with a Du Barry, having been fascinated by the plump charms of Madame Poudens, wife of a rich jeweller at Versailles, attempted to seduce her. The lady estimated her virtue at a rich abbey, and finally parted with it for that of Bernay, which was made over *in commendam* to a son, whether by Poudens or Louis was not clearly known, but who, at the age of seven, in defiance of the concordat of Francis I with the Pope, was made abbé of Bernay, father superior of Benedictine monks, and entitled to draw an income of fifty-seven thousand livres per annum, left by Duchess Judith to God and the poor. The case was by no means uncommon, Charles of Valois, bastard of Charles IX and Marie Fouchet, at the age of thirteen was invested with the revenues of Chaise-Dieu, and Henry IV bartered an abbey for a mistress.

Thomas Lindet was cur é of S. Cross.

The introduction of the power-loom from England had

produced much want and discontent in Normandy, and in Bernay many hands were thrown out of work. The sickness and famine which had periodically afflicted that town of late years became permanent, and the poor priest was condemned to minister in the presence of want and disease, without the power of alleviating either, whilst the revenues of the Church were drained to fill the purse of the non-resident abbé, and by him to be squandered on luxuries and vanities.

Lindet had more than once expressed his opinion upon the abuses regnant in the Church. In 1781, in a discourse addressed by him to the general assembly of his parish, he had said :—' We desire that justice should be brought to bear upon these abuses, which outrage common sense and common right, at once. But is there any hope in the future of an accomplishment of our desires ? At present, all is dark; but never let us despair. We groan under oppression. But be sure of this,—wrong-doing revenges itself in the long run. We wish to abolish the intolerable privileges which burden some, that others may trip lightly through life. Alas ! the privileged classes are jealous of our jealousy of them. They scarce permit us to pray the advent of a rectification of abuses, which will prove as glorious to religion as it will prove beneficial to society. Who will put salt upon the leeches, and make them disgorge the blood of the poor ? '

For having used this language the curé had been severely

reprimanded by his bishop; for bishops were then, as they are frequently now, the champions of abuses.

At the present date, Lindet was again in trouble with his diocesan. For three days in succession the sanctuary lamp in his church had remained unlighted. The reason was, that the curé's cruse of oil was empty; and not the cruse only, but his purse as well. He had neither oil by him, nor money wherewith to buy any; the lamp therefore remained dark. Lindet hoped that some of his parishioners would come forward, and furnish the sacramental light with a supply of oil, and this eventually took place; but, in the meantime, three days and nights of violation of the rubric had elapsed. The *officiel* or inquisitor of the bishop heard of this, and called on Thomas Lindet, the day before the opening of this tale, to inform him that it was at his option to pay down twenty-five livres for the misdemeanour, or to be thrown into the ecclesiastical court.

Under the *ancien régime*, a large portion of a bishop's revenues was derived from ecclesiastical fines imposed by his court, and into this court cases of immorality, heresy and sacrilege among the laity, and of infringement of rubrical exactness, and breach of discipline among the clergy, were brought. As the prosecutor was also virtually the judge, it may be supposed that judgment was usually given against the defendant, who might appeal to the archbishop, or from

him to the pope,—all interested judges, but who was debarred
from carrying his wrong before a secular tribunal.

The sun was declining behind the pines, and was painting
with saffron the boles of the trees, and striping with orange
and purple the forest paths, as Thomas Lindet prepared to
part from his friend Jean Lebertre, curé of the pilgrimage
shrine of Notre Dame de la Couture, at the brow of the hill
where the path to the Couture forked off from the main road
to Bernay. At this point the trees fell away towards the valley,
and the shrine was visible, lit in the last lights of evening which
turned the grey stone walls into walls of gold.

La Couture is a singularly picturesque church, with lofty
choir rising high above the nave roof, and with numerous
chapels clustered about the chancel apse. The spire of lead
with pinnacled turrets, in that setting glare, seemed a pyramid
of flames.

The priest of Bernay was a tall thin man of forty-five, with
colourless face, sunken cheeks, and restless, very brilliant eyes.
His face, though far from handsome, was interesting and
attractive. It beamed with intelligence and earnestness. His
long hair, flowing to his shoulders, was grizzled with care
rather than with age,—the care inseparable from poverty,
and that arising from the responsibilities attending on the
charge of a number of souls. His brow was slightly retreating
and wanted breadth, his cheek-bones were high. The nose

and mouth were well moulded, the latter was peculiarly delicate and flexible. The thin lips were full of expression, and trembled with every emotion of the heart.

Lindet's hands were also singularly beautiful—they were narrow and small; a lady would have envied the taper fingers and well-shaped nails. Malicious people declared that the priest was conscious of the perfection of his hands, and that he took pains to exhibit it; but this was most untrue. No man was more free from vanity, and had a greater contempt for it, than Thomas Lindet. He had contracted a habit of using his right hand whilst speaking, in giving force to his words by gesture, and whilst thinking, in plucking at the cassock-buttons on his breast, but this trick was symptomatic of a highly-strung nervous temperament, and was in no degree attributable to personal vanity.

Lebertre was somewhat of a contrast to Lindet. He was a middle-sized, well-built man, with a face of an olive hue, hazel eyes, large, as earnest as those of his friend, but not like them in their restlessness; they were deep, calm wells, which seemed incapable of being ruffled by anger, or clouded with envy. His black hair was flowing and glossy, without a speck in it of grey. 'I would not do so,' said he, holding Lindet's arm; 'you should bear meekly, and suffer patiently.'

'Bear and suffer!' repeated the curé of S. Cross, his eyes lightening and his lips quivering; 'True. "Suffering is the badge of all our tribe." What the English poet puts into the mouth of a Jew is a motto meet for a French curé. But, my brother, tell me—are not wrongs and sufferings crushing us, destroying our self-reliance, ruining our independence, and obliterating our self-respect? How can a priest be respected by his flock when he does not respect himself; and how can he respect himself when he is trodden like dirt under the feet of his spiritual superiors?'

'Bearing wrongs and suffering injustice without a murmur is the badge of a Christian; above all, of a priest. He who suffers and endures uncomplainingly is certain to obtain respect and reverence.'

'A pretty world this has become,' exclaimed Lindet; 'the poor are ground to powder, and at each turn of the wheel we are bidden preach them Christian submission. They look around, and see everywhere labour taxed, and idleness go free. Toil then like a Christian, and pay, pay, pay, that the king may make fountains for his garden, the nobles may stake high at cards, and the bishops and canons may salary expensive cooks. Say the little farmer has a hundred francs. Out of this he is obliged to pay twenty-five for the taille, sixteen for the accessories, fifteen for his capitation, eleven for tithe. What remains to him for the support of his family, after he has paid his rent? Truly of this world may be said what is said of hell: "*Nullus ordo, sempiternus horror inhabitat.*"'

Lebertre did not answer. With the steadfastness of purpose that was his characteristic, he returned to his point, and refused to be led into digression by his vehement and volatile companion. 'You must not go to Evreux, as you propose,' he said.

'I shall go to the bishop,' returned Lindet; 'and I shall give him the money into his hand. I shall have the joy, the satisfaction, may be, of seeing, for once in my life, a bishop's cheek burn with shame.'

'Is this a Christian temper?'

'Is it the part of a Christian bishop to consume his clergy with exactions and with persecutions, and to torture them with insults? Our bishop neglects his diocese. He receives some four hundred and fifty thousand livres per annum, and can only visit Bernay, with five thousand souls in it, once in three years, to confirm the young and to meet the clergy. When he comes amongst us on these rare occasions he takes up his abode at the Abbey, and receives us, the priests who seek advice and assistance, at a formal interview of ten minutes, into which we must condense our complaints; and then we are dismissed without sympathy and without redress.'

Lindet took a few steps along the path to La Couture. 'I will accompany you, Jean,' he said; 'and I will tell you how I was treated when last I had access to Monseigneur. He sat at a little table; on it was a newspaper and a hand-bell, and his large gold watch. He signed to me to stand before him; I did so, holding my hands behind my back like a boy who is about to be scolded. He asked me some trifling question about my health, which I did not answer. I could not afford to waste one out of my ten minutes thus; so I broke out into an account of our troubles here. I told him there was no school for the children; that I had no parsonage house. God knows! I would teach the poor children myself if they could be crowded into my garret, but the good woman with whom I lodge will not permit it. I told him of the want and misery here, of the exactions under which the poor are bowed. I spoke to him of the hollow-eyed hungry work-men, and of the women hugging their starving babes to their empty breasts.' The priest stopped, gasping for an instant, his trembling white hand working in the air, and expressing his agitation with mute eloquence. 'All the while I talked, his eye was on the newspaper; I saw that he was reading, and was not attending to me. What he read was an account of a fête at Versailles, from which, alas! he was absent. Then he touched his bell. "Your time is up," he said; and I was bowed out.'

'You forget that the time of a prelate is precious.'

'I grant you that,' answered Lindet, with quivering voice; 'too precious to be spent amidst a crowd of lackeys in dancing attendance on royalty; too precious to be wasted on fêtes and dinners to all the lordlings that Monseigneur can gather about his table in the hopes that they may shed some lustre on his own new-fledged nobility.'

'I will not hear you, my friend,' said Lebertre, turning from him; 'you are too bitter, too vindictive. You would tear our bishops from their seats, and strip them of their purple.'

'Of their purple and fine linen and sumptuous faring every day, that Lazarus may be clothed and fed!' interrupted Lindet, passionately.

'You would abolish the episcopacy and convert the Church to presbyterianism,' said the curé of La Couture with a slight tone of sarcasm.

'Never,' answered the priest of S. Cross; his voice instantly becoming calm, and acquiring a depth and musical tone like that in which he was wont to chant. 'No, Lebertre, never. I would preserve the ancient constitution of the Church, but I would divest it of all its State-given position and pomp. I would have our bishops to be our pastors and overseers, and not our lords and tyrants. I reverence authority, but I abhor autocracy. David went forth in the might of God to fight the Philistine; Saul lent him his gilded armour, but the shepherd put it off him—he could not go in that cumbrous painted harness. With his shepherd's staff and sling he slew the giant. Woe be it! the Church has donned the golden armour wherewith royalty has invested her, and crushed beneath the weight, it lies prostrate at the feet of the enemy.'

Lindet walked on fast, weaving his fingers together and then shaking them apart.

'But let me continue what I had to tell you of the bishop's visit here,' he said. 'I was walking down the Rue des Jardins an hour after my reception, with my head sunk on my bosom, and—I am not ashamed to add—with my tears flowing. I wept, for I was humbled myself, and ashamed for the Church. Then suddenly I felt a sting across my shoulders, as I heard a shout. I started from my reverie to find myself almost under the feet of the horses of a magnificent carriage with postilions and outriders in livery, that dashed past in a cloud of dust. I stood aside and saw my bishop roll by in conversation with M. Berthier, laughing like a fool. My shoulders tingled for an hour with the lash of the post-boy's whip, but the wound cut that day into my heart is quivering and bleeding still.' As he spoke, he and his friend came suddenly upon a wayside crucifix which had been erected at the confines of the parish as a station for pilgrims, in a patch of clearing. The pines rose as a purple wall behind it, but the setting sun bathed the figure of the Saviour in light, and turned to scarlet the mat of crimson pinks which had rooted themselves in the pedestal.

Lebertre pressed the hand of his agitated companion, and

pointed up at the Christ, whilst an expression of faith and devotion brightened his own countenance. He designed to lead the thoughts of Lindet to the great Exemplar of patient suffering, but the curé of S. Cross mistook his meaning. He stood as one transfixed, before the tall gaunt crucifix, looking up at the illumined figure. Then, extending his arms, he cried, 'Oh Jesus Christ! truly Thou wast martyred by the bishops and aristocrats of Thy day; smitten, insulted, condemned to death by Annas and Caiaphas, the high priests, and by Pilate, the imperial governor. Verily, Thy body the Church bleeds at the present day, sentenced and tortured by their successors in Church and State.'

Before the words had escaped his lips, a cry, piercing and full of agony, thrilled through the forest.

Lindet and Lebertre held their breath. In another instant, from a footpath over which the bushes closed, burst a peasant girl, parting the branches, and darting to the crucifix, she flung herself before it, clasping her arms around the trunk, and in so doing overturning a flower-basket on her arm, and strewing the pedestal and kneeling-bench with bunches of roses.

She was followed closely by a large man, richly dressed, who sprang towards her, cast his arms round her waist, and attempted to drag her from her hold. 'Sacré! you sweet little wench. If persuasion and flattery fail, why, force must succeed.' And he wrenched one of her bare brown arms from the cross. She cast a despairing look upward at the thorn-crowned head which bowed over her and the seducer, and uttered another piteous wail for help.

At the same moment, the sun passed behind some bars of fog on the horizon, and the light it flung changed instantly from yellow to blood-red. The figure of the Christ was a miserable work of art, of the offensive style prevalent at the period, contorted with pain, the face drawn, and studded with huge clots of blood. In the scarlet light it shone down on those below as though it were carved out of flame, and menaced wrathfully.

The girl still clung to the cross with one arm. She was dressed in a short blue woollen skirt that left unimpeded her ankles and feet, a black bodice laced in front, exposing the coarse linen sleeves and shift gathered over the bosom about the throat. Her white frilled Normandy cap, with its broad flaps, was disturbed, and some locks of raven hair fell from beneath it over her slender polished neck. The oval sun-browned face was exquisitely beautiful. The large dark eyes were distended with terror, and the lips were parted.

'Mon Dieu! do you think that those frail arms can battle with mine?' asked the pursuer with mocking composure, as he drew the other arm from the stem of the cross, and holding both at the wrists, pressed them back at the girl's side so as to force her to face him.

'Look at me,' he said, in the same bantering tone; 'can your pestilent little village produce so wealthy and promising a lover as me? Your Jacques and Jeans have but a few liards in their purses, and can only offer you a pinchbeck ring; but I'—he disengaged one hand, whilst he felt in his pocket and produced a purse; 'whilst I—Ha! listen to the chink, chink, chink! You do not know the language of money, do you? Well, I will interpret; chink, chink—that means silk dresses, satin shoes, dainty meats, and sweet bonbons. Now then!' he exclaimed, as she made a struggle to escape.

'Now then,' repeated Thomas Lindet, who, quick as thought, strode between the man and his prey. He released the child; and placing her beside him, with a lip that curled with scorn, he removed his huge shovel hat, and bowing almost double, with a sweep of the hat, said, 'M. Berthier! the little one and I bid you good evening!'

Then he drew back, extending his arm and hat as an ægis over the girl.

The gentleman stood as if petrified, and looked at them. He was a tall man, largely made, very big-boned, with his hair powdered and fastened behind by a black silk bow. His face was closely shaven, the nose short, the upper lip very long and arched. But the most conspicuous feature of his face were his eyes, set in red and raw sockets. As he stood and looked at the priest, he mechanically drew a handkerchief from his pocket, and proceeded with a corner of it to wipe the tender lids.

His coat was of maroon velvet edged and frogged with gold braid, his waistcoat was of white satin, and his hat was three-cornered and covered with lace. He wore a rapier at his side; and he was evidently a man of distinction.

'Come, Lebertre, my friend,' said Lindet, cheerfully, without taking any more notice of the gentleman; 'I will accompany you and help to protect this damsel.' The girl had lost one of her sabots, but in the excess of her fear she walked along unconscious of her loss. The curé of La Couture strode on one side of her, and the priest of Bernay paced on the other, supporting her with their hands, for her limbs shook with agitation, and, if unassisted, she would have fallen.

'I know her,' said Lebertre to his friend, 'she is little Gabrielle André, and lives down by the river with her father, who is a farmer of the Abbey.'

Lindet looked across at his companion, with a glad light dancing in his eyes, and raising one hand heavenwards he exclaimed: 'Did I not say that the Church in all her members suffers and bleeds? Would, dear friend, that, as we have rescued this poor child out of the hands of a betrayer, we might also rescue the poor Church from her seducers!'

Lebertre did not answer; but after a while he said solemnly, and with an air of deep conviction: 'Lindet! did you mark how, at the cry of the child, the head of the Christ shook and frowned?'

CHAPTER II.

THE Charentonne in its meanderings forms a number of islets. The stream is in itself inconsiderable, but it spreads itself through its shallow valley like a tangled skein, and cuts up the meadows with threads of water easily crossed on plank-bridges.

Much of the land in the bottom is marsh, into which a rill dives and disappears, but other portions are firm alluvial soil, producing rich crops of grass, flax, and here and there patches of corn.

On one of these islands, if islands they may be called, above the hamlet of La Couture, stood a cottage, in style resembling those we meet with in the southern counties of England, constructed of black timber and white plaster, and thatched. To the south, at its back, lay a dense growth of willow and poplar, screening the house from the sun, and giving it in winter a moist and mouldy appearance, but in summer one cool and refreshing. A considerable flower-garden occupied the front of the cottage, filled with superb roses, white, yellow, and red. Tall white and scarlet lilies leaned against the house, whose thatch was golden with house-leek, so that in the flower season the Isle des Hirondelles attracted the admiration of all who passed along the road to Ferrières.

In this cottage lived Matthias André, father of Gabrielle, whom the two priests are conducting across the foot-bridge towards him.

He was cleaning out the cow-house as they approached, littering fresh straw in the stall from which he had forked the manure. He was a middle-sized man, clad in knee-breeches and blue worsted half-stockings that covered the calves, but were cut short at the ankles. His sabots, which shod his otherwise bare feet, were stained and clotted with soil. His coarse linen shirt was open at the throat, exposing his hairy breast, and the sleeves were rolled to the elbows, so as to give free play to his brown muscular arms. A large felt hat, out of which the sun had extracted the colour, lay on the bench before the door, and his head was covered with a blue knitted conical cap, the peak and tassel of which hung over his right ear.

Labour and exposure had bronzed and corrugated the features of Matthias, oppression and want had stamped on them an expression of sullen despair. His brow was invariably knit, and his eyes were permanently depressed. He muttered to himself as he worked: he never sang, for his heart was never light. How can the heart be light that is

weighed down, and galled with chains? The life of the
peasant before the French Revolution was the life of a slave;
he could not laugh, he could not even smile, for he had to
struggle for bare existence with exactions which strangled
him. He and his sons were like Laocoon and his children
in the coils of the serpent that was laced round their limbs,
that breathed poison into their lungs, and sucked the life-
blood from their hearts; and that serpent was the *Ancien
Régime.*

Louis VI had enfranchised the serfs on the royal domain,
and the nobles, after his example, gradually released theirs,
finding that the peasant, with liberty and hope, worked
better than the slave, and made the land more valuable. To
them they sold or rented some of their acres. In 1315
appeared the order of Louis X, requiring all the nobles to
emancipate their serfs, because 'every man should be born
free; therefore let the lords who have rights over the persons
of men, take example from us, and bring all to freedom.'

The nobles, determined by their interest, obeyed; but
down to 1789 serfs remained in France;—it was from the
hands of the Church that the Revolution liberated them. To
the last, the canons of the Cathedral of S. Claude, in
Franche-Comté, refused to emancipate their slaves from the
feudal right of *main morte*, which placed human beings, ran-
somed by the blood of Christ, on a level with the cattle.

In Jura there were as many as ten thousand; but in Normandy serfage had disappeared in the thirteenth century. The serf became a small farmer, and free;—but at what price? The land was his on condition of paying a rent. Charges also, *real*, that is, paid in money or in fruits, and *personal*, that is, acquitted by service rendered free of expense to the landlord, weighed on the agriculturist.

The imposts which oppressed him were these :—First, the *Taille* or tax. Of this there were two kinds, the *taux* and the *taillon.* From these taxes the nobles and the churchmen were exempt. Of nobles there were in France some 83,000, and of churchmen some 200,000. The capitation was an impost direct and personal, which touched all. Calculated upon the presumed value of land and property which was taxable, it was arbitrary, and those who had access to, and credit with, the officers of comptrol, were lightly rated, whilst those without interest were obliged to pay according to an exaggerated estimate. By a succession of injustices, also, the capitation of some was fixed, whilst that of others varied. The duty of tenth was levied nominally on all; but nobles and ecclesiastics were privileged, and paid nothing on their woods, meadows, vines, and ponds, nor on arable land belonging to the home farm.

The *Corvée*, also, weighed only on the peasant. The name, according to etymologists, indicates the posture of a man bowed at the hardest labour. He who was amenable to the *corvée* was required to work himself, and make his horses and oxen work, for his landlord and for government. By this means the roads and other public works were kept in repair.

Two grand sources of public revenue were the *Gabelle* and the *Excise.* The gabelle, or monopoly of salt, pressed upon the peasant in two ways. The father of the family, obliged to pay for salt which he needed a price fifty times its value, was also required, under pain of imprisonment, to purchase a certain amount, determined by the clerks, and fixed according to the presumed consumption of his family. If he failed to purchase the requisite amount, or if he was suspected of being in possession of contraband goods, at any time of the day his house might be invaded by the officers of the Excise, and its contents examined.

The feudal rights to grinding the corn, and pressing the grapes and apples, were also grievous restrictions on the liberty of the farmer and peasant. His landlord might imprison him for crushing the wheat he grew in a hand-quern, and for squeezing enough apples to fill a bottle with cider.

The *Champart* was another feudal right. The farmer was bound to yield to his lord not only a share of his harvest, but also he was not permitted to reap and garner his own corn till the portion due to the proprietor had been removed from his field. In addition to all these burdens came the *Tithe;* wheat, barley, rye, and oats were at first alone tithable. But the conversion of arable land into pasture and into fields of lucerne, sanfoin, and clover, to escape this tax, affected the income of the clergy, and they claimed the right of taking the tenth of cattle and of tithing wool. Nobles and roturiers resisted this claim, and numerous law-suits were the result,—suits rendered so expensive by the corruptions existing in courts of justice, that the vast majority of sufferers paid the tenth of their goods to the clergy rather than risk all to the lawyers.

Matthias André removed his blue cap to the curés as they approached. He bore them no grudge,—they were fellow-sufferers; but he was wont to grind his teeth as the nobleman or the provost drove by, and he would curse the monk who came to exact the convent dues.

'Good evening to you, neighbour André,' said Jean Lebertre; 'we have brought you your daughter. She is a little upset, frightened by the impertinence of a—well, of a gentleman.'

'Of a rascal,' interrupted Lindet.

'She shall tell you the story,' said the priest of La Couture, thrusting the girl forward; 'she can do so better than I; all I know of it is, that my friend here rescued her from a gentleman who was treating her with insolence.'

'How was it, child?' asked Matthias, casting his fork from him with such violence that it stuck into the soil and remained upright.

Gabrielle moved towards the seat.

'Yes, sit down,' said Lebertre; 'poor child, you are greatly overcome.'

Gabrielle sank upon the bench. She still trembled in all her limbs. Removing her white cap, which was disarranged, her beautiful dark hair fell in waves down her back and touched the seat she occupied. The fear which had distended her eyes had now deserted them, and the irises recovered their usual soft and dewy light. The peachy colour also returned to cheeks that had been blanched, but the delicate rosy lips still quivered with excitement. Clasping her hands on her lap, and shaking the locks from her temples, she looked up beseechingly at her father, and said, in gentle entreaty,—

'My father! Let me not go to the château again.'

'Tell me what took place.'

'It was M. Berthier, my father. You know how I have feared him. Why did you send me to the château?'

'Go on, child.'

She suddenly clasped her hands over her brow, threw her head forward, and resting her elbows on her lap, said:—

'Promise me! I am not to go near that place again.'

'Is time so common an article that I can afford to waste it thus?' exclaimed André. 'Go on with your story, or I shall return to littering the cow-stall.'

'My father!'

'Well!'

'I am not to go there again!'

With a curse the peasant flung himself towards his fork, tore it out of the ground, and recommenced his work. He continued carrying into the cow-shed bundles of straw and spreading them, with apparent forgetfulness of his daughter, and indifference to her trouble. She remained with her head in her hands, crying. Lebertre spoke to her, but her grief had now obtained the mastery over her, and she could not answer him.

'Let her cry herself out,' said Lindet.

After the first paroxysm was over, she sprang up, ran to her father, cast her arms about him, and placing her chin upon his breast, looked up into his eyes. This was an old trick of hers. Matthias never looked any one in the face, and when his daughter wished to meet his gaze, she acted thus.

'I will tell you all now,' she said. 'Come, sit by me on the bench.'

'I have no time at present,' he answered, sullenly. 'Besides, I can guess a great deal.'

'You shall listen to me,' said the girl; 'I will not let you go till you have heard everything.'

She removed the manure-fork from his hand, and led him to the door of the cow-shed. He would not go farther, he would not seat himself beside her, as she had asked. He yielded to her request in one particular, but not in another. It was his way,—his pride, to do whatever he was asked with a bad grace. He supported himself against one side-post, with his head down, and the knuckle of his forefinger between his teeth; she leaned against the other jamb.

'I went round to the houses, as usual, selling my bunches of roses; I sold one to Madame Laborde, and two to the Demoiselles Bréant; and M. François Corbelin, the musician, bought one, but he did not pay me,—he had no money with him to-day, but he promised for next time. Then I went to the château of M. des Pintréaux, but the ladies did not want any of my roses; and then I walked on with my basket to the Château Malouve. The lackeys told me that Monsieur was not in, but that he was a little way along the road, and that I was to take him my roses, as he particularly wished to purchase them, he wanted them all; so I walked on, but I was distressed, for I did not like to meet M. Berthier alone. He always addresses me in a way that gives me pain, and he makes his jokes, so that I am ashamed.'

'Well, well, go on.'

'So, my father, after I had shown him my basket——'

'Then you found him?'

'Yes; he was at no great distance. He laughed when I came towards him. He did not seem to care much for the roses, but looked at me with his horrible eyes, and he put his hand to my chin, and asked for a kiss, then I was frightened and ran from him; but he followed me, and I was so frightened that I could not run with my usual speed; my head was spinning, and I scarcely knew whither I was going; then, just as he caught me up, M. le Curé rescued me from him. God be praised!'

Matthias turned from the door-post to resume his pitchfork, but his daughter intercepted him once more.

'My father,' she entreated, 'say that I am never to go again with my roses to M. Berthier!'

'Did he pay you for the bunches he took?'

'No; I ran away before he paid for them.'

'You are a fool; you should have taken the money, and then run away.'

Lebertre now stepped forward to interfere.

'It is not right, Matthias, that the poor child should be sent into such peril again.'

'M. Berthier buys more bunches than any one else,' answered André, moodily.

'Dear father, I have too often to suffer the looks and smiles and jokes of those to whom I offer my bunches of flowers,' said the girl, emboldened by finding that the priest took her part. 'Let me work in the field every day with you. Let us dig up the garden, and turn it into a potato-field.'

'Remember the risk to a young and pretty child,' continued the curé, 'in sending her round the country alone with her basket of flowers. The young gentlemen are gay and reckless; shame and sin enough have been wrought in this neighbourhood by them, and M. Berthier is notorious for his debaucheries. You are thrusting your child over a precipice.'

'We must live,' answered the peasant, fiercely. 'Answer me this. Does not the sailor risk life for a small wage; does not the soldier jeopardy his for a gay coat and a liard a day? Is it not the mission of men—I do not mean of nobles, they are not men, they are gods—to labour and struggle for a subsistence in the midst of perils? Shall not my child, then, run some risks to win enough to satisfy the gnawing hunger in our vitals? Does not the doctor venture his health for the sake of a fee, and shall not this girl risk her honour to save her life?'

'You imperil both your soul and hers.'

Matthias shrugged his shoulders.

Lindet strode up to him, caught his shoulders in his palms, and jerked his head upwards; their eyes met for a second, and in that second Lindet mastered his dogged humour.

André threw it aside, and straightening himself, he beat his hands together, and cried out in an altered tone, full of bitterness and pain,—

'My God! what are we poor but the cattle of the rich? We are theirs; what is the good of our attempting to resist their will? They possess our earnings, our labour, our life, our honour; ay! our souls are theirs, to ruin them if they like. Can anything I may do protect poor Gabrielle from M. Berthier, or any other great man who shall cast his lustful eyes on her? No. Let things take their course. Perhaps God will right our wrongs at the judgment. I wait for that. Thy kingdom come!' he exclaimed, throwing up his hands to the sky. 'And till then,—if it be God's will that we should be the prey of the powerful,—that they should eat us up, and pollute our honour,—why, His will be done, we must even bear it.'

'Do you love your daughter?' asked Lebertre.

'As much as I can afford,' answered André, relapsing into his moody humour.

'You do love her,' said Lindet; 'but you love yourself better.' Matthias looked furtively at him.

'I love her, indeed,' he said, sadly; 'but I have no thoughts for anything but how to stave off the great enemy.'

'What great enemy?' asked Lebertre.

'Hunger,' answered the peasant, passionately.

'The child shall not take her flowers to the Château Malouve any more,' said Lindet, firmly. 'She shall take them
instead to my brother Robert, and he will buy them. Mind,
instead, not besides.'

'Yes, monsieur!' answered André. 'Indeed, I do not
desire that evil should befall my dear child, but hunger is
imperious; and oh! last winter was so terrible, that I dare not
face another such, so destitute of means as I have been.'

Dusk had by this time settled in, and the curés walked
homewards. Their roads lay together as far as La Couture,
which is almost a suburb of Bernay, and was, according to
antiquaries, the original parish church of that town, before
the erection of S. Cross.

'See,' said Lindet to his friend, as they parted at the door
of the presbytery of La Couture; 'see how want and poverty
dry up the natural springs of love and virtue; and how the
nobles, the Church, and the king, by their oppression of the
peasant, are demoralising him. Believe me, if ever a day of
reckoning should come, those natural feelings, which oppression has turned into gall, will overwhelm the oppressors. If
once the people get the upper hand, mercy must not be expected; wrong-doing has long ago destroyed all the tenderer
feelings of our poor.'

But he was wrong in thinking that they were destroyed.
Frozen over they were, but not dried up.

That night, after André had gone up his ladder to the bed of straw on which he lay, and after several hours of darkness, Gabrielle woke up at the sound of sobs, and creeping lightly from her attic chamber to her father's door, she saw him by the moonlight that flowed in at the unglazed window, kneeling against his bed, with his head laid upon his arm, and the moon illumining it, weeping convulsedly, and the white light glittered in his tears.

CHAPTER III.

THE west front of Évreux Cathedral occupies one side of a small square, of which the south side is formed by a high wall pierced by the arched gate that conducts into the court-yard of the bishop's palace.

Above this arch was wont to be erected the arms of the prelate occupying the see, impaled with those of the diocese. The Bishop of Évreux in 1788 was Monseigneur de Narbonne-Lara, and the arms borne by him displayed a ramping and roaring lion. As those of the bishopric were a S. Sebastian bound to a pillar, and transfixed with arrows, the combination was peculiar, and was seized on by the wags to point a moral. They observed that the saint typified Religion, bound hand and foot by establishmentarian thongs, and pierced through with many sorrows, whilst Monseigneur's lion, which seemed bent on devouring the martyr, symbolized the greed and ambition of the episcopacy.

Monseigneur de Narbonne had scrambled from a counter to a throne. He was one of those few prelates of the French Church who were not members of great families. Tell it

not in Gath! his father made and sold goose-liver pasties at
Strasbourg; but Strasbourg is a very long way from Évreux.

The bishop's father called himself Lara, his mother had
been a Demoiselle Narbonne; by combining the names, and
prefixing to the maternal cognomen a *De*, the bishop was able
to pass himself off as a member of the nobility, and to speak
disparagingly of roturiers. Above the parental shop at Strasbourg hung a wooden and painted figure of a plucked goose,
the badge of the family profession, and the only heraldic
device of which old Lara boasted. The lion, says Æsop,
once assumed an ass's skin; but on the shield of Monseigneur de Narbonne-Lara, bishop of Évreux, abbot *in commendam* of three religious houses, the ancestral goose ramped
and roared as a lion or out of a field gules.

The bishop was ambitious of becoming an archbishop and
a cardinal; he had therefore to pay his court at once to
Versailles and to Rome—a course he was perfectly competent
to pursue, for, though filled to the brim with pride, he had
not a drop of self-respect. He was a tall, stout and handsome
man, but his good looks were marred by the redness and
fleshiness of his face, and his proportions were disguised by
the pomposity of his carriage.

Being a man of consummate shrewdness, he had succeeded
in making himself a favourite at Court. His knowledge of
German had won him first the bishopric of Gap, and after-

wards the more important one of Evreux, when, during the late reign, the Dauphiness had set Austrian fashions. For the same reason, he was now private chaplain to the Queen. He gave capital dinners, and hoped by the choiceness of his cookery and wines to buy the favour of those who had the ear of royalty. By fussy officiousness in the diocese, by worrying his clergy, he hoped to obtain credit for energetic discharge of his episcopal duties, and by favouring the Jesuits, he made sure that his acts would be favourably reported at Rome.

Monseigneur was now about to achieve a triumph. Prince Louis-Stanislas-Xavier, commonly called ' Monsieur,' the brother of the King, Duke of Anjou, Alençon and Vendôme, Count of Perche, Maine, and Senonches, having business to transact in Normandy connected with the bailiwicks of Bernay and Orbec, of which he was lord, had been invited to the palace by the Bishop of Evreux, and the prince had accepted the invitation.

Monseigneur de Narbonne was in a flutter of excitement at the prospect. The same may be said of Mademoiselle Baptistine, his sister, who lived with him. The grand old palace was turned inside out. Painters, gilders, and upholsterers had taken possession of the house, and had banished the bishop into the turret overlooking the garden.

The prelate sat in his purple cassock and cape, pen in

hand, making imaginary calculations of the expenses the visit of the prince would entail upon him. He had ordered the withdrawing room to be furnished with blue silk hangings powdered over with silver lilies, and having ascertained from his sister the price per yard of silk, and having allowed a margin for the fleurs-de-lis, he measured the room when no one was looking, and had just estimated the cost. He added to this the blue velvet divan, and the chairs gilt and covered with blue velvet, and the painting and gilding of the ceiling, the carpets and the mirrors. He had pretty well satisfied himself that the income of the see would not bear such an expenditure as he contemplated. But it was worth the sacrifice. Three archbishops were then infirm. His own immediate superior at Rouen had been reduced very low by a virulent attack of gastric fever, brought on by immoderate eating of peaches; and, according to the last account from Rouen, the archbishop, immediately on his recovery, had again attacked the fruit of which he was passionately fond, in opposition to the express orders of his physician. If the archbishop were to be again prostrated, there was every chance of his vacating an archiepiscopal throne, and also of placing a cardinal's hat at the disposal of the Pope. M. Ponce, the *officiel*, was with the Bishop of Evreux.

'My good Ponce,' said the bishop, 'you must procure me money somehow. Between ourselves, the expenses which I shall be compelled to incur, in order adequately to entertain royalty, are so considerable, that I must have my coffer replenished, or I shall be involved in difficulties.'

'I think, my Lord,' answered the confidant, 'that some of the cases for your lordship's court might be compromised, and that would at once produce a sum of ready money.'

'My excellent friend, I shall esteem it a favour if you will do so. Are there many cases in hand?'

'My Lord, I think there are some other cases coming on, but they are not ripe yet. But, if your lordship will take my advice, I should advise attention to be directed rather to the clergy than to the laity. The times, as your lordship is well aware, are somewhat uncertain. A spirit of antagonism to constituted authority is abroad; there is much restlessness, much impatience of the rights of those, whom Providence has ordained masters and governors, in Church and State.'

'It is but just that the shepherd should live of the milk of the flock,' said the bishop with dignity.

'Your lordship is theoretically right; but, unfortunately, the flock will not submit to be milked with as great equanimity as heretofore. Since the local parliaments, to the detriment of the liberties of the Church, have assumed to receive appeals from our courts, we have lost the hold upon the laity that we possessed formerly. I think—but here I bow to your lordship's superior judgment—that it would not be advisable, just at present—I only urge at present, to draw off too much milk from the laity. Now as for the *prêtrisse*, that is quite another matter. The priests are at your disposal, your lordship can do with them almost what your lordship likes. They are, in fact, mere servants of the bishop.'

'True, Ponce,' said the prelate, blandly; 'I say to this man go, and he goeth; and to another do this, and he doeth it.'

'And the most satisfactory point is this, they have no appeal against their bishop. The law——'

'I am the law,' interrupted Monseigneur; 'to the diocese in all matters ecclesiastical, I repeat the expression, I am the law.'

'Your lordship is right,' continued the officer; 'and therefore I would urge that the most ready source of money is to be found in the Church. You have but to fine a priest, and he cannot escape you. He cannot evade your court, he cannot appeal to the crown, he dare not throw himself on public opinion. He is completely at your mercy. He is your slave. If he refuses to comply with your requirements, you can inhibit him, or suspend him. Whilst suspended, the income of the living goes to your lordship, and you have only to provide out of it for the ministration of the sacraments; a small tax, for there are always indigent or disreputable clergy glad enough to take temporary duty for a trifling fee. But the curé knows better than to resist his diocesan. He has been bred to consider it a matter of conscience to yield to his ecclesiastical superior; and, even if conscience does not influence him, common prudence will act upon him, when he considers that every other profession is legally shut against him, so that he must be his bishop's slave, or starve.'

'I have no wish for a moment to act with undue severity towards my clergy,' said Monseigneur de Narbonne; 'indeed, I am incapable of any such action; but discipline must be maintained, and when a spirit of defiance manifests itself, even amongst the clergy, it is high time that they should be made to recognise who is master in the Church. The curés dare to call my episcopal acts in question, and to oppose the execution of my projects. Is the Church a constitutional government? Certainly not; it is a monarchy of which every prelate is sovereign in his own see. The laity may have eluded his crook, but with the spike he can transfix his recalcitrant clergy.'

'I can give your lordship an instance of insubordination corroborative of what you have just stated. I have just returned from Bernay——'

'Ah! there you have one of these new lights,' interrupted the bishop. 'I know his sentiments; he is a leader of disaffection, a man of ungovernable vehemence, huge pride, and insolent demeanour.'

'Quite so, my Lord,' said M. Ponce. 'According to your

honoured instructions, he has been closely watched, and, as I learned that he had neglected to light his sanctuary-lamp during three days, he has rendered himself amenable to justice. I have, however, offered him to compromise the matter on the receipt of a fine of twenty-five livres. He has refused me the money, and declares that he will speak to your lordship about it, face to face.'

'The fellow must be humbled,' said the prelate; 'he forgets that he has no legal status, that he is a mere salaried curate, and that I have it in my power to ruin him. I am glad that he is coming here; I shall have an opportunity of cautioning him to exhibit decorum in his conduct and respect in his behaviour.——Well, Mademoiselle!' he suddenly exclaimed, as the door opened, and his sister entered, embracing a large deal box.

'I have brought you your letters, Monseigneur, and——'

'Well, my good sister, and what?'

'Oh, nothing, nothing!'

'May I ask what that box contains?' enquired the bishop blandly, whilst he took the letters.

'Nothing in the world, brother, but——'

'But what, eh?'

'Oh! nothing at all.'

'Shall I retire?' asked M. Ponce, who had risen from his seat on the lady's entry.

'By no means, my Ponce, by no means;' and he began to tear open his letters.

'Ha! begging appeals. The priest of Semerville is restoring his church, and entreats help; the people are too poor, the landlord too chary of giving, and so on.' Away fluttered the note, torn in half, and the *officiel* obsequiously picked it up and placed it with a score other dead appeals in the waste-paper basket.

'The curé of S. Julien entreats me to interfere—some widow who has been wronged—bah!' and that letter followed the first.

'"I have allowed nine months to elapse since the *vicaire* of Vernon was appointed, and the licence has not yet been forwarded; wherefore, knowing the uncertainty of the post, he is confident that the omission is due to the neglect of the postman, and not of the forgetfulness of the bishop." Humph! inclined to insolence. That is the way these young curates behave! You shall await my convenience, M. Dufour.' This letter was crumpled up, and thrown at the basket.

'An altar to S. Joseph! The clergy of Louviers are desirous—and so on. Well, Louviers is a large place. S. Joseph the patron of the Jesuits; at any other time than this, my good friends.' Away sped this appeal. '"The curé of Beaumont ventures to observe that it is two years since the last confirmation, and that the children are growing

up and leaving the district." Confound his impudence! My
rule is plain enough, to hold a confirmation every year in
the large towns, Évreux and Louviers; one every second year
in the smaller towns; and one every third year in the rural
districts. Sister! enclose a printed slip with· that notice to
the curé of Beaumont.'

' Yes, brother.'

' What have we here? So, ho! a note from M. Berthier,
Intendant of Paris, written at his country seat, near Bernay,
about Thomas Lindet, who has behaved to him without proper
respect, and whose revolutionary principles render him a
dangerous person to be the curé of a large and important
town. Pass me my paper-case, Ponce, my good fellow, I will
send him a note in return to thank him for the information,
and to promise that the curé shall be reprimanded and
cautioned. Intendant of Paris! a man of consequence, is he
not, Ponce, eh?'

' A man of very great consequence, my Lord; his father-
in-law is M. Foulon, a great person at Court, as your lordship must know.'

If the bishop had attended to his sister instead of to his
letters, he would have observed that she was carefully placing
the deal box underneath the divan or sofa, which occupied
one side of the little room.

' Can I assist you, Mademoiselle?' asked M. Ponce.

'On no account,' replied the lady with evident alarm and agitation.

She made several ineffectual attempts to attract her brother's attention, but he was too absorbed in his letters to notice her. And the moment he had despatched his answer to M. Berthier, he plunged at once into a discussion as to the guests who were to be invited to meet His Royal Highness, at a fête on the evening of his arrival.

'I am in doubt whether to ask M. Girardin,' said the prelate; 'what is your opinion, my Ponce? He is Lieutenant-General of the bailiwick, which should weigh against his lack of nobility; his views are too liberal to please me, he is a bit of a philosopher, has read Rousseau and Voltaire, perhaps, and thinks with Montesquieu. I do not like to introduce a herd of roturiers to the Duke; and, if one admits two or three, all the burghers of the place will be offended at not having been invited.'

'As you have done me the honour of asking my opinion,' said the functionary, 'I would recommend you to invite M. Girardin. Feed well those who are not favourably disposed towards you; dazzle those who are your enemies, and you render them powerless.'

'I quite agree with what you say,' said the bishop. This was not extraordinary, as his official merely repeated a sentiment he had heard Monseigneur express several times before;

'those whom I cannot suppress I dazzle, those whom I cannot dazzle I invite to my table.'

'There is sound worldly wisdom in that,' said M. Ponce.

'And it works admirably,' the bishop continued; then, turning to his sister, he said, 'Well, Baptistine, what about the box?'

The lady gave a little start, frowned, and shook her head.

'Well,' paused the bishop; 'what is in it? Where have you put it?'

Mademoiselle Baptistine at once seated herself on the sofa, and spread her gown, as a screen, to cover it, whilst she made several cabalistic gestures to signify that the presence of a third party prevented her from saying what she wanted. M. Ponce caught a glimpse of these signs, or guessed that he was no longer wanted, for he rose, and, after having formally saluted the bishop, and asked permission to retire, he walked sideways towards the door, repeatedly turning to bow.

As his hand rested upon the latch, the door was thrown open, and a large black retriever bounded into the room, between the legs of a powdered footman in purple livery, who announced, 'M. le Marquis de Chambray.'

The gentleman who entered was tall and thin, with a solemn face, adorned with a pair of huge grey moustaches. His hair was powdered, and the dust covered the collar of

his velvet coat. He was elaborately dressed, and had the air
of an ancient dandy. The Marquis was a man of some
fortune, and of illustrious family. He acted for the prince
as his deputy in the bailiwicks of Orbec and Bernay. Scarcely
less stiff and formal than his appearance was his character.
He was an aristocrat of the aristocrats, filled with family pride,
and rigid in his adherence to the rules of etiquette of the
reign of Louis XIV. He was never known to have made
a witty remark, certainly never a wise one. But though
neither witty nor wise, he was a man who commanded respect,
for he was too cautious ever to act foolishly, and too well-
bred ever to behave discourteously.

'Ah! sapristi!' exclaimed the Marquis; 'my naughty dog,
how dare you intrude? I must apologise, my Lord, for the
bad conduct of my dog. I left it in the courtyard, but it has
found its way after me.'

'Let him remain,' said the bishop; 'fine fellow, noble dog!
The doors are all open, my dear Marquis; the workmen are
engaged in getting the palace just a little tidy for our
distinguished visitor. Never mind the dog—it would be
impossible to shut him out, whilst the house is in confusion.
I am so sorry that you should be shown into this little
boudoir; but really, I am driven to it as my only refuge in
the midst of a chaos.'

'I have come to inform you, my lord bishop, that Monsieur

will be with you on Thursday next, if that will suit your convenience. I received a despatch from him to-day, and, amongst other matters, was a notice to that effect, and a request that the announcement should be made to you immediately.'

'We shall be proud to receive him, and everything shall be in readiness,' said the bishop.

'The weather is exceedingly fine,' observed the Marquis, turning courteously towards Mademoiselle Baptistine.

'It is charming,' answered the bishop's sister, nervously. Mademoiselle Baptistine was a lady of forty-five, with an aquiline nose, of which, as an aristocratic feature, she and her brother were proud. Her complexion was fair, her eyes very pale, and starting from her head, so that she had always, except when asleep, the appearance of being greatly surprised at something.

'It is also hot; Mademoiselle doubtless finds it hot,' said the Marquis.

'Very much so. I have been quite overcome.'

'But it is seasonable,' observed the visitor. And so on.

Presently, however, the conversation brightened up a little; for the Marquis, turning sharply on the bishop, said: 'By the way, I met a member of your family the other day.'

A scarlet flush covered the bishop's face, and Mademoiselle Baptistine turned the colour of chalk.

'I met the old Countess de Narbonne in Paris; she is doubtless a cousin. I told her I was acquainted with your lordship, but she did not seem to know you; probably her memory fails.'

'The De Narbonne and the De Narbonne-Lara families, though remotely connected, are not the same,' answered the bishop, wiping his hot face; 'the branches separated in the reign of Saint Louis, and therefore the connection between them is distant. Mine crossed the Pyrenees and settled in Spain, where they fought valiantly against the Moors. The castle of Lara is in Andalusia; the family assumed the territorial name of Lara, in addition to the De Narbonne, on their receiving the Spanish estates from a grateful monarch in recognition of their services. My grandfather, unfortunately, gambled half the property away, and my father sold the rest to pay off the debts his father had contracted; an honourable proceeding, which reduced the family, however, greatly. With the remains of his fortune he came to France, retaining possession only of the ancestral castle in Spain.'

Suddenly Mademoiselle Baptistine uttered a scream. From under the sofa darted the retriever with a huge pasty in its mouth. In its efforts to secure the dainty morsel, it flung the lid of the box from which it had extracted the pie, half way across the room.

'What is the dog at?' exclaimed the bishop.

'Rascal!' shouted the Marquis, 'bring that here instantly.' He threatened the brute with his stick, and the dog crawled to him with the pasty in its mouth.

'What manners!' cried the nobleman; 'I am so grieved at the ill-conduct of my dog—No, Madame!' as the lady stooped towards the cover of the box, which had contained the delicious tempting pie. 'Never, Madame; allow me.'

'Allow me!' said the bishop, bending his knee, and stooping towards it. But Mademoiselle Baptistine was as active as either of the men; and thus it came to pass that the three heads met over the lid of the box; and at the same moment the bishop and the Marquis read a printed shop-label, pasted upon it, and directed in manuscript to the bishop, from—

'Jacques de Narbonne-Lara (formerly Lara),
Maker of the celebrated Strasbourg Goose-liver Pasties.
Rue des Capuchins, 6; Strasbourg.'

'Sapient dog!' said the nobleman, rising, and blowing his nose. 'My wise Leo knows what is good. Ah! the pasty is utterly gone, he has eaten it. I quite envy him the mouthful. Pray accept my deepest regret for his misconduct.'

'Do not mention it,' answered the bishop, with his eyes still on the hateful label.

'I am so glad to have the address,' said the Marquis, with a slight tinge of sarcasm in his voice; 'I will write to the shop and order some of these pasties for myself—I dote on the paté de foix gras.'   And he bowed himself out of the room.

'What has that fool Jacques been about?' asked the bishop, throwing himself back in his chair, and clasping his hands in the air above his head.

'My dear brother!' answered Baptistine, 'Jacques has assumed the same name as you have; he is proud of being brother to a bishop, that is why—and he has sent you the pasty as an offering of brotherly love—so he says in his letter. I found the box on the table in the hall, and all the servants round it, laughing. I snatched it from them, and brought it up here, when——' the rest was drowned in tears.

'He had better have sent me a halter,' said the bishop.

CHAPTER IV.

FAMINE reigned in France, for the resources of the country were drained off to sustain the court in luxury and vice. In seven years, Louis XV added seven hundred and fifty millions of francs to the two billions and a half of debts left by Louis XIV. Archbishop Fénélon wrote to the Grand Monarque: 'At length, France is become one great hospital, desolate and unprovided with the necessaries of life. By yourself alone these disasters have been created. In the ruin of France, everything has passed into your hands; and your subjects are reduced to live upon your bounty.'

Louis the Well-Beloved was hunting one day in the forest of Sénart. He met a peasant carrying a coffin. 'For whom is that coffin?' asked the king. 'For a man.' 'What did he die of?' 'Hunger.' France was dying: in a few years, but for the Revolution, it would have been dead and buried, killed by famine.

'In my diocese,' said the Bishop of Chartres, 'men browse with the sheep.'

Taxes innumerable were paid. But there was not money

E 2

enough.   Hundreds perished, that the beasts of Æsop's fables
might squirt water in the duck-ponds of Versailles.   The royal
mistresses sparkled with jewels, and each jewel cost a human
life.   One hundred millions of francs went in pensions, the
Red Book told on whom.   Exemption from taxes was given
liberally; the king created nobles, the revenue created em-
ployés, all these were exempt.   Thus, whilst the sum required
of the people increased every year, every year the number of
payers decreased.   The load weighed on fewer shoulders, and
became more and more oppressive.

At Versailles, fifteen thousand men and five thousand horses
were supported at the public cost to give splendour to the seat
of royalty; they consumed sixty million livres per annum.
The king's house cost eighteen millions, that of the queen
four millions, and those of the princes nine millions, though
they possessed as their apannages a seventh part of the territory
of France.   The Church drew an annual income of four
hundred and fifty millions; the tithes were worth eighty
millions, and its buildings were estimated at five hundred
millions.   Of the land in France, one-fifth belonged to the
Church.

What was the condition of the peasant ?   It has been already
described; it was he who bore the burden and heat of the day.
On his toils the court, the nobles, and the Church lived.   It
was his blood that they sucked.   The peasant might not plant

what he would in his fields; pastures were required to remain pastures, arable land was to be always arable. If he changed his field into meadow, he robbed the curé of his tithe; if he sowed clover in his fallow land, the landlord or the abbot turned in his flock of sheep, to crop off it what he deemed his share. The lord and the abbot sent out their cattle to pasture an hour before those of the peasant; they had the right to keep huge dovecots, and the pigeons fed on the grain of the farmer. The tenant worked for his landlord three days in the year for himself, three days for each of his sons and servants, and three for each horse and cart. He was bound to cut and make and stack his lord's hay in spring, and to reap and garner his wheat in autumn; to repair the castle walls, and make and keep up the castle roads. Add to all this the tax to the king, twelve sous per head for each child, the same for each servant, the subvention for the king; the twentieth for the king, that is, the twentieth portion of the fruits of the earth, already tithed for the Church.

When we hear folk declaim against the French Revolution, do not let us forget what was the state of the people before that event. The Revolution was a severe surgical operation, but it was the salvation of France.

To the beautiful gothic church of Notre Dame de la Couture, the people of Bernay and the neighbouring villages went in procession, on the Feast of the Assumption, to entreat the

Blessed Virgin to obtain for them relief from their miseries. Human succour seemed in vain. If they appealed to the king, his answer was, *Give !* If they besought the nobility, they also answered, *Give !* If they threw themselves at the feet of the Church, her response was also, *Give !*

Now, throughout the land a cry went up to Heaven. At Bernay it took the form of a pilgrimage.

The origin of the Church of La Couture was as follows. Far away in the purple of antiquity, when first the faith of Christ began to dawn in Gaul, a shepherd-boy found himself daily deserted by his flock, which left him as he entered the forest in the morning, and only returned to him at nightfall. Impelled by curiosity, he followed the sheep one day, and they led him through bush and brake till he emerged on a pleasant sunny glade upon the slope of the hill, where the pasture was peculiarly rich, and where also, resting against a magnificent wild rose, leaned a black statue of the Blessed Virgin.

This discovery led to a concourse of pilgrims visiting the image, which had been thus unaccountably placed in the heart of a forest. The clergy of the ancient city of Lisieux sent a waggon to transport the image to their church; but no sooner was it placed upon their altar than it vanished, and was found next morning in the glade of Bernay. A chapel was erected over it, and was served by a hermit, but the afflux of pilgrims made the shrine rich, and a church was built in the forest, and about the church a village soon arose. The trees were cut down, and the bottom of the valley was brought into cultivation, from which fact the church obtained its name of La Couture, or Ecclesia de Culturâ Bernaii.

The church is beautifully situated on the steep side of the hill, with its west front towards the slope, and its apse standing up high above the soil, which falls away rapidly from it into the valley. The western doorway is richly sculptured and contains a flamboyant window, occupying the tymphanum of the arch. Above this portal is a large window, which, at the time of our story, was filled with rich tracery, and with richer glass that represented Mary, the Queen of Heaven, as the refuge of all in adversity. In the central light, the Virgin appeared surrounded by flames and rays, her face and hands black, whilst angels harped and sang around her. A fillet surmounted her, bearing the text 'Nigra sum, sed formosa, sicut tabernacula cedar.' (Cant. i. 4.) On one side, cripples and sick persons stretched forth their hands to the sacred figure; on the other, were peasants trampled on and smitten by the servants of nobles in armour, whilst above in the tracery might be seen houses and barns in conflagration, and ships about to be engulfed in waves [1].

---

[1] The window is described from one existing in the north aisle of the church of S. Foy, at Conches, the stained glass in which church is perhaps the finest in Normandy.

From the west door, a flight of fifteen steps leads down into the nave, so that on entering, the appearance of the church is almost that of a magnificent crypt.

On the 15th of August, in the afternoon, the church presented an imposing spectacle. Eight parishes had united to visit the shrine, and supplicate the protection of the Blessed Virgin. The day had been hitherto very fine, and the sight enjoyed from the churchyard of the processions arriving from different quarters, in the bright sunshine, had been singularly beautiful. Each parish procession was headed by its banner ; the clergy, by crucifix and candles. Various confraternities, with their insignia, united to give picturesqueness to the scene. From the interior of the church the effect was striking, as the line,—endless it seemed,—rippled down the flight of western steps, with tapers twinkling and coloured banners waving; whilst the organ thundered, and the people shouted the refrain of a penitential litany. The illumined figures in the yard contrasted with those in shadow, as they flowed through the portal : this was epecially noticeable when a band of girls in white, with white veils, and lighted taper in hand, preceded by their white banner emblazoned with a representation of the Assumption, moved through the doorway. The leading ribbons of this banner were held by two maidens in white ; one of these was Gabrielle, and her appearance in this pure garb was most beautiful. A wreath of white roses

encircled her head, and clasped the muslin veil to her temples.
As the shadow of the arch fell upon her, a slight puff of wind
extinguished her candle, but on reaching the foot of the steps
a taper was held towards her, and she was about to re-light
hers at the flame, when, raising her eyes, she encountered those
of M. Berthier, who, with a smirk, proffered her his burning
candle.　She shrank away, and kindled her light at the candle
of a girl who followed her.

M. Berthier was in company with an old gentleman, very
thin, with a hatchet face, white hair, and black eyes active and
brilliant.　He was dressed in an old brown riding-coat, with
high collar, over which protruded a short wiry pig-tail, fastened
with a large bow.　He took snuff, at intervals of a few minutes,
from a large gold box; and he took it in a peculiar manner,
not from his fingers but from the palm of his hand, into which
he shook the tobacco dust, and from which he drew it into his
nostrils by applying the palm to his face.　This method of
snuffing might be economical, but it was ungainly and dirty,
for it left crumbs of tobacco upon the lips, nose, and cheeks
of the old man.

'That is the wench,' said Berthier, after he had politely
returned the taper, which he had unceremoniously snatched
from the hand of a peasant, that he might offer it to
Gabrielle.

'A pretty little darling,' the old man replied.　'Is this the third flame this year, and we only in August? Bah! my lad, you are positively shocking.'

'Are you going to remain here among these rascals?'

'A moment or two, my friend; I want to see who are the malcontents. Bah! these people ask Heaven for food. Let Heaven give them rain and sunshine, and the earth yield her increase; who will profit thereby? Not they. Bah! Famine is not the result of the seasons, it is no natural phenomenon. It is good for the people to be kept on low diet, it humbles them; America bred fat cattle, and they have thrown off the yoke. What makes the famine, my boy? Why, *we* make famine, and keep up famine, because the people must be retained in sub-jection.'

Berthier touched the old man to silence him; Lindet was close to them, and his glittering eye rested on the Intendant and his father-in-law. But Foulon took no notice of the touch, and he continued:—'Bah! If they are hungry, let them browse grass. Wait till I am minister, I will make them eat hay; my horses eat it.'

Thomas Lindet heard the words as distinctly as did Berthier. A flush, deep as ruby, suffused his face, and he clenched his teeth, whilst a flame darted from his eyes.

'Who is that devil?' asked Foulon, with imperturbable calm-ness, of his son-in-law.

'He is the priest of S. Cross, at Bernay. I owe him a grudge. Come out of this crush into the air, I am stifled.'

Berthier drew his father-in-law to the door.

The weather was undergoing a change. To the west, above the hill, a semicircle or bow of white cloud, in which the sun made prismatic colours, edged a dense purple-black mass of darkness. It was like gazing into a hideous cavern whose mouth was fringed with fungus.

'A storm is at hand,' said Berthier; 'it is approaching too rapidly for us to escape. We must remain here.'

An ash with scarlet berries grew opposite the west door, on high ground. This tree stood up against the advancing clouds like a tree of fire, so intense was the darkness within the bow of white. The leaves scarcely rustled; at intervals a puff of wind swept over the churchyard and shook the tree, but between the puffs the air was still. Gradually a peculiar smell, very faint, like the fume of a brick-kiln at a great distance, filled the air. The white vapourous fringe dissolved into coils of cloud, ropy, hanging together in bunches, and altering shape at each moment. A film ran over the sun, which was instantly shorn of its rays; a chill fell on the air, and a shadow overspread the ground; the ash turned grey, and everything that had been golden was transmuted into lead.

From the church within sounded the organ, and the people

chanting the Magnificat; and incense rose before the altar, on which six candles burned.

From over the western hill came the mumble of distant thunder, a low continued roll like the traffic of heavy-laden vehicles on a paved road. A few large drops fell and spotted the flagstone on which Berthier and Foulon stood. They looked up. The sky was now covered with whirling masses of vapour, some light curl-like twists flew about before the main body of lurid thunder-cloud, which was seamed and hashed with shooting lights.

The wind arose and moaned around the church, muttering and hissing in the louvre-boards of the spire; the ash shivered and shook, the willows and poplars in the valley whitened and bent, and the long grass in the cemetery fell and rose in waves; the jackdaws flew screaming around the tower, a martin skimmed the surface of the ground, uttering its piercing cry.

Foulon had been scratching his initials listlessly on the flag on which he stood, with the ferule of his walking-stick. Drops like tears falling about it made him say:—'Come in, Berthier, my boy. The rain is beginning to fall, and you will have your smart coat spotted and spoiled.'

The two men re-entered the church. Vespers had just concluded, and Lindet ascended the pulpit. From where he stood he saw them in the door-way, with the sheet-lightning flashing and fading behind them. At one moment they appeared encircled with flame, at another plunged in darkness.

'As I came into this church to-day,' spoke Lindet with distinctness, 'I heard one say to another: *If the peasants are hungry, let them browse grass. I would make them eat hay; my horses eat it.* As I stand in this pulpit, and the lightning illumines yonder window, I see painted there a lean, famished peasant, trampled under the hoofs of the horse of some noble rider, and the great man has his staff raised to chastise the peasant. Under these circumstances, the poor man lifts his hands to heaven, as his only refuge. That is what you do this day,—you, the down-trodden, scourged, and bruised; you who are bidden browse the grass, because that is the food of brute-beasts. Just Heaven! the importunate widow was heard who cried to the unjust judge to avenge her on her adversary, and shall not God avenge His own elect, though He bear long?'

The rain burst with a roar upon the roof,—a roar so loud and prolonged that the preacher's voice was silenced. The vergers closed the great doors to prevent the rain from entering, for the wind began now to blow in great gusts. The fountains of heaven seemed to have burst forth, the rain rattled against the west window, loudly as though hail and not rain were poured upon it. Dazzling flashes of lightning kindled up the whole interior with white brilliancy, casting no shadows. The congregation remained silent and awed, the clergy in their tribune opposite the pulpit sat motionless. The candles flickered in the draughts that whistled round the aisles; their flames seemed dull and orange.

Suddenly the bells in the tower began to peal. According to popular belief their sound dispels tempests, and the ringers were wont to pull the ropes during a storm. The clash and clangour of the metal alternated with the boom of the thunder. The darkness which fell on the church was terrible, men and women on their knees recited their beads in fear and trembling. Scarce a heart in that great concourse but quailed. Once a child screamed. Then, as for one instant, the bells ceased, the sobbing of a babe at its mother's breast was heard. The water began to flow down the hill, collect into a stream in the churchyard, and to pour in a turbid flood down the steps into the nave. It boiled up under the closed door, it rushed into the tower and dislodged the ringers, who were soon over shoe-tops in water.

A startled bat flew up and down the church, and dashing against the altar-candles extinguished one with its leathern wings.

All at once the rain ceased to fall, and the wind lulled. None stirred; all felt that the tempest was gathering up its strength for one final explosion ere it rolled away. Then a tall thin woman in black, with a black veil thrown over her

head, was observed to have stationed herself immediately before
the altar, where she knelt with outstretched arms and uplifted
face. Those who were near observed with horror that the
face, from which the veil was upthrown, was of a blue-grey
colour. When she had made her way to her present situation
none knew; none had observed her in the procession, for then
she had been, probably, closely veiled. She threw her arms
and hands passionately towards the black Virgin above the
altar, and in the stillness of that lull in the storm her piercing
cry was heard pealing through the church, 'Avenge me on
my adversary.'

'My God!' whispered Berthier to his father-in-law, as he
pointed to the excited worshipper, 'look at my wife, Foulon!
she has gone mad.'

'Bah!' answered the imperturbable old man; 'nothing of
the sort, my boy; she is invoking vengeance upon you and
me.'

Instantly the whole church glared with light, brighter than
on the brightest summer day. No one present saw any
object, he saw only light—light around him, light within him,
followed by a crash so deafening and bewildering that it was
some minutes before any one present was able to perceive
what had taken place, much less to realize it.

The lightning had struck the tower, glanced from it, bringing part of the spire with it; had rent the west wall of the

church, and had shattered the slab on which, some minutes previously, Foulon and Berthier had been standing.

This was the last effort of the storm; the sky lightened after this explosion, the rain fell with less violence, and gradually ceased.

The congregation left the church. The torrent, which had rushed down the hill, had in some places furrowed the graves and exposed the dead. The grass was laid flat, and much of it was buried in silt. Every wall and eave dripped, and the valley of the Charentonne lay under water.

CHAPTER V.

MATTHIAS ANDRÉ did not join the procession. He had been to mass in the morning, for the Assumption was a day of obligation. And now he sat smoking bad tobacco out of an old brown clay pipe, on the seat before his door, facing due north, towards Bernay; there was a corn-field on his right, cut off from the Isle of Swallows by a rivulet of water—a field he had ploughed whilst his daughter Gabrielle drove the horses, which he had sown with his own hands, and which he had reaped. Gabrielle had bound the sheaves after him, and now the shocks stood in goodly array, waiting to be garnered. They had been waiting thus twelve days. The harvest was late this year, owing to the cold spring. Much corn was down in the country, and the tithe-cart of the monastery had been round to farm after farm, and had come last to his. He did not dare to remove a sheaf till the Abbey had taken its tenth; and after the monks came the revenue officers, taking their twentieth. What the palmer-worm had left, the locust devoured. Now came the feast-day, on which all work ceased, so the good wheat remained a thirteenth day unstacked.

Sullen, with downcast eyes, sat the peasant without his coat, but in his red velvetine waistcoat, drawing long whiffs from his pipe, and blowing them leisurely through his nostrils.

Beside him sat a little wiry brown man, with coarse serge suit of snuff-brown, face and hands, stockings and cap, to match. His eyes were sharp and eager. This was Etienne Percenez, the colporteur.

'You have not joined the procession, Matthias, my friend,' said the little man, filling a pipe.

'For five and forty years I have supplicated God, our Lady, and the Saints, to assist me in my poverty, and the answers to my prayers have been doled out in such scant measure, that I have almost given up prayer,' answered André.

'You must work as well as pray,' quoth the little man, with his pipe in his mouth.

'Do I not work?' asked the peasant-farmer, turning almost fiercely on his friend; 'I work from morning till night, and from the new year to the new year. But what does that avail when the season is bad? A hard winter, a late summer, and then fiery heat from June to August, without a drop of rain. The grass is hardly worth mowing; the clover is short and scanty, and the corn-crops are poor. When we thrash out the wheat, we shall find the greater part of the ear is husk.'

'Things may mend,' said the colporteur; 'they always reach their worst before they right themselves. When we have the States-general, why then we shall see, we shall see !'

. Matthias shrugged his shoulders. 'What did the Notables do for us last year?'

'The Notables are very different from the States-general. The Notables were all chosen out of the nobility—one hundred and forty oppressors met together, to decide how much greater oppression we could be made to bear. But in the States-general, the oppressed will have a voice, and can cry out.'

'The Notables are summoned again.'

'Yes, my friend, they are summoned by Necker, but not to consult on the deficit, but to deliberate on the form of election to the States-general, and on their composition.'

'How great is the deficit?'

'At the end of last year the expenditure surpassed the receipt by one hundred and ten millions, and the deficit now amounts to sixteen hundred and thirty millions. The exchequer cannot borrow money, for Necker has discredited loans by publishing the state of the finances. Do you think the Notables, the princes of blood-royal, the chiefs of the nobility, the clergy and the magistracy, will pay the debt out of their own pockets? No, no; they like to spend and not to pay. Now, the king is going to call together the

States-general. The Notables pay! they saw only in Calonne's scheme the spoliation of the nobility and clergy, that is why they drove Calonne away, and brought in Loménie de Brienne, the bishop, in his stead; they brought a churchman into the ministry to bury the public credit, dead long ago. De Brienne finds that there is no other resource but to take possession of Calonne's plans, and ask the Parliament of Paris to consent to a vast loan. But the Parliament is made up of judges, men grave and economical, and they are indignant at an impost on their lands. Why should they be made to pay for Monsieur the Count d'Artois' fêtes, and the queen's follies? Why consent to a debt ever accumulating, and acquiesce in the ruin of France? Tell me that, my friend Matthias. When the walls crack, we do not paste paper over the rents to hide them—we dig down to the foundations, and we relay them. Perhaps the Parliament of Paris thought this, my André, so they appealed to the States-general. The States-general we shall have; and then, Matthias, we, the oppressed, the tax-payers, the hungry—we shall have a voice, and shall speak out; and, Matthias! we shall make ourselves heard.'

'Go on,' said the farmer; 'tell me the rest.'

'The king declares that he will convoke the States-general.'

'We shall speak out?' asked André, hesitatingly.

'Our own fault, if we do not.'

'But they will punish us if we do.'

'What, Matthias, punish all France! Remember, all France will speak.'

'And we can tell the good king that the tax-gatherers, and the excise, and the nobles, and the abbés, are crushing us? that they are strangling us, that we are dying?'

'Surely.'

'And the tax-gatherers, and the excise, and the nobles, and the abbés, cannot revenge themselves on us for saying that?' André leaned back and laughed. He had not laughed for many years, and his laugh now was not that of gaiety.

'A storm is rising,' said Percenez, pointing over the hill.

'Will the king listen to us?'

'Yes, he will listen.'

'But will he redress our wrong?'

'We shall make him. He has put the means into our hands.'

The first roll of thunder was heard.

'We shall be relieved of the taxes, the *gabelle*, the *corvée*?'

'I do not say that; but the taxes will be levied on all alike.'

'What! will the abbé and the noble pay six sous a livre for salt, and pay the taille?'

'Certainly, we shall make them pay. We pay, so must they.'

Again André leaned back and exploded into laughter, whilst from over the hill the forked lightnings darted, and the thunder boomed.

The two men watched the approach of the tempest. The mutter of the thunder was now unceasing, and the vault was illumined with continuous flashes.

'I must hasten home,' said Etienne Percenez, 'or my old dame will die of fright at being alone in the storm.'

'And I will go in,' said André. But he did not go in at once; he stood in his door. As Percenez crossed the foot-bridge, he heard his friend bellow. Thinking he was calling, the little brown man turned his head; he saw that André was laughing.

'I cannot help it,' roared the peasant; 'to think of the nobles, the intendants, and the abbés, paying taxes!' and he roared again. Then he signed to Percenez.

'The storm is coming on.'

'Very, very fast,' cried the other, beginning to run.

Matthias went inside the house, and seated himself before the fireless hearth, and listened to the wind growling round the eaves. The rain splashed against the little window, glazed with round panes. There was a leak in the roof, and through it the water dribbled upon the floor of the bedroom overhead. It became so dark in the chamber, that Matthias would have lit a candle, had not candles cost money. The water swept down the window in waves; the house trembled at each explosion of the thunder. Going to the door, the peasant saw by the lightning no part of the landscape, for the rain falling in sheets obscured everything. He shut the door; the flashes-dazzled him. Then he threw himself down on a bench, and put his hands to his ears, to shut out the detonations of the thunder, and began to think about Necker and the States-general, and the probability of the nobles and clergy paying taxes, and this idea still presented itself to him in such a novel and ludicrous light, that again he laughed aloud. All at once an idea of another kind struck him, as his hand touched the floor and encountered water. He leaped with a cry to his feet and splashed over the floor. He rushed to the door. The darkness was clearing, and by the returning light, as the rain began to cease, and the surrounding hills to become visible, he observed every lane converted into a torrent of brown fluid; the roads had become watercourses, and were pouring turbid streams through the gates into the fields and meadows. The Charentonne had risen, and was rising every moment. The water was level with the bridge which conducted into his corn-field, and that was above the surface of the ground, for it rested on a small circumvallation raised to protect the field from an overflow. For a moment he gazed at his wheat; then he burst away through the sallows and willow-herbs which grew densely together behind his cottage, drenching himself to the skin, and for ever marring the crimson velvet waistcoat; and struggled through the rising overflow and dripping bushes to the south point of his isle, where usually extended a gravelly spit. That was now submerged; he plunged forward, parting the boughs, and reached a break in the coppice, whence he could look up the valley. At that moment the sun shot from the watery rack overhead, and the bottom of the vale answered with a glare. Its green meadows and yellow corn-fields were covered with a sheet of glistening water, its surface streaked with ripples, pouring relentlessly onwards, and lifting the water-line higher as each broke. Clinging to a poplar, from which the drops shivered about him, up to his middle in water, stood Matthias André, stupefied with despair. Then slowly he turned, and worked his way back.

The few minutes of his absence had wrought a change. His garden was covered, and the flood had dissolved or overleaped the dyke of the corn-field, and was flowing around his shocks of wheat.

Nothing could possibly be done for the preservation of his harvest. He stationed himself on the bench at his door, and watched the water rise, and upset his sheaves, and float them off. Some went down the river, some congregated in an eddy, and spun about; others accumulating behind them, wedged them together, and formed a raft of straw.

'Go!' shouted he to his corn-sheaves; 'sodden and spoiled, I care not if ye remain. Go! now I must starve outright, and Gabrielle—she must starve too.'

Gabrielle!

Instantly it occurred to him that she was at the church, and would need protection and assistance in returning.

He went inside and put on his coat, took a strong pole in his hand, and bent his steps towards the foot-bridge. It was not washed away, but it was under water. He felt for it with the pole, found it, and crossed cautiously. Then he took the road to La Couture. Many people met him. Recovered from their alarm, their tongues were loosened, and they were detailing their impressions of the storm to one another. André accosted a neighbour, and asked him if he had seen Gabrielle. He had not; but supposed she was behind;—many, he said, were still in the churchyard, waiting for the flood to subside.

Some old women, who lived in a cottage only a hundred paces beyond the stile across which André strode into the road from his islet, now came towards him.

'Neighbour Elizabeth, have you seen my child?'

'No, Gaffer André.'

A little farther on he met a girl-friend of Gabrielle's, in

white, with her wreath somewhat faded, and her candle extinguished.

' Josephine ! where is my little one ? '

' I do not know, father André; I have been looking for her amongst the girls of our society, but I could not find her.'

' Do you think she is still in the church ? '

' That may be, but I do not think it is likely; you know that the lightning struck the spire.'

' Was any one killed ? '

' No; but we were all dreadfully frightened.'

Matthias pushed on. He questioned all who passed, but could gain no tidings of Gabrielle. Several, it is true, had seen her in the procession; some had noticed her in the church; but none remembered to have observed her after the fall of the lightning.

André was not, however, alarmed. He thought that possibly his daughter was still in church, praying; probably she was with some friend in a cottage at La Couture. Gabrielle had many acquaintances in that little village, and nothing was more probable than that one of them should have invited the girl home to rest, and take some refreshment, till it was ascertained that the water had sufficiently subsided to permit of her return to the Isle of Swallows.

When he reached La Couture, he went direct to the church. He was shocked to see the havoc created there by the bursting of the storm; workmen were already engaged in filling the graves that had been ploughed up by the currents, and covering the coffins which had been exposed; head-crosses lay prostrate and strewn about, and the sites of some graves had completely disappeared. A knot of people stood at the west end of the church, gazing at the ruin effected by the lightning; the summit of the spire was cloven, a portion leaned outward, the lead was curled up like a ram's horn, and a strip of the metal dissolved by the electric fluid exposed the wooden rafters and framework of the spire. The stroke had then glanced to the apex of the nave gable, thrown down the iron cross surmounting it, had split the wall, shattered the glass, and then had fallen upon and perforated the threshold.

Matthias André entered the church, and sought through its chapels for his daughter. She was not there. No one was in the sacred building.

Then he entered the village, and visited one house after another. No one had tidings to tell of Gabrielle. The father became anxious. He enquired for the girl who had borne the banner of the Blessed Virgin. He asked her about his daughter, who had stood near her, holding the leading ribbon.

She had seen Gabrielle, of course she had, when they entered the church; she sat near her in the aisle during vespers.

When the storm came on, Gabrielle seemed to be greatly alarmed; she must have fainted when the lightning fell, because two gentlemen had carried her out of church.

Whilst the girl spoke, she stood in the doorway of her cottage, holding the trunk of a vine which was trellised over the front of the house and a small open balcony, to which a flight of stairs outside the dwelling gave access.

The girl was the sister of Jean Lebertre, curé of the church, and she kept house for her brother. During the conversation, a priest stepped out of the upper room that opened on to the balcony, and leaning his elbows on the wooden rail, looked down on André.

' What is the matter ? ' he asked.

Matthias turned his face to the questioner. It was Lindet.

' I cannot discover what has become of my daughter, Monsieur le Curé. Pauline, here, asserts that she fainted in church at the great thunder-clap, and that she was carried out by two gentlemen.'

In a moment, Lindet strode down the stairs, and said, looking fixedly with his bright eyes on the girl :

' Answer me, Pauline, who were those gentlemen ? '

' I do not know, monsieur.'

' What were they like ? '

' Ma foi ! I was so dazzled that I hardly know.'

' Are you sure they were gentlemen ? '

'Oh, monsieur! of course they were. One had on a velvet coat.'

'Of what colour?'

'Reddish-brown, I think.'

'And is that all you observed of him?'

'He wore a sword.'

'And the other?'

'The other gentleman was quite old.'

'Did you see the face of the first?'

'I think so.'

'And did you notice any peculiarity? Consider, Pauline.'

'His eyes were strange. The sockets seemed inflamed.'

Lindet beat his hands together; André folded his arms doggedly, and his chin sank on his breast, whilst a cloud settled on his brow.

'That is enough,' he said, in sullen tones; 'I am going home.'

Lindet caught his arm.

'Are you going home, man?'

'Yes, I am tired. I have lost my crops, I have lost my daughter, and, what is worst, I have spoilt my best waistcoat.'

'What! will you not make further enquiries? Your daughter will be ruined,' said Lindet, vehemently.

'Why make further enquiries? I know now where she is.'

'And will you make no effort to recover her?'

'Why should I? I can do nothing. The poor cannot resist the great. The storm came on just now, and the lightning smote yon spire. Why did you not make an effort to protect the spire? Because you were powerless against the bolt of heaven. Well! that is why I make no attempt to protect my child; what could I do to oppose the will of an Intendant, a great man at Court, and very rich?'

'The child will be ruined. Make an attempt to save her.'

André shook his head.

'No attempt I could make would save her; no attempt I could make would save my corn either. I shall go home and wipe my waistcoat; perhaps I may save *that* from utter ruin.'

CHAPTER VI.

THOMAS LINDET was not satisfied. Some effort must be made to rescue the girl. If the father would not move, he must. He started immediately for the château. He was an impetuous man; what he resolved on doing he did at once, as quickly as he could.

In half an hour he was at the Château Malouve.

The house was small and modern. It stood by itself, with the woods for a background, on the slope of the hill, facing south-east. The ground before it fell rapidly away towards the valley, and was in field and pasture. A terrace had been formed in front of the house, with a pond in the midst, and a triton to spout water from a conch-shell. But as the château occupied high ground, and there was little water on a higher level, the triton maintained in wet weather an inconsiderable dribble, which not even the storm of that day could convert into a jet; but in hot weather it was dry.

The château was flanked by two square blocks, the roofs of which were capped with tower-roofs and weathercocks. The body of the building had the high exaggerated roof of

Louis XIV's time, pierced with attic louvres. Every window was provided with emerald green shutters, and the walls being of a chalky whiteness, the house had a gay and smiling appearance.

M. Berthier had a large house in Paris, in which he resided the major portion of the year, only visiting Malouve in the summer for a month or two.

At the back of the château was a yard, one side occupied by stables, another by servants' offices; access to this yard was obtained through an iron gate painted green and gold, set in a lofty iron railing, very gay with paint, very strong and insurmountable, the spikes at the summit being split and contorted so as to form a pretty, but, at the same time, an eminently practical chevaux-de-frise.

As Thomas Lindet approached the gate, two hounds rushed out of their kennels before the coach-house door, and barked furiously. One was chained, but the other, by accident, had got loose, the staple which fastened the chain having given way; and the brute now flew to the gates, dragging the clanking links after him, and leaped against the iron bars.

The shovel hat and black cassock were an unusual sight to the dog, and the costume of the priest excited it to a pitch of fury. First it set its head down, with the paws extended, rolled back its lips exposing the pink gums and white fangs, and growled; then it leaped up the iron rails, as though desirous of scrambling over them, started back, barked furiously; its chained brother assisting vociferously. The eyes of the hound became bloodshot. It flung itself again and again at the gate, it ran along the line of rails, leaping on the dwarf wall in which they were fixed, and slipping instantly off it, scrambling up again, and catching at the bars with its teeth, searching along the whole length for a gap, through which it could force its way; sometimes thrusting its head between the rods, and then, nipped by them, becoming more furious; racing back to the great gates, scraping at the earth under them with intent to burrow a way to get at the priest, but always unsuccessful.

Lindet rang the great bell.

A rakish-looking footman opened the glass doors of the house, looked out and called 'Poulet! Poulet!' to the hound, but it paid no attention, so the footman sauntered to the stable and then to the coach-house, in search of a groom. As he passed the kennel, he kept at some distance from the chained dog, but addressed it in a conciliatory tone—'Eh bien! Pigeon, mon ami! Soyez tranquil, cher Pigeon.' But the Pigeon paid no more attention to this advice than did the Chicken to his calls.

Not being able to find the groom, the footman leisurely visited the garden, and called, not too loudly, 'Gustave!' Gustave, the gardener, having at last turned up, a little conversation ensued between him and Adolphe, the footman, which ended in both appearing in the court, and making towards the hound from opposite quarters, Adolphe keeping unduly in the rear.

Having approached the dog—which by this time had worked itself into a mad rage, apparently quite ungovernable—within such distance as Gustave, on one side, and Adolphe on the other, respectively thought consistent with prudence, 'Come on, my brave fellow, excellent dog, worthy hound, trustiest of chickens!' called Adolphe, 'come, don't be a naughty child. Come, be docile once more, and all shall be forgotten.'

'Come this way, you rascal!' roared Gustave authoritatively, 'come and let me chain you up, or, sapristi! I'll dash your brains out, I'll tear the liver out of you, I'll poke your red eyes out, I'll cut off your bloodthirsty tongue. Sacré! I give you three minutes by the clock, and, ventre gris! if you don't obey me, I'll be the death of you. Come, you insolent, audacious ruffian. Come this moment!'

But the dog paid not the slightest attention to the entreaties of Adolphe and the threats of Gustave.

Lindet folded his arms, and looked on the men contemptuously. They were both afraid of the hound, but pretended that they were not.

'You must give him rein,' said Adolphe; 'he will exhaust himself, and the poulet will be an angel once more.'

'Not for a moment,' roared Gustave; 'suffer that demon an inch of liberty; never! He shall be chained to a block of stone,—he shall not move a paw, he shall not open his mouth, he shall not wink an eye. He shall have no meat for a thousand days, till the devil in him is expelled!'

'I will fetch the dear fellow a sponge-cake. I know he loves sweets, do you not, my Poulet? And above all sweets, sponge-cake; yes, in one moment! Be gentle till my return.'

'I will get my double-weighted whip, with lead in it, and fifty thousand knots in the lash, and nails in each knot, and the nails rusty, and crooked, and spiked. Ah! ha! they will make the devil jump; they will make the devil bleed! Sapristi! I will cut and chop and mangle his accursed hide.'

'Bah!' said a creaky voice.

M. Foulon was there. He had heard the noise, which was indeed deafening, and had descended to the yard from his room. He was in his brown topcoat, and the little wiry pigtail with its huge bow protruded over it like a monstrous dragon-fly that had alighted on his collar.

'Bah! you are three fools,' said he; then, drawing his great gold snuff-box from his breast pocket, he poured some of the dust into his hand, snuffed it up himself, strewing his face with particles of tobacco, then he emptied half that remained in the box into his hand, and walked leisurely up to Poulet.

'Eh bien, Poulet!' said he, with a tone of mingled banter and defiance. The hound turned its head instantly, snarled, cowered, and the old man flung the snuff into its face.

'Now you may go and wink and sneeze your superfluous spirits away, you chicken, you!' Foulon continued; 'now you may go to your darling brother Pigeon, and you may tell him that you do not like snuff, that snuff is expensive, because of the excise; that we have a monopoly of tobacco, and that the revenue gains by tobacco. Do you understand, Poulet? Well, go and tell Pigeon all about it. Here, I will help you.' He caught the end of the chain, and drew the dog after him to its kennel. The brute's attention was engrossed by its own distress, the snuff in its eyes blinded it, the snuff up its nose afflicted it with sneezing, and down its throat choked it.

Foulon called to Gustave for a hammer. Adolphe ran with alacrity to look for one, Gustave brought one. The old man calmly snuffed again, then took the hammer and riveted the staple. 'Now, then, you rascal,' said he, turning abruptly upon the footman; 'do you not see that you have left Monsieur le Curé outside the gate? How thoughtless, how unmannerly!'

Adolphe bounded to the railing and unlocked the iron

gate. Thomas Lindet walked past him, and went straight towards Monsieur Foulon.

The old gentleman removed his hat and bowed courteously; the priest, absorbed in the purpose of his visit, had forgotten these courtesies. He now bent towards Foulon stiffly, and raised his shovel hat.

'You have done me an honour I never hoped to have enjoyed. This day you have made me a proud man; hitherto I have been humble. Beware, my dear curé, or you will blow me up into extravagant conceit.'

Lindet looked at him with surprise.

'You did me the honour of preaching an observation I made within your hearing to my excellent son-in-law, the good Berthier. I did not know that my remarks were so valuable, so deserving of repetition.'

'I have come to speak of quite another matter,' said Lindet.

'Indeed! I thought your visit was one of congratulation to the poor old man, Foulon, on having made a shrewd and pertinent remark at last—at last, after so many years of stupidity, Foulon has given promise of being witty and wise. But allow me to observe that you did not give my remarks exactly as they were made. Not that a word or two is of consequence, but still accuracy is a point—a point, you understand, we revenue farmers learn to appreciate.'

'Sir, I came here——'

'Pardon me, my dear curé, we will stick to the point. The expressions I used were these. "Bah!—" you did not render that interjection in your version. Now, that interjection is expressive; besides, it is characteristic; I always use it. Well, I said, "Bah! if the peasants are hungry, let them browse grass. Wait till I am minister, I will make them eat hay; my horses eat hay." You left out the words "wait till I am minister." Be exact, my good friend; exactness is a virtue.'

'M. Foulon, I have come here——'

'One moment, my good curé; here is a little lesson of Christian forgiveness for you to take home with you. This day you desired to turn loose these hungry peasants on me; this day I have chained up a savage bloodhound that was ravening to be at your throat. Now, what have you to say?'

'I want to know where is the girl Gabrielle André, whom your son-in-law, M. Berthier, and you, M. Foulon, carried out of church this afternoon?'

'Bah! I am ashamed of my good, model curé. He is as bad as we naughty laymen, and runs after pretty girls and petticoats.'

Lindet clenched his hands and teeth.

'She is your charming niece, is she not? Ah, ha! my sad scapegrace of a curé!'

'M. Foulon, I will not have this,' said the priest, passionately; 'this insult is intolerable.'

'Then you can always leave the court,' answered the old man; 'see! the door is open. But we will not quarrel. Come along into the hall and have some refreshment.'

Lindet stamped. The imperturbable coolness and insolence of the old gentleman exasperated his fiery spirit.

'Come, come, cool down,' said Foulon; 'I did not mean to irritate you. Is the girl your relative?'

'No.'

'Of course, then, she is one of your parishioners?'

'No, she is not.'

'Then, pardon me, but I am surprised at your taking so much trouble, and running the risk of being torn to pieces by those villanous dogs, to make enquiries about her. I will answer all your enquiries with the utmost frankness, if you can assure me that her father authorized you to come here and demand her.'

Lindet's face became crimson. He bit his lips with vexation. That he was completely at the old man's mercy, he felt; and he was conscious that the revenue-farmer was making him ridiculous.

'I insist on knowing whether the girl is here. I know her father and her, and I have a perfect right to make these enquiries. I now ask to see her. You dare not keep her here against her father's and her own will.'

'You are the most inconsequent of curés,' exclaimed

Foulon, laughing gently; 'you ask to see her, and you ask at the same time whether she is here. I neither say that she is here, nor that she is not here. As to your seeing her, that is out of the question. If she be not here, how can I show her to you? If she be here, I do not bring the chambermaids into the courtyard to receive pastoral exhortations.'

Whilst speaking with Lindet, the old gentleman had moved slowly towards the gates of the yard: Lindet had followed him, without observing whither he was conducting him. Thus Foulon had drawn him outside the rails. Now, having finished this last insulting speech, spoken with an air of politeness and cordiality, he suddenly turned on his heel, stepped within, slammed and locked the iron gates of the enclosure, leaving Lindet without.

The curé attempted to speak again; but Foulon retired, waving his hand and hat, and bowing courteously. Then he made the circuit of the house, in hopes of finding another door, but was baffled. It is true there was a small door in a high wall, which led into the garden, but it was fastened from within. The terrace was so raised, being built up from the slope, that it could not be reached, and on every other side the château was enclosed by walls and rails.

Lindet wasted a few minutes in making the round of the premises, feeling all the while that he should be at a loss what course to pursue, even if he did penetrate once more within. At last he desisted and retired, satisfied that the only person who could claim access to the girl, with any chance of obtaining it, was her father; and Lindet was convinced that he could not be stimulated to make the attempt.

Had Lindet accompanied André home to les Hirondelles, instead of rashly going himself in quest of Gabrielle, he would have done her a greater service.

When Matthias André returned to les Hirondelles, he found that the water had subsided almost as rapidly as it had risen. The plank-bridge was no longer submerged, and the garden and house were clear. The corn-field presented the appearance of a large pond, but that was because the dyke retained the water; there being no gap in it, there was no drainage.

To his amazement, he saw M. Berthier seated at his door. André scowled at him, but deferentially removed his bonnet.

'Good evening, man!' said the Intendant, nodding, but not rising from his seat. 'Your name is Matthias André, is it not?'

'Yes, monsieur.'

'Ah! your daughter was at the church this afternoon?'

'She was, monsieur, and I cannot find her——'

'I know, I know,' interrupted Berthier; 'I can tell you more about her than you could tell me.'

'Monsieur, I heard that you and your honoured father-in-law

had removed her from the church, when she fainted during the thunderstorm.'

'You heard aright,' said Berthier. 'There was evident danger in remaining within. The spire might fall at any moment and bury those in the church under its ruins. We saw a girl near us fall, and thinking she had been injured by the lightning, we carried her out and transported her to my house. We did not know where was her home. She is now with my wife, Madame Berthier, who has taken great interest in her.'

André remained standing before him with his eyes on the ground. He knew that Berthier was deceiving him, and the Intendant did not care to do more than give his account of what had really taken place, a superficially plausible colour.

'I see your wheat is under water,' said the stout gentleman, pointing with his thumb towards the submerged field, and then, drawing his handkerchief from his pocket, he twisted the corner into a little screw and ran it round the lids of his eyes in succession.

'Yes, monsieur, all my crop is destroyed.'

'And what have you to subsist upon now?'

'Nothing!'

'Can you pay the tax?'

'I do not know.'

'Have you any money laid by, to help you out of your

difficulties? Of course, in prosperous times, you have put aside a nice sum to fall back upon?'

'Monsieur! how can a peasant lay by? The revenue absorbs all his profits, and leaves him barely enough for his subsistence. He may live in times of plenty; in times of scarcity he must die.'

'Then what do you intend doing?'

Matthias shrugged his shoulders.

'All depends on the winter. I have a few potatoes. I must sell this wet corn—it will all be mouldy—for what it will fetch. Ah! if I could have garnered it three days ago, or even yesterday. I shall starve.' He groaned.

'And your daughter will starve with you!'

André answered with a scowl.

'Do you owe any money?'

'Yes; I owe Jacob Maître, the usurer, four hundred crowns.'

'You cannot pay him?'

'No. I have been in debt a long while; he threatens, and I had hoped to pay him off a part this year.'

'And now he must wait?'

'He will not wait.'

'How so?'

'He will put me in prison.'

'And whilst you are in prison, what will your daughter do?'

'God knows!' André bowed his head lower, and began to mutter to himself.

'What are you saying?' asked the Intendant.

'Nothing,' answered the peasant, doggedly.

'But I will hear,' said Berthier.

'I said if God would not provide, then the devil must.'

'Goodman André, that is a somewhat shocking sentiment. Besides, it is not altogether true; there may be a half measure, you know. Now madame, my wife,—a very worthy, pious woman—a little of heaven one way, but a deuced black and ugly one—a little of hell the other way,—she is the person to do it. She has commissioned me to ask you to allow her to retain your child as her servant. That is her message. She wants an active girl to wait upon her, and she has taken a fancy to your daughter. I do not interfere in household matters—understand that—but my good wife, being unable, or disinclined, to come here and see you on the subject, has persuaded me to do her work. I am goodnatured, I am fat; fat people are always goodnatured, so I yield to my wife in everything. I am her slave—her factotum. It is a pity to be goodnatured; one is imposed upon, even by the best of wives.'

André did not speak; through the corner of his eyes he was contemplating his submerged corn-field. He knew still that Berthier was deceiving him, and he was calculating the chances

of the approaching winter. Would his potatoes last, even if
Jacob Maître did not come down upon him? Would not the
usurer seize on everything,—his cow, his horse, his cart, his
potatoes, his bed and furniture, his very clothes?

Berthier took some money out of his pocket, and made
twelve little heaps on the seat beside him.

'What do you say to me, in my generosity, giving you six
months' wage for your girl in advance? This is very reckless
of me, because I really do not know whether she will suit
madame or not. Madame is capricious, she sometimes sends
away a dozen servants in the year. However, as you are in
great distress, and I am constitutionally liberal—fat people are
always liberal—I say, well, I will risk it. You shall have six
months' wage in advance, and the wage is good; it is high,
very high. Count.'

André touched one of the little heaps with his finger, and
upset the silver pieces, that he might reckon their number;
then he counted the heaps, and multiplied the sum in one by
six; then he doubled that.

He would not speak yet.

Berthier substituted gold for some of the silver. Rarely had
gold passed through the peasant's fingers. He took the piece
up in his trembling palm, turned it over, and looked at it
fixedly. His hand shook as with the palsy, and the gold piece
fell from it into the mud. André's brow became beaded with

perspiration. He stooped, and picking it up hastily, went to a pitcher and washed it reverently, and then replaced it on the bench.

' Well, man !' said the Intendant, taking his pocket-handker-chief and spreading it on his knee. It was stained.

Matthias moodily entered the stable, produced a pick, and walked into his potato-croft. Berthier stared after him, uncertain whether by this action he designed in his boorish manner to express his determination to break off the transaction. Matthias began to dig up a row of potatoes, and Berthier saw him take up the roots, and count the tubers on each, and measure them with his eye.

Presently he returned with a lap-full; these he measured in a bushel, and made a rough calculation of the number he should gather from his little croft.

The gloom on his face became deeper. Then he went into the cow-house and remained there a few minutes. After that he entered the little orchard of some dozen trees, and estimated the yield of apples; then he returned to the house, opened the clothes-chest, and threw all the articles of wearing apparel on the table and bench, and made a mental valuation of them. There were some silver ornaments,—round perforated buttons and a brooch that Gabrielle wore on great fêtes; an heirloom. The peasant was unable to estimate their value, so he brought them out to the Intendant, and said, sulkily:

'What are these worth?'

Berthier weighed them in his hand, laughed, and said:

'The value of the silver is trifling—five or eight francs, at the outside.'

The wretched father carried them back into the house.

Presently he came out in a vacillating, uneasy way—his mind hardly made up.

'You promise me that it is only madame who will have anything to do with my Gabrielle?' he said.

'I promise you that! of course I will. She will be with madame night and day; will scarcely be out of her sight.. Will that content you?'

André still mused, and refrained from giving a decided answer.

Just then he caught sight of the money-lender, Jacob Maître, a short-built, red-whiskered and bearded man, with thick overhanging red brows, standing on the dyke, contemplating the havoc made in André's field by the flood.

That sight determined him. He bent, gathered up six of the heaps of silver between his palms, rushed with it into his cottage, and bolted the door.

CHAPTER VII.

AFTER Berthier had seen Gabrielle safely locked up in one of the towers that formed the extremities of his house, at Foulon's advice he had visited the Isle des Hirondelles.

Madame Berthier had returned from the church, and was in her own chamber, at the farther end of the house.

This unhappy woman was Foulon's daughter; towards her he had never shown the least paternal love. Possibly it was not in his nature to exhibit love. She had never been beautiful, having inherited her father's hatchet-face; in addition to her plainness was her colour; her complexion was of an ashen blue-grey, the result of having taken much nitrate of silver medicinally. Her plainness and her complexion being neither of them attractive, Berthier made no pretence of loving her, ' and Foulon did not exact it of him. Berthier, the Intendant, or Sheriff of Paris, a man of humble extraction, being descended from a race of provincial attorneys, had worked his way into prominence and power by his shrewdness and unscrupulousness. He had married Foulon's daughter for the sake of some money she inherited from her mother, but chiefly in hopes of one day possessing his father-in-law's large fortune.

Foulon had begun his career as an intendant of the army, and had amassed immense wealth by victualling badly and charging high. The soldiers fasted or fed on garbage, that Foulon might fatten. He was both a contractor for the army, and one of the commission appointed to watch and check the contractors.

Madame Berthier was naturally a woman of a warm and affectionate disposition; but meeting with no response from her husband or her father, and, through repeated humiliations to which she was subjected by her profligate husband, all that warmth had accumulated into a fire which burned in her bosom, consuming her, disturbing her intellect, and wrecking her constitution.

She was a tall thin woman, dressed wholly in black. Her hair was grey, a silvery grey, contrasting painfully with the blue-grey of her face. Her large hazel eyes were clear and bright, but their brilliance was unnatural, and impressed a stranger with a conviction that they betokened a mental condition on the borders of insanity.

Her sitting-room was quite square, with a window to the east, another to the west, and a third to the south. It was painted yellow throughout; the curtains were of orange damask, and a patch of yellow rug occupied the centre of the polished floor.

In the midst of this chamber sat Madame Berthier, making cat's cradles, her favourite amusement, and one with which she would occupy herself during long hours of loneliness. By constant practice she was able to accomplish all the usual changes with the threads very rapidly, and she was frequently puzzling out new arrangements with an interest and application completely engrossing.

On her shoulders couched a Persian cat, of great size, with long hair. It had been white originally, but Madame Berthier had dyed it saffron; the saffron stains were on her grey hands, as she wrought with her threads. The appearance of the cat was unpleasant, for being by nature an Albino, its eyes were pink, and they seemed unnaturally faint, when contrasted with the vivid colouring of its coat. The cat sat very composedly on her shoulder, with its round yellow face against hers, and its paws dangling on her bosom.

'Be patient, Gabriel,' said she to the cat, who moved uneasily on her shoulder, as his quick ear caught the sound of steps in the corridor. 'We must all acquire patience; it is a heavenly virtue, but it is, oh! so hard to obtain.'

Berthier tapped at the door, opened it, and introduced himself and Gabrielle. •

The cat rose, balancing itself nicely where it had been

reposing, set up its back and tail, stretched itself, and then re-settled.

'Well now, madame,' said Monsieur Berthier; 'making cradles still, I see.'

The lady worked vigorously with her threads, and did not look up or answer her husband.

'Look this way, Madame Plomb.'

She threw up her head, bit her lower lip, and stamped her foot impatiently. As her eye lit on Gabrielle it remained fixed, and her complexion became more deadly.

'I have brought a new servant to attend on you,' continued Berthier. 'Are you listening to me, Madame Plomb?'

Again she stamped, but she would not speak.

'You will take great care of her, my Angel! and you will pay especial regard to her morals, mind that, my Beauty! I have promised her father that she shall be under your charge, and that you shall take care that she be virtuous and pious.'

Madame Berthier would neither look at him, nor speak to him. He knew that she struggled daily with herself to maintain composure, and to restrain her tongue, in his presence, and he amused himself inventing a thousand means of insulting and irritating her, till he had wrought her into frenzy.

'I am sure you will like this new addition to your little

staff,' continued the Intendant, placing his large hands on Gabrielle's shoulders, and thrusting her forward.

The girl cowered under his touch, and an expression of horror and loathing passed across her face. Madame Berthier, whose eyes were fastened on her, saw this and laughed aloud.

'What! not a word for your Zoozoo! Cruel madame, not to look at, or speak to, your own devoted husband.'

No; not a look or a word. The poor wife sought to ignore him. She began diligently to weave her cat's cradles, though her eyes still rested on Gabrielle. Maybe she trembled a little, for the yellow cat mewed fretfully, and shifted its position slightly, then rubbed its head against her blue cheek, as if beseeching not to be disturbed.

'This little mignonne is a gem—a beauty of the first water. You must be very careful of her; such pretty little faces would bewitch half mankind. Look, madame! what a ripe luscious tint, what a rich and glowing complexion, like a peach, is it not? It is flesh—actually warm, soft, rosy flesh; it is not *lead.*'

Madame Berthier uttered a cry at this coarse insult, and covered her face with her hands.

'You should wear gloves, Madame Plomb,' continued her husband, 'and then you might cover your face with some prospect of concealing your complexion. But what do I see?

You have been dyeing your hands with saffron. Actually trying to gild lead.'

The wretched woman threw down her cat, sprang to her feet and fled out of the room, down the corridor which extended the length of the house, from one tower to the other. She was caught almost instantly in her father's arms.

'How now!' exclaimed the old man. 'How is this, my little Imogène? In a pet! one of your little naughty tantrums! Naughty Imogène!'

'My father!' cried the unhappy woman, 'why did you marry me to that man?'

'Tut, tut,' said M. Foulon, disengaging himself from her. 'You ask me that so often, that I am obliged to formularize my answers and your questions into a sort of catechism. How does it begin? Ah! Where were you married? *Answer:* At S. Sulpice. Who by? *Answer:* By Father Mafitte. What were you asked? *Answer:* Wilt thou have this man to thy wedded husband? *Answer:* I will. Now, then, whose doing was it that you were married to Monsieur Berthier? Why, your own, child!'

'Father, take me away.'

'Imogène, what nonsense! May I offer you my arm to conduct you back to your yellow chamber?'

'Father,' she wrung her hands, 'he insults me.'

'He has his little jokes about your complexion, eh? Bah!

you should not be such a baby as to mind his playful banter. He is a boy, gay at heart, and very facetious.'

'It is not that,' moaned the wretched woman; 'he brings young girls here,—and I his wife have to receive them, and—— Oh, father! take me away, or I shall go raging mad!'

'Bah! young men will be young men—not that Berthier is such a youth, either! You must not exact too much. Look at your face in the glass, and then say,—can he find much satisfaction therein? Is it not natural that the butterfly should seek brighter and fairer flowers?'

'You have no heart.'

'Imogène, I never pretended to possess those gushing sentiments which make fools of men and women. I am a man of reason, not sentiment. I have no passions. You never saw me angry, jealous, loving,—never! I think, I reason, I calculate, I do not feel and sympathize; I am all intelligence, not emotion. Bah! Take things coolly. Say to yourself, What is reasonable? Is it reasonable that Berthier should profess ardent passion for me, who am plain and blue? No, it is preposterous; therefore I acquiesce in what is natural.'

'You take his part against me.'

'I take the part of common sense, Imogène. I cannot say to Berthier, be a hypocrite, go against nature. I always accept human nature as I find it, and I never attempt to force the stream into a channel too strait for it.'

Madame Berthier stood looking from side to side distractedly. 'I find no help anywhere!' she moaned.

'Imogène, you have plenty to eat, good wine to drink, first-rate cookery; you employ an accomplished milliner; your rooms are handsomely furnished; you can drive out when it pleases you. What more *can* you want?'

'Love,' answered the poor woman. 'I am always hungry. I am always in pain here,' she pointed to her breast; 'I want, I want, I want, and I never get what I desire.' Then uttering another cry, like that which had escaped her when her husband insulted her, and running along the corridor from side to side, like a bird striving to escape, she beat the walls on this side, then on that, with her hands, uttering at intervals her piercing wail.

Berthier came into the corridor and joined his father-in-law. 'There is nothing more offensive to persons of sentiment than fact,' said Foulon, brushing the tobacco from his nose and cheeks. 'Before fact down go Religion, Poetry, Ethics, Art. People live in a dream-world, which they people with phantoms. Show them that all is a delusion, and they are wretched—they love to be deceived. Bah! I hate sentiment. It is on sentiment that Religion and Morality are based. What is sentiment? On my honour, I cannot tell.'

On reaching the end of the corridor, Madame Berthier stood still, and turning towards her husband and father, she raised her hands, and cried, as she did in church:

'Avenge me on my adversaries!'

Then, becoming calmer, she called:

'Gabriel!' For the cat was standing at her door, and was mewing. The strangely-dyed beast, hearing her call, darted past the two men, and seating itself before her, looked up into her face.

'My faithful Gabriel!' she said. Then with a single bound it reached her shoulder, and placing its fore paws together balanced itself, whilst she walked slowly up the passage. The appearance of the woman in the dusk, in her long black gown and shawl, with her frightful head on one side to give room for the cat to stand comfortably, was wild and ghostly.

She approached her husband and her father slowly. As she passed them, she turned her face towards Foulon, and said: 'I have looked to you for help,' she touched him with her stained finger. 'I have looked to you for help,' she touched Berthier on the breast, turning to him; 'I find none.' Throwing her hand up and pointing out of the window towards the evening star, that glittered above the horizon,—'Queen of heaven, I have looked to you! And,' she continued in a low voice, hoarse with suppressed emotion, 'if she gives me none, I shall seek help in myself.'

'That is sensible, Imogène,' said Foulon; 'one should find resources in one's self.'

'Mind,' she said, sharply; 'I ask for love. If I do not get it, I take revenge.' Then she swept into her room, and shut the door.

Gabrielle was there in her white dress and veil, scarcely less pale than her garments. The roses in her wreath exhaled a strong odour as they faded. She stood where she had been placed by Berthier, nearly in the middle of the room. The evening was rapidly closing in. The sun had set, but through the west window the light from the horizon glimmered.

Madame Berthier threw herself into a seat and looked at Gabrielle.

'Are you a bride?' she asked, in a harsh voice.

'No, madame,' answered the girl, trembling.

'Ah! no. You were one of those in procession to-day.'

'Yes, madame.'

'How came you here?'

'Madame, I think I fainted at the thunderclap, and I remember no more, till I was brought through the yard into this house.'

'Have you been here before?'

'Madame, I have been to the Chateau sometimes with my roses.'

'What roses?'

'The bunches that I sell.'

'Then you are the flower-girl, are you, whom I have seen at the gate sometimes?'

'Yes, madame.'

'Why have you been brought here, do you know?'

Gabrielle burst into tears, threw herself on her knees, and stretching out her hands towards the lady entreated :— 'Oh madame, dear, good madame! send me home, pray let me out of this dreadful house. Madame, I want to go home to my father; pray, good madame, for the love of Our Lady!'·

'Child,' said Berthier's wife, 'are you not here by free choice?'

'Oh no, no!' cried Gabrielle. 'Only let me go, that I may run home.'

'Where do you live?'

'At Les Hirondelles.'

'What is your name?'

'Gabrielle André.'

'Gabrielle?'

'Yes, madame.'

The strange woman uttered a scream of joy; caught her cat in her hands, and held it up before the girl.

'See, see!' she said; 'this is Gabriel, my own precious Gabriel!'

She softened towards the poor child at once.

'Come nearer,' she said. 'What have you let fall? Ah!
your taper. They brought that with you, did they?'

'Madame, I think I had it fast in my hand.'

'Wait,' said the lady. She struck a light, and kindled the
taper, which Gabrielle had raised from the floor.

. 'Just so,' continued she; 'hold the light before you, and
remain kneeling, that I may see your face; but do not kneel
to me; see! turn yonder, towards the western sky, and the
dying light, and the evening star.'

Gabrielle slightly shifted her position, too frightened to do
anything except obey mechanically.

'You are very pretty,' said Madame Berthier. 'How very
beautiful you are! Do you know that?'

'Madame!' Gabrielle was too much alarmed to colour.

'Now, tell me, do you know M. Berthier?'

'Oh, madame!' the girl said, with a sob, as her tears began
to flow; 'I dread him most of all. He frightens me. He is
wicked; he pursues me with his eyes. Father had just promised that I should never come to this house again, because,
because——' she was interrupted by her tears.

'Go on, Gabrielle.'

'Because he ran after me in the forest, and the curé saved
me from him, just as he caught me up.'

'You do not like Berthier; I saw it in your face.'

'Oh, madame! how could I?'

The lady laughed a little, chuckling to herself.   Presently she addressed Gabrielle again.

' Do you know me ? '

' No, madame.'

' Do you know my name ? '

' You are called Madame Plomb,' said Gabrielle, hesitatingly.

The woman stamped passionately on the floor, and jerked the yellow cat off her shoulder.

' Who told you that ?   Why do you call me that ? '

' Oh, madame !   I am so sorry, but I heard Monsieur Berthier address you by that name.   I meant no offence.'

' Listen to me, child.'   The lady drew her chair towards Gabrielle.   ' Give me your light.'   She snatched the taper from her trembling hand, and waved it before her face.   ' Look on me,' she said ; ' yes, look, look.   Now you know why they call me the Leaden ! ' · She blew out the candle, and continued : ' It is only those who hate me who call me by that name ; only those, remember, whom I hate.   Beware how you call me that again.'

She leaned back, and remained silent for some minutes. Gabrielle's tears flowed fast, and she sobbed heavily.   She was not only frightened, but weary and faint, and sick at heart.

' Shall I protect you ? ' asked the lady, at length.

' Madame ! I pray you,' pleaded Gabrielle, through her tears.

'Then I will. He shall not touch you. You shall sleep in my little ante-room.'

'May I not go home?'

'Alas! poor child, how can you? The gates and doors are locked. The walls are high; and if you scaled the walls, the bloodhounds would be after you. Perhaps you may go home soon, but not now; you cannot now!'

After another pause, she said:

'Gabrielle, stand up.'

The girl instantly rose.

'Gabriel, Gabrielle, my cat and you! I love my cat, why not you? Will you kiss me?'

Passionately she caught the girl to her bosom, and kissed her brow and lips and cheek. Then laughing, she said:

'Yes! Gabrielle, you must be here awhile, and you shall hold the threads, and help to make cat's cradles.'

CHAPTER VIII.

THE moon, in her first quarter, hung in a cloudless sky over the valley of the Charentonne, reflected from every patch and pool of water. The poplars, like frosted silver, cast black shadows over the white ground. The frogs were clamorous, for their domain had been unexpectedly extended.

Thomas Lindet, in his attic, was putting together a few clothes into a bundle, to take with him to Évreux, as he was about to start next morning, after the first mass at six. He occupied two rooms in a small cottage opposite the church. It was an old house, in plaster and timber, with a thatched roof, and consisted of a ground-floor and an upper storey. The ground-floor was occupied by an old woman, and the priest tenanted the rooms above. His sitting-room, in which he was making up his bundle, was clean; the walls were laden with whitewash, as was also the sloping ceiling. The window was covered with a blue-and-white striped curtain of bed-ticking; the chairs were of wood, unpolished, with wooden seats. Over the chimney-piece were a crucifix and two little prints, one of Jean Jacques Rousseau, the other of S. Jerome.

His small library occupied a few deal shelves on one side of the
fireplace. Besides his breviary, there were few books in binding,
except an old copy of Atto of Vercellæ on the 'Sufferings
and Persecutions of the Church,' and a Geoffrey of Vendôme
on 'Investitures.' But there were many pamphlets and pole-
mical tracts, such as were circulated at that time in France,
and in paper covers, torn and dirty, were Montesquieu's
'Esprit des Lois,' and Rousseau's 'Emile.'

Having completed his preparations, the priest blew out his
candle, drew the curtain, and looked out of his window, pierced
through the thatch. The church of S. Cross was exactly opposite, on the other side of the small square, and the moon
brought its sculpture into relief. The gothic tower, surmounted by an ugly bulbous cap, cut the clear grey sky; the
delicate tracery of the windows stood out like white lace
against the gloom of the bell-chamber.

The west front had been remodelled in 1724, and, though
Lindet, with the taste of the period, admired it, no one at the
present day would approve of the stiff Italian pedimented
doorway, with its four pillars incrusted in the wall, or of the
niche in the same style, containing the effigy of the Empress
Helena bearing the cross, which intrudes upon the elegant
gothic west window.

After the excitement of the day, a reaction had set in, and
Lindet felt dispirited, and disposed to question the judicious-

ness of his purpose. He leaned on the window-sill listening
to the trill of the frogs, sweetened by distance, and to the
throbbing of the clock in the tower. From where he stood,
he could see the rosy glimmer of the sanctuary lamp, through
the west window of the church. At this window, looking
towards the light which burned before the Host, he was wont
every evening to say his prayers, before retiring to rest.

He put his delicate hands together. The mechanism of
the clock whirred, and then midnight struck. The notes
boomed over the sleeping town, and lost themselves among
the wooded hills. All at once Lindet's mind turned to the
poor child for whose preservation he had laboured ineffectually
that day. Then, fervently, he prayed for her.

She was seated at the window in Madame Plomb's ante-
chamber, fast asleep, with her head on her hands. The
window was wide open, and the shutters were back, so that
the moon and air entered, and made the chamber light and
balmy.

About nine o'clock, the cook had been to madame's room
to tell Gabrielle that she was to sleep with her at the other end
of the house; but Madame Berthier, full of violence, had struck
and driven the woman out of the room, and she had retired,
very angry, and threatening to tell 'Monsieur.' The woman
had been as good as her word; but Berthier and Foulon being
together in the billiard-room playing, she had not ventured

to interrupt them till they left, which was at midnight. The cook was very angry, and, like an insulted servant, threatened to leave the house.

'Ah! so so!' exclaimed Berthier. 'We shall see. You were right to obey my orders. Gustave! come here; follow me, Antoinette; the girl shall be removed immediately, awake or asleep, by gentleness or by force.'

The silver light struck across the face of the sleeping girl, still wet with tears, and streaked the floor. An acacia intercepted some of the light, and as a light wind stirred, it produced an uneasy shiver over the floor. A leaf, caught in a cobweb, pattered timidly against one of the window-panes. A ghost-moth fluttered about the room, its white wings gleaming in the moonlight, as it swerved and wheeled, while its shadow swerved and wheeled in rhythm, on the sheet of Gabrielle's couch, as though there were two moths, one white, the other black, dancing up and down before one another. The shadows of the acacia foliage made faces on the floor. Dark profiles, hatchet-shaped, with glistening eyes and mouths that opened and shut, faces of old women munching silently, silhouettes of demons butting with their horns, or nodding, as though they would say,—Wait, wait, wait! We shall see!

The white veil of the sleeping girl lay on the floor, in a line. The flickering lights crossed it, and the shadows of the leaves resembled black flat insects, and long slugs, scrambling over

it, in a mad race.   The foliage of the acacia whispered, and
·the pines of the forest close by hummed as the wind stirred
their myriad vibrating spines.   The air laden with the fragrance
of the resin, was not balmy only, but warm as well.   An owl
in the woods called at intervals to-whoo! and waited, expecting
an answer, then called again.   Then the night-hawk screeched,
and fluttered among the trees.   In the garden-plots whole
colonies of crickets chirped a long quivering song in a thousand parts, perfectly harmonized, all night long, with a rapidity
of execution perfectly amazing.

From Bernay sounded distant, yet distinct, the chime of
midnight.   At the same moment the hounds in the yard became restless, and gave tongue spasmodically.   The girl sighed
in sleep, and turned her head from the light; then she woke,
started up, and uttered a scream.   The door of the room was
open, and Berthier stood in it, looking at her, with the cook
and Gustave in the background.   At the same moment,
a black figure glided from behind the window-curtains, and
stood between him and her.

'Sacré! Madame Plomb, you are up late,' observed the
Intendant, advancing into the chamber, and shutting the door
behind him upon the two servants.   'May I trouble you,
Madame Plomb, to retire to your couch?'   He stepped
towards her.

The woman drew herself up, raised her arm, and the moon flashed along a slender steel blade she brandished.

' Nonsense, my charmer ! ' said Berthier; ' no acting with me. Put down that little toy and begone.'

' Stop ! ' she exclaimed. ' Do you see that veil there ; there, beast, there on the floor ? '

' Perfectly well, my angel.'

' Pass over it, if you dare.'

' I dare ! ' he said scornfully, but without advancing.

' If your foot transgresses that limit, I swear, beast ! it will be your death.'

He looked at her; the moon was on her blue-grey face, and she looked at him. Her countenance was terrible: in that light, it was like the face of a fiend.

' You are a devil,' he said.

' You have made me one,' she answered.

Deadly hatred glared out of her wild black eyes; there was resolution in the set lips and hard brow, and Berthier felt that what his wife threatened, that she would execute. He could not endure the flash and glitter of her eye-balls, and he lowered his.

' I hate you,' she muttered; ' I hate you, beast ! Do you think I should shrink from *your* blood ? Is your blood so dear to me ? Should I shrink from your corpse—from your dead face ? I have only seen the living one, and that is to me so odious, that I long to see the dead one; it is sure to be more pleasant. Those red inflamed eyes of yours, are they so bewitching that I should not wish to close them for ever? Those lips, which I have never kissed, beast! I promise to kiss them one day. I promise it, remember. They shall be stiff and cold then. That shall be my one and only kiss.'

The hounds barked furiously without, so furiously that they disturbed the house. Adolphe opened his window and called: 'Be quiet, my children; be good boys, there! Pigeon and Poulet!'

Gustave roared from the window of the corridor: 'A thousand devils! shall I not murder you to-morrow, if you are not quiet this instant?'

The acacia creaked and crackled.

Berthier moved towards the window, he was determined to disarm his wife, if possible.

'Where are you going?' she asked, sharply.

'I am going to look out, and see why the dogs are so furious.'

'You cannot see into the yard from this window.'

'No, but I can see if anyone is without.' Next moment— 'Imogène! I believe that there must be some one.'

She lowered her knife, with the fickleness of her disorder; the idea distracted her attention.

'Where?'

'Come and look.'

She stepped towards the window. Instantly, quick as thought, he struck her wrist, and sent the knife flying from her grasp, across the room.

Gabrielle in an agony of terror cried, 'My father! Oh, my father!'

Madame Berthier uttered a moan of pain and rage. Her husband would have grappled with her at once, but that something whizzed in at the open window, and struck him in the eye with such force that he staggered backward, and the blood burst from the lid and streamed over his cheek.

Madame Berthier recovered her knife, and threatening him with it, drove him, blinded with pain and blood, out of the room.

Who can describe the horror of conscience to which Matthias André was a prey that night? He remained after the departure of Berthier, for some hours half stupefied, looking at the money which he held in his hand; then he tied it up in a piece of rag, and placed it in his bosom; but it was too heavy there, it seemed to weigh him down, so he fastened it to the belt of his blouse, which he now put on. To distract his mind, he began to replace in the boxes the clothes he had drawn from them, but, as he huddled them in, unfolded, they would not all go in. In the dusk, the garments which were not thus disposed of looked like bodies of human beings waiting to be buried. He threw out all the clothes from the trunks again, and began to fold them, but he did this work clumsily, and there remained still one of Gabrielle's dresses uncoffered. The sight of this distressed him, it reminded him of his daughter too painfully, so he hid it under the table. Then he could not resist the desire to peer at it where it lay, and the fancy came upon him that she lay there dead, and that he had killed her; so he fled up the ladder into his loft, and cast himself upon his bed.

But there was no rest there. The transactions of that evening haunted him. He tried to calculate what had best be done with the money; but no! all he could think of was that this was the price of his child's honour and happiness.

Remembering that he had not taken any supper, he descended the ladder and sought in the dark for a potato pasty; but when he had found it he could not eat it, for he considered that it had been made by *her* fingers. He tried to uncork a bottle of wine, but could not find the screw, so he broke the neck, and drank from it thus; the broken glass cut his lips, for his hand shook. Gabrielle's old gown under the table he could not see, it was too dark, but he was constrained by a frenzied curiosity to creep towards it, and feel if it were there. Yes; he felt it, and he shrank from the touch.

The moon shone in at his bed-room window. The light distressed him, when he returned to his couch; so he tried to block up the window by erecting his coat against it, supported by a pitchfork and a broom. It remained thus for just five minutes, and then the structure gave way, and the moonlight flowed in again.

André could bear the house no longer. He again descended the ladder, stole past the table, and opening his door, went outside. He took the path across the foot-bridge and entered the forest. He resolved to ascend the hill, and see the outside of the château in which lay his child. The way was dark, the shadows of the pines and beech-trees obscured it, but the wretched man knew it well, and he walked along it, trembling with fear. He heard voices in the forest, he saw faces peeping from behind the tree-boles. The rustle of birds in the pine-tops made him start; but he held on his way.

When he reached the castle Malouve, he stood still. His brow was dripping. The clock of Bernay parish church struck twelve. At the same time the dogs scented him, and began to bark.

The unhappy father prowled round the building, looking up at every window, his every limb shaking with apprehension.

Suddenly, from an open casement he heard a cry. He knew the tone of that voice. The cry pierced his heart.

He ran to the foot of the building which rose from the sward at this spot, and looked up at the window. An acacia-tree stood at a little distance from the wall, and he proceeded to scramble up it. The trunk was smooth, and presented no foot-hold. He was a clumsy man, and could not mount well; the branches were brittle and broke with him. He heard voices in the chamber whence his daughter's cry had reached him, he grappled with the tree and worked himself up a little way with his knees. The leaves shook above him as though the acacia responded to every pulsation of his heart.

'Father! Oh, my father!'

That call to him—it seemed denunciatory, reproachful—burst upon his ear. He tore the money from his belt, and with all his force, he hurled it through the window; then he slid down the tree and fled.

He fled, but the cry pursued him; it echoed from every wall of the château. He heard it in the bay of the bloodhounds; it came to him from the dark aisles of the forest, the wind swept it after him; the owl caught it up and towhoo'd it, the night-hawk screamed it.

He put his hands to his ears to shut it out. But the cry was within him, and it echoed through and through and through him—

'Father! Oh, my father!'

The cry of a child betrayed by its own parent,—the cry

of a slave sold by its own father,—the cry of a soul given up to devils by him who had given it being,—the cry of a loving heart against him it had loved, against him for whom the hands had worked gladly, the feet tripped nimbly, the lips smiled sweetly, and the eyes twinkled blithely—

'Father! Oh, my father!'

As he sprang over the stile, as he raced to the foot-bridge, as he traversed it, from the white face that glared up at him from the water, from the rustling reeds, from the soughing willows, from his own white and black home as he reached it —

'Father! Oh, my father!'

In his horror and despair he threw himself in at the door, and ran towards the ladder. He scrambled up it; and drawing it up after him fastened a rope that lay coiled on his floor to it, and he noosed the other end about his neck, and he crawled to the hole in the floor through which he had mounted and drawn the ladder, and the cry came up to him from below.

He leaped towards it, and so sought to silence it.

CHAPTER IX.

ALL Evreux was out of doors, as Thomas Lindet, travel-soiled and weary, entered the city. The double avenue of chestnuts before the church and seminary of S. Taurin was thronged with people, and a large triumphal arch spanned the road just beyond the square, the sides adorned with pilasters of gilt paper and banks of flowers, and the summit crowned with a banner emblazoned with the lilies of France. In the tympanum of the arch was a niche lined with crimson cloth destined to contain a statue of S. Louis, lent for the occasion by the superior of the seminary. The raising of the pious king to his destined position was an operation which engaged all eyes, and provided conversation for all tongues.

It is wonderful how much noise and commotion attends the execution of a very simple performance in France. Every spectator is by the fact of his presence constituted an adviser, and those engaged on the work which attracts observation harangue and expostulate and protest at the top of their voices.

Those whose task it was to translate S. Louis from the

ground to his elevated pedestal, proceeded with their duty in a somewhat clumsy and unworkmanlike manner. A pulley had been erected at the apex of the gable above the arch, and a cord ran over it into the midst of the crowd which pulled promiscuously and with varying force at the rope. The other end of the rope was attached to the neck of the monarch, and as he was raised he dangled in the centre of the archway, much more like a felon undergoing the extreme penalty of the law, than a canonized saint. In the meanwhile, two vociferous men in blue blouses and trowsers, half way up two ladders, were supposed to steady the king, but on account of the jerky manner in which the crowd hauled at the rope, they were unable to achieve their object, and they vented their displeasure in oaths. All at once there was a crash. The head had separated from the body—the statue was in plaster; and first down fell the trunk and then the crowned head. The catastrophe caused a sudden silence to fall on the multitude, but it was soon broken by execrations and invocations of 'mille diables.' Then a general rush was made to inspect the remains of the decapitated king.

'There was absolutely no piece of wood or wire to keep head and trunk together!' exclaimed one of the workmen, elevating the fragment of head. 'Of course it broke off. Who ever heard of a plaster cast without a nucleus of solid wood or iron in the middle!'

'Out of the way! make room,' shouted a coachman, cracking his whip; and the crowd started aside to allow a handsome lumbering coach to roll by, and pass under the triumphal arch. Two heads were protruded from the windows, to see what caused the commotion and throng; and Lindet, happening to look in that direction, saw the faces of Foulon and Berthier.

'Why are all these preparations being made?' asked Lindet of a shopman near him.

'Ah!' exclaimed the man; 'don't you know that Monsieur the Prince is coming?'

Lindet pushed up the street, passed the Palais de Justice, a handsome, massive Italian building, and walked straight to the bishop's palace. Having reached Évreux, he would do his business and leave it.

The gate to the palace was decorated with evergreens and banners, the arms above the archway had been re-gilt and re-coloured; S. Sebastian was very pink, exuded very red blood from his wounds, and the lion of monseigneur ramped in a refulgent new coat of gold leaf.

The wooden doors were wide open, displaying the interior of the quadrangle; a long strip of crimson carpet conducted from the gate over the pavement to the principal entrance to the house; footmen in episcopal purple liveries, their hair powdered, skipped hither and thither.

Lindet walked straight into the court, and asked to see the bishop.

'You must wait in the office, yonder,' said the servant he addressed, with impatience.

'Please to tell the bishop that I desire to see him.'

'You're mighty imperious. Perhaps he may not want to see you.'

'Never mind. Tell him that Thomas Lindet, curé of Bernay, has walked to Évreux on purpose to see him, and see him he must.'

'Well, well, sit down in the office.'

Lindet entered the little room, and waited. He waited an hour, and no bishop came; he rang a bell, but it was not answered; then he stepped out into the court, and catching a servant by the arm, insisted on his message being conveyed to monseigneur.

'This is a mighty inconvenient time,' said the man; 'don't you know that the Prince is expected?'

'But not here.'

'Yes, here; he stays at the palace.'

Lindet stepped back in astonishment.

'What does the priest want?' asked the butler, who was passing at that moment.

'I have come here desiring to speak with monseigneur. I have come from Bernay on purpose.'

'Get along with you,' said the butler; 'what do you mean by intruding at this time? Don't you know that his lordship only sees the parsons on fixed days and hours? Get out of the court at once, you are in the way here.'

'I shall not go,' said the curé, indignantly; 'I shall not move from this spot till my message has been taken to the bishop. He may be just as indisposed to receive me to-morrow as to-day.'

'Ay! he won't see any of you fellows till the latter end of next week. So now be off!'

'What is the matter?' asked a voice from an upper window. 'Chopin, who is that?'

The butler and the priest looked up. At an open window stood Monseigneur de Narbonne-Lara, in a bran-new violet cassock and tippet, his gold pectoral cross rubbed up, his stock very stiff, and his dark hair brushed and frizzled. 'What is all this disturbance about, Chopin, ay?'

'Monseigneur!' replied the butler, bowing to the apparition, 'here is a curé from Bernay, who persists that he must see your lordship.'

'Tell him, Chopin, that I am engaged, and that this is not the proper day.'

'Monseigneur,' began the butler, again bowing; but Lindet interrupted him with—

'I want to speak for one moment to your lordship.'

'Who are you ?'

'I am Thomas Lindet, curé of S. Cross.'

'Oh! indeed. Friday week, at 2 P.M.,' said the bishop, shutting the window and turning away.

Lindet remained looking after him. The bishop stood a moment near the window, with his back towards the light, meditating; then he turned again, opened the casement, and called—

'Chopin, you may give him a glass of cider, and then send him off.'

'Yes, monseigneur.'

He slammed the window, and walked away.

Lindet had much trouble in finding an inn which had a spare bed to let. The Grand Cerf was full and overflowing; the Cheval Blanc, nearly opposite, seemed to be bursting out at the windows, for they were full of heads protruded to a perilous distance, gazing up the Paris road; the Golden Ball at last offered an attic bed, which Lindet was glad to secure. This little inn stood in the Belfry Square, a market-place, named after an elegant tower containing a clock and curfew bell, in the purest Gothic of the fourteenth century, surmounted by a spire of delicate lead tracing, in the same style as that on the central tower of the Cathedral, but smaller considerably. The square was tolerably free from people, as monsieur was not expected to pass through it, and the comparative quiet was acceptable to the weary priest. After having taken some refreshment, and rested himself for an hour on his bed, his restless, excited spirit drove him forth into the street.

The bells of the Cathedral and S. Taurin were clanging and jingling, flags fluttered from every tower and spire, musketry rattled, men shouted, a band played the Descent of Mars, as Lindet issued from a narrow street upon the square before the Cathedral and saw that it was crowded, that a current was flowing in the midst of that concourse, and that the current bore flags and banners, and followed the music. The priest, mounting upon a kerbstone, saw that the civic procession was conducting the Prince to the episcopal palace. He saw the town gilds pass, then the confraternities or clubs, in their short loose cassocks, knee-breeches, and caps, with sashes tied across their breasts, emblazoned with their insignia. Three principal confraternities appeared—that of Évreux, preceded by a banner figured with S. Sebastian, that of S. Michael, and that of S. Louis. A band of Swiss soldiers in red uniform followed, and in the midst of these guards rolled the gaily-painted carriage of Louis-Stanislas-Xavier, son of France. Lindet saw a portly young man, of good-humoured but stolid appearance, bowing acknowledgment of the acclamations which greeted him. That was the Prince. Lindet saw nothing of the reception at the gate, presided over by the ramping lion

and the wounded saint; he could hear a pompous voice reading, and he knew that monseigneur was delivering an address
from the Clergy to the Royal Duke, but what was said, how
many titles were rehearsed, how much flattery was lavished,
how many expressions of devotion and respect were employed—all this was lost in the buzz of the crowd.

What was he to do? He could not wait for more than
a week, as required by the bishop. The journey had cost
him more than he could well afford, and the expense of the
inn at Évreux would far exceed what his purse contained,
if he deducted the twenty-five livres due to the bishop. He
had determined not to give the money to the *officiel*, but to
the prelate himself, and to explain to him the reason of his
having broken the requirements of the Church.

Entering the Cathedral, he seated himself in the aisle, where
he could be alone and in quiet, to form a plan for seeing
the bishop and coming to an explanation with him; but he
could not hit upon any to his mind. He walked round
the church, admiring its height, and the splendour of its
glass. In the Lady Chapel he stood, and his lip curled
with a smile as he observed, in one of the north windows,
a bishop vested in cope and mitre, holding the pastoral staff
in one hand, whilst with the other he threw open the cope
to grasp a sword girded at his side, and exposed a suit of
knightly armour, in which he was entirely enveloped. .

'Ah!' said Lindet to himself, 'when these panes were pictured it was as now, the shepherd's garb invested the wolf. And what marvel! If the Church may not appoint her own pastors, how can she be properly shepherded? "Qui præfuturus est omnibus ab omnibus eligatur," said S. Leo.'

The priest lingered on till late in the church. He was weary, and the Cathedral was more attractive than the little bedroom at the 'Golden Ball.' He took a chair in the chapel of S. Vincent, and was soon asleep.

It was afternoon when the prince arrived, and the afternoon rapidly waned into evening dusk, and the dusk changed to dark.

At nine, the Cathedral doors were locked, after a sacristan had made a hasty perambulation of the church to see that it was empty. Lindet did not hear his call, as he walked down the aisles crying 'All out!' and the verger did not observe the slumbering priest in the side chapel. Thus it happened that the curé was locked up in the church.

It was night when he awoke; slowly his consciousness returned, and with it the recollection of where he was. He was much refreshed. The walk of many miles every day in hot sun had worn him out, and this quiet nap in the cool minster had revived him.

The moon glittered through the windows, and carpeted the aisle floors.

He rose from his chair, and leaving the chapel, bent his knee for a moment before the High Altar, where the lamp hung as a crimson star, and tried the north transept door which opened into the square. It was locked. He then sought the west doors, but found them also fast. Returning down the south nave aisle, he saw lights from without reflected through the windows on the groined roof, and strains of instrumental music were wafted in.

Near the south transept he found a small door: it was the bishop's private entrance. Lindet pushed it, and the door yielded. He found himself in a small cloister leading to the palace. The lights were brighter, and the music louder. They issued from the palace garden, of which the priest obtained a full view.

The garden occupied the whole south side of the Cathedral, and was well laid out in swath and flowers. A beautiful avenue of limes extended the whole length of the garden, above the broad moat which separated the palace precincts on the south from the city. This moat has been turned into a kitchen-garden in our own day, but in that of which we are writing it was full of water. The avenue, therefore, formed a terrace above a broad belt of water, not stagnant, as in many moats, but kept fresh by a stream flowing through it.

The modern traveller visiting Évreux, should on no account

fail·to walk on the city side of this old moat, for from it he
will obtain the most striking view of the magnificent Cathedral
and the ancient picturesque palace, rising above the lime-trees.
A couple of lines of young trees have been planted, and the
half-street turned into a boulevard; but in 1788, this side of
the moat was bare of trees, and a row of tall houses faced
the water, with only a paved road between, and a dwarf
wall pierced at intervals with openings to steps that descended to the moat, where all day long women soaped
and beat dirty clothes, with much diligence, and more
noise.

Lindet found the garden brilliantly illuminated. Lamps
were affixed to the old walls of the Cathedral, and traced
some of its most prominent features with lines of coloured
fire. The statues which, in imitation of Versailles, the bishop
had set up in his flower-garden, held lanterns. A pond of
gold-fish, in the centre of the sward, surrounded a vase, in
which burned strontian and spirits of wine, casting a red
glare into the water, and producing a wild contrast to the
calm white moonlight that lay in flakes upon the gravelled
walks.

The avenue was, however, the centre of light. In it tables
were laid, brilliant with candelabra supporting wax candles,
and with coloured lanthorns slung between the trees, and
lamps attached to every trunk. At intervals also were sus-

pended brass rings, sustaining twenty candles. Wreaths of artificial flowers, banners, mirrors, statues holding lights, transparencies, occupied every conceivable spot and space, and transformed the quiet old lime avenue into a fairy-land palace.

The tables were laden with exquisite viands in silver, and glittered with metal and glass.

The higher end of the tables was towards the west, and a daïs, crimson carpeted, raised a step above the soil, supported the board at which sat the prince, the bishop, and all the most illustrious of the guests.

On the opposite side of the moat, a crowd of hungry women and children strained their eyes to see the nobles and high clergy eat and drink, which was only next best to themselves eating.

'So we are going to have the States-general, after all,' said the Duke de la Rochefoucauld, a noble-looking man, with a frank, open countenance, full of light and dignity.

'Yes,' answered the prince; 'His Majesty cannot withdraw his summons.'

'You speak as if he wished to do so,' said M. de la Rochefoucauld.

'I am not privy to his wishes,' answered Louis Stanislas with a smile on his heavy face; 'let us not talk of politics, they are dull and dispiriting subjects.' Then, turning to the bishop, he said: 'Monseigneur, I think you could hardly choose a more delightful retreat than this of yours. To my taste, it is charming. You are really well off to have such a capital palace and such delightful gardens. If I were you, nothing would induce me to change them. Why, look at the Archbishop of Rouen——By the way, how is the arch-bishop?' he turned to the duke, whose kinsman the prelate was. 'I heard he had been seriously unwell.'

The Duke de la Rochefoucauld assured 'monsieur' that the cardinal was much better; in fact, almost well.

'That is right,' said the prince. Then again addressing his host, he continued: 'No, I assure you, nothing in the world would induce me, were I you, my Lord Bishop, to desert this see for another.'

'I am hardly likely to have the chance put in my way,' said the bishop.

'And then,' pursued Louis, 'who, having once built his nest in charming Normandy, would fly to other climes? You are a brave Norman by birth, I believe, monseigneur?' Louis had an unfortunate nack of getting upon awkward subjects. This arose from no desire of causing annoyance, but from sheer obtuseness. He resembled his brother the King in being utterly dull, with neither wit nor vice to relieve the monotony of a thoroughly prosaic character.

'No, your grace,' answered the bishop, slightly reddening,

'I belong to a Navarre family. The family castle of Lara is in Spain. The name Lara is territorial, and was adopted on the family receiving the Spanish estates and Castle——'

'Excuse me,' said the prince, interrupting him; 'but I think, my dear Lord, we have a ghost before us.'

The bishop looked up from his plate, on which his eyes had rested whilst narrating the family history, and saw immediately opposite him, standing below the daïs, in ragged cassock, with the buttons worn through their cloth covers, with dusty shoes, and with a pale, eager face quivering with feeling, Thomas Lindet, curé of S. Cross at Bernay.

The bishop was too much astonished to speak. He stared at the priest, as though he would stare him down. The guests looked round almost as much surprised as the prince or the bishop, so utterly incongruous was the apparition with the place. The look, full of pain, stern and passionate, contrasted terribly with the faces of the banqueters, creased with laughter. The pale complexion, speaking too plainly of want and hunger—why did that look upon them as they sat at tables groaning under viands and wines of the most costly description? The dress, so ragged and dusty, was quite out of place amongst silks and velvets. The bishop waved his hand with dignity, and his episcopal ring glittered in the lights as he did so. But Lindet did not move. Then, addressing his butler over the back of his chair, the prelate said: 'Chopin, tell the fellow to go quietly. If he is hungry, take him into the servants' hall and give him some supper.'

Lindet put his hand into his bosom, and drew forth a little moleskin purse,—a little rude purse, made by one of the acolytes of Bernay out of the skins of the small creatures he had snared, and given as a mark of affection to his priest. He emptied the contents of this purse into his shaking palm, and with agitated fingers, he counted twenty-five livres, put the rest—it was very little—back into the mole-skin bag; and then, holding the money, he mounted the daïs.

'Go down, sir, go down!' said the indignant prelate; and several footmen rushed to the priest to remove him.

'Leave me alone,' said Lindet, thrusting the servants off; 'I have business to transact with my diocesan.'

'What do you want?' asked the bishop, his red face turning purple with wrath and insulted pride; 'get you gone, and see me at proper times and in proper places!'

'Monseigneur,' answered Lindet in a clear voice, 'I have walked through dust and heat from Bernay to speak to you, and I am told I cannot see you for a whole week.'

'Go, go!' said the bishop; 'I do not wish to have an unpleasant scene, and to order you to be dragged from my table. Go quietly. I will see you to-morrow.'

'No,' Lindet answered; 'you would not receive me privately this afternoon, now you shall receive me publicly, whether the time suits or not. You have fined me, unheard, for not having lit my sanctuary-lamp. I had neither oil nor money; therefore I must pay you a heavy fine. There is the money—' he leaned across the table, and placed it in the bishop's plate. ' Count it,—twenty-five livres; and next time your lordship gives a feast, spend what you have wrung from me in buying—' he ran his eye along the table, and it lit on a pie,— ' goose-liver pasties for your distinguished guests.' It was a random shot, a bow drawn at a venture, but it went in at the joints of the mail, and smote to the heart.

Lindet turned from the table and walked away.

The guests sprang to their feet with a cry of dismay. Monseigneur de Narbonne-Lara had fallen out of his chair in an apoplectic fit.

CHAPTER X.

'COME here, children—my angels, Gabriel and Gabrielle!' said Madame Plomb, standing in the corridor at an open window. 'Come and see what is to be seen.'

The yellow cat, who had been seated on a little work-table in the lady's boudoir, bounded lightly to the floor, and obeyed its mistress's call. Reaching her, the cat leaped to her shoulder, that being the situation in which it would obtain an uninterrupted view of what it was called to witness. Gabrielle followed, still in white, for she had no other clothes with her, looking very pale, with dark rings round her eyes.

Madame Berthier made no allusion to the occurrences of the night; they seemed to have faded from her recollection, and her attention had been concentrated on cat's cradles, which she was able to execute with great ease, now that she had Gabrielle's fingers on which to elaborate the changes.

In the courtyard was Berthier's travelling carriage, with the horses attached, and the coachman standing beside them. Foulon and his son-in-law were near the carriage.

'Adolphe! my dressing-case,' said the old man.

'Monsieur, you will find it in the well under the seat.'

'Are the pistols in the sword-case?' asked Berthier.

'Monsieur will find them in the sword-case.'

'You have packed up my green velvet coat, and you have provided silk stockings?' asked Foulon.

'Monsieur will find everything in his trunk.'

'But you have forgotten the canister of snuff.'

'Monsieur, I ask pardon, it is under the seat.'

'Ah!' said Foulon, pointing up at the window, and nudging Berthier; 'contrasts,—see!'

The Intendant looked up, and caught sight of the three faces looking down on the preparations,—the yellow-faced cat, the blue-faced wife, the pale-faced peasant-girl.

'You are surely going to salute the cheeks of your lady, before you start, my friend,' said Foulon. Then, in a loud voice to his daughter,—'Well now, Imogène, how are you this morning? eh! In rude health and buoyant spirits. Capital! And how is my little darling? What! pale as the moon. The naughty dogs must have disturbed your innocent slumbers. Oh, Poulet! oh, Pigeon! you rascals,' he shook his forefinger at the dogs,—'how shall I forgive you for having broken the rest of my little mignonne! for having robbed her of her roses! for having filled her maiden breast with fear! Oh, you dogs! oh, oh!'

'Is everything ready?' asked Berthier of Adolphe.

'Everything—everything,' replied the footman.

'See that the dogs be properly fed, Gustave.'

'Certainly, monsieur.'

'What is the matter with my boy's eye?' asked Foulon. 'It has been lacerated; it is unusually tender; it is bruised.' Then, elevating his voice, and addressing those at the window, 'Ah! who has been striking and scratching my good Berthier? I know it was that cat. Oh, puss! you sly puss, how demure you look! but that is all very well by day. At night, ah! then you show your claws.'

The sheriff, finding that everything necessary was in the carriage, mounted the steps to the house, and making his way to the corridor presented himself before his wife, Gabrielle, and the cat. He stood before them with his eyes down, and with a sullen expression of face. His right eye was discoloured and cut; it both watered and bled, and he repeatedly wiped it.

'Madame,' said he, with less of his usual insolence of manner, 'your father and I shall be absent for some days.'

'Look me in the face,' said his wife. He lifted his eyes for an instant; the wounded organ evidently pained him, for it was glassy, and the lid closed over it immediately; the other fell before the glance of the lady.

'Madame,' he continued, 'we are about to visit Conches on business, and, after a delay there of a day, we proceed to

Evreux to meet the Count of Provence. He visits the bishop, and we dine with him at the palace on Thursday evening.'

'What is that to me?' asked his wife.

'I thought you would like to know, madame.'

'Why do you not call me Madame Plomb?'

His eyes fluttered up to hers and fell again.

'Because you are a coward,' said the lady. 'I know you for a bully and a coward.'

'Madame, I shall retire,' he said, scowling. 'I came here in courtesy to announce to you our departure, and I meet with insult.'

'What is to become of this child?' asked the lady, touching Gabrielle.

'She remains here,' answered Berthier; 'I have engaged her to be your servant. I have hired her of her father.' A look of triumph shot across his flabby countenance: 'he has received six months' wage in advance.'

Gabrielle uttered a faint cry and covered her face.

'I doubt not he has returned the money,' said Madame Berthier. 'See! in this soiled rag is a sum; it was cast in at the window last night. If I mistake not, this blood which discolours the linen is yours. It looks like yours, it feels like yours—ugh! it smells like yours.'

'Madame, I know nothing about that money. I know

that I have agreed with the girl's father, that he has received payment for her services, and that I keep her here.'

'Whether she remains here or at home,' said Madame Berthier, 'she is safe from you, as long as I am here to protect her.'

'As long as you are here,' answered Berthier, as he walked towards the stairs. Then turning to her, with his foot on the steps, he said, with a coarse laugh: 'As long as you are here to protect her! Quite so, Madame Plomb. But how long will you be here?' He disappeared down the stairs, and entering the carriage with Foulon, drove through the gay iron gates, and was gone.

'Gabrielle,' said Madame Berthier; 'my dear child, we will seek your father, and ask him whether this is true. I do not believe it, do you, Gabriel, my angel!' she turned her lips to the cat's ear. The animal rubbed its chin against her mouth and purred. 'I understand, my sweet! you wonder how the money came in at the window, do you not? Well, perhaps the good man was deceived by that beast, and, when he found out what sort of a man the beast was, he brought the money back; he could not get into the house at night, so he cast the silver through the window. Was it so, Gabriel? You are awake at night, you walk about in the moonlight, you can see in the dark; tell me, my seraph! was it so?' Then catching the girl's arm, she whispered, 'Wait, I have

not shown you the cat's castle. You have seen his net and
his coffer, his parlour, his pantry, and now you shall see his
castle, in which we shall shut him up when he is naughty.
That is his Bastille. Have you ever seen the Bastille,
Gabrielle? No, of course you have not. Now come with
me, and I will build you the cat's Bastille.'

The unfortunate woman drew the little peasant-girl into her
yellow room, seated herself in her high-backed chair, and in
a moment had her fingers among the strings.

'Take it off, Gabrielle,' she said. 'Come, Gabriel! sit
quiet, and you shall see the pretty things we shall construct
for you.'

The cat obediently settled himself into an observant attitude,
with his head resting between his paws; Gabrielle drew
her chair opposite Madame Berthier, and held up her fingers
to receive the threads.

'So,' said the lady; 'that is the net.'

She worked nimbly with her fingers.

'I have such trouble when I am alone,' she said; 'I have
to stretch the threads on this winding machine, or lay them
on the table. Gabriel is so selfish, he will not make an
attempt to assist me. But then all these contrivances are
for him, you know, and he would lose half the pleasure, if
he were made to labour at their construction. See! this, now,
is the cat's cabinet. I should so much like to do something,

that is, to dye your white dress saffron. You do not know how becoming it would be. I love yellow and black. I wear black, but Gabriel wears yellow. There! we have the basket. They used to dress the victims of the Inquisition in yellow and black, and torture and burn them in these colours. This is the cat's parlour. And Jews, as an accursed race, were obliged to wear yellow, so I have heard. Among the Buddhists, too, the monks wear saffron habits, in token that they have renounced the world. This, my dear, is the pantry. And the Chinese wear it as their mourning colour—their very deepest mourning. But I like it; it suits my complexion, I think. There! Do you observe this? How your fingers tremble! This is my own invention. Put up your fingers, so. Up, up! There, now. You have the cat's Bastille, a terrible tower for naughty pusses, when we shut them up. Ah! what have you done with your shaking, quaking fingers? You have pulled down, you have utterly dissolved my Bastille, and all the imprisoned cats will get out!'

At the same moment, Gabriel bounded from his perch.

'Why, how now!' exclaimed Madame Berthier; 'you are crying, my poor girl! Why do you cry? You lack patience. Ah! that is a great and saintly virtue, very hard to acquire. Indeed, you can only acquire it by constant prayer and making cat's cradles. That is my experience. Yes, it is patience that you want. We poor women have much to bear in this world from the wicked men. If we had not religion and trifling to occupy our thoughts and time, we should go mad. I am sure of it. Sometimes I feel a burning in my head, but first it comes in my chest, a fire there consuming me; then it flames up from my heart into my brain, and sets that on fire, and I should go crazy but for this. I say my rosary and then I make cradles, and then I say my chaplet again, and then go back to my threads. Why are you crying?'

' Madame !' entreated Gabrielle; ' may I go to my father?'

' But, my dear, I think the beast said your father had engaged you to him as my servant and companion.'

' Oh, dear madame ! you are so kind, pray let me see him and speak to him.'

' You shall,' answered the lady; ' I will accompany you. I like to walk out, but I go veiled. I frighten children sometimes, and even horses are afraid of me. Yes; we will go together, and I shall see your papa ! Ah ! I long to see your papa ! You are Gabrielle, and my cat is Gabriel. Both were quite white, till I dyed my angel yellow, and I want to dye your white clothes, and then you will be both just alike. Who knows, when I see your papa, perhaps we may be alike !'

The strange woman went into her bed-room to dress for going out; presently she came from it, bearing some black garments.

'You should have waited,' said she to Gabrielle; 'after the
Bastille comes the grave. I was going to make the grave
for puss, and then you pulled my tower down.'

When ready for the walk, Madame Berthier parted with
many expressions of tenderness from the yellow cat. It
was some time before she could resolve on going, for she
stood in the door wafting kisses to her 'angel Gabriel,' and
apologising to him with profuse expression of regret for
her absence.

'But we shall return soon, my Gabriel! do not waste your
precious affections in weeping for my absence. Soon, soon!
And now, adieu! come on, my Gabrielle.'

The walk was pleasant, and Madame Berthier enjoyed it.
She insisted on picking yellow and blue flowers as they went
along, and showing them to her companion.

'See!' she would say; 'the colours harmonise.'

The plantation of pines was soon passed, and then their
road traversed beech copse. The leaves were beginning to
turn, for the drought had affected the trees like an early frost.
Among the beech were hazels, laden with nuts, hardly ripe;
fern and fox-gloves grew rank on the road-side.

The day was warm, the air languid, being charged with
moisture that rose from the heated and wet earth, so that a
haze veiled the landscape. The flies were troublesome,
following Madame Berthier and Gabrielle in swarms. A

squirrel darted across the path and disappeared up one of the trees.

'Oh!' cried Madame Berthier; 'if Gabriel had only been here. How he would have run, how he would have pounced upon that red creature! Gabriel is so nimble.'

'Ah, madame!' exclaimed the girl, as they came within sight of the valley and the Island of Swallows, 'my poor father has lost his corn.'

'What is the matter?'

'See! the water has been out, and it has flooded our field in which the wheat was standing uncarried.'

'Alas! the pretty yellow corn,' said Madame Berthier, 'your father must buy some more.'

'He has no money.'

'Yes, child, he has; did not the beast give him your wage? Ah! I forgot, and he returned it.'

They crossed the little foot-bridge. Gabrielle stood still, with her hand on her heart, and looked round.

'I do not see him,' she said, anxiously.

'Oh, the papa is indoors, doubtless.'

They reached the front of the cottage.

'The garden must have been very gay,' said Madame Berthier; 'what roses! but ah! how the rain has battered them, and the flood has spoiled the beds. Why do you grow so many pink and white roses? I like this yellow one.'

Gabrielle put her hand on the latch and gently opened the door. She looked in; it was dark, for the little green blind was drawn across the window.

'Go in, my child,' said the lady; 'I will look about me, and then I shall come to you. I want to see the papa, so much.'

The girl stepped into the room, and called her father.

How silent the house seemed to be! the air within was close and hot.

'Father, where are you?' she called again.

Madame Berthier was picking some roses, when she heard a scream. She ran to the cottage-door, sprang in, and saw Gabrielle standing against the wall, her eyes distended with horror, her hands raised, and the palms open before her, as though to repel some one or something she saw.

'What is the matter?' asked madame. 'It is so dark in here.' She drew back the window-curtain.

'Ah!'

There, in a corner, where the ladder conducting to the upper rooms had stood, hung Matthias André, with his head on one side, his eyes open and fixed, the hands clenched and the feet contracted.

'Mon Dieu! is that the papa?' exclaimed Madame Berthier. 'Why, really, he is not unlike me. See! our faces are much alike. I am Madame Plomb, and he is Monsieur Plomb.'

The girl was falling. The strange woman carried her out into the open air.

'His complexion is darker than mine,' she said, musingly; 'but we are something alike.'

CHAPTER XI.

THE shock was too much for Gabrielle's already excited nerves to bear, and she remained for several days prostrated with fever. During this time, Madame Berthier attended her with gentle care and affection. She administered medicines with her own hand, slept in the room beside her, or kept watch night and day. The unfortunate woman having at length found a human being whom she could love, concentrated upon her the pent-up ardour of her soul. The cat attracted less attention than heretofore, and for some days his cradles were neglected.

If Madame Berthier had been given a companion whom she could love, in times gone by, and had been less ill-treated by her husband and neglected by her father, she would never have become deranged; it is possible that a course of gentle treatment and forbearance from irritating conduct on the part of M. Berthier might eventually have restored her already shaken intellect; but such treatment and forbearance she was not to receive.

Madame Berthier was walking in the court-yard one day, when Gabrielle was convalescent. Her husband and father had returned, but she had seen little of them. The former carefully avoided the wing occupied by the invalid and his wife, out of apprehension of infection, for he was peculiarly fearful of sickness; and Foulon did not approach them, not having occasion.

As she passed the kennel, she halted to caress the hounds. Poulet and Pigeon were docile under her hand, and never attempted to fly at and bite her. She and her father were the only persons in the château who had the brutes under perfect control; they feared Foulon, but they loved Madame Plomb. Animals are said to know instinctively those persons who like them. The poor woman exhibited a remarkable sympathy with animals, which they reciprocated. The dogs would never suffer Berthier to approach them without barking and showing their fangs, because he amused himself in teasing and ill-treating them; they slunk into their kennels before Foulon's cold grey eye, Madame Berthier they saluted with gambols. She patted the dogs, and addressed them by name.

'Well, Pigeon! well, Poulet! how are you to-day? Are you more reconciled to Gabriel? Ah! when will you learn to love that angel? He fears you; he sets up his back, and his tail becomes terrible to contemplate; and you—you growl at him, and you leap towards him, and I know if you were loose you would devour him. Alas! be reconciled, and love as brethren.' Turning to Adolphe, who approached, she asked, 'Have they been good boys lately?'

'Madame, their conduct has been superb.'

'That is nice, my brave dogs; I am pleased to hear a good account of you.'

'Madame, I must except Poulet for one hour. For one hour he misconducted himself; but what is an hour of evil to an age of good? it is a drop in an ocean, madame.'

'Did he misconduct himself, Adolphe? How was that?'

'Alas! madame, that I should have to blame him; and yet the blame does hardly attach to him,—it rests rather on the staple,—the staple of his chain. It gave way that day that the curé came.'

'What curé?'

'Ah! madame does not know? Monsieur the Curé of Bernay arrived at the gate, and the brave dog rushed towards him, and would have devoured him, doubtless, but for the rails. The staple, madame, was out; but Gustave and I, assisted by your honoured father, secured the dog once more, and no blood was shed.'

'What brought the curé here?'

Adolphe fidgeted his feet, and platted his fingers.

'Tell me, Adolphe,' persisted madame, 'tell me why

M. Lindet came to this house. These gates are not usually visited by Religion.'

'Madame,' answered the servant in a low voice, and with hesitation, 'I think he came here to enquire after the young girl——'

'I understand,' said the lady. 'Who spoke to him?'

'It was M. Foulon, your honoured father, who dismissed him.'

'Did the priest seem anxious to obtain information?'

'Madame, I believe so; he seemed most anxious.'

'Thank you, Adolphe. Open the gate for me; I am going to Bernay.'

'Madame will, I am sure, not mention what I have said,' the man began, nervously.

'Be satisfied; neither M. Berthier nor M. Foulon shall know that you have mentioned this to me.'

'Madame is so good!' exclaimed the man, throwing open the gate.

The unfortunate lady, having gathered her veil closely over her face, so as completely to conceal it, took the road to Bernay, and, entering the town by the Rue des Jardins, crossed the square in front of the Abbey, and speedily made her way to the Place S. Croix, where dwelt the priest.

The day being somewhat chilly, Thomas Lindet was seated before the fire in the kitchen; his brothers, Robert and Peter, were with him.   Robert was an attorney in practice at Bernay, Peter was supposed to help him in the office, but as the practice was small, and Peter was constitutionally incapable of attending to business, or of doing anything systematically, his value was nil.   The brothers were remarkable contrasts.   Some years later, when the events of the Revolution had developed their characters, they were nicknamed Robert le Diable, Thomas l'Incredule, and Pierre le Fou.   It is needless to say that these names were given them by their enemies.   Only in the first dawn of Christianity do we find a nickname given in a spirit of charity—Barnabas, the Son of Consolation.   These names were partly just and partly unjust.   Robert was never a devil; Thomas was, perhaps, a doubter; Peter was certainly a fool. Robert had an intelligent face, much like that of his brother the curé ; his lips were habitually arched with a smile; it was difficult to decide whether the smile was one of benevolence or of sarcasm.   An ironical twinkle in his eye led most who had dealings with him to suspect that he was internally jesting at them, when they received from him some mark of courtesy or esteem.   A thorough professional acquaintance with the injustice of the *ancien régime,* had made him, as desirous of a change as his brother Thomas.   He had the same passionate love of right and liberty, the same vehemence, but his strong clear judgment completely governed and modulated his impulses.   He was scrupulously honest and truthful.   The

Revolution rolled its course around him, and he became one of its most important functionaries, without compromising his character, without losing his integrity; under every form of government he served, being found an invaluable servant in the interest of his country, true to France and to his conscience. He had no love for power; he dreaded its splendour: he loved only to have work and responsibility. He was less a man of politics than of administration. His extreme caution was a subject of reproach, but it saved his neck from the guillotine in the Reign of Terror, and his probity, which left him unenriched by the public moneys which had passed through his hands, preserved him from exile in 1816. Of him the great Napoleon said: 'I know no man more able, and no minister more honest.' The innumerable difficulties with which he had to deal in administrative and financial practice during the Revolution, occupied his close attention, and he shunned public discussion, in which he knew he should not shine, that he might be the soul of committees. The Girondins, mistrusting him, thrust him into the arms of Robespierre, who received him, saying, 'We shall found Salente, and you shall be the Fénélon of the Revolution.'

Jean Baptiste Robert, to give him his name in full, was little conscious of the part it was his destiny to play, at the time our story opens. He and Peter were smoking.

'Well, Thomas! what have you gained by this move?' asked Robert, alluding to his brother's expedition to Evreux.

'To my mind,' put in Peter, 'you have acted very wrongly, and have not exhibited that respect to constituted authority, which the catechism enjoins.'

Thomas had his own misgivings, so he did not answer.

'You should have waited,' said Robert.

'That is your invariable advice,' said Thomas, impatiently; 'always wait, wait, wait—till doomsday, I suppose.'

'Till the election of deputies,' said Robert, between his whiffs; 'it is the same.'

'You will be inhibited, brother Thomas,' Peter observed, as he shook some of the ashes from his pipe on to the floor; 'as sure as eggs are eggs, Monseigneur the Bishop will withdraw your licence, and inhibit you from preaching and ministering the sacraments. And quite right too.'

'Why right, Peter?' asked Thomas.

'Because you have gone against constituted authority. I say, reverence constituted authority; never thwart it. Constituted authority, in my eyes——'

'Is constituted despotism,' said Thomas.

'No; it is right. Obedience is a Christian virtue; obedience is due to all who are set over us in Church and State. You have revolted against constituted authority, brother, and constituted authority will be down on you. You will be inhibited. Mark my words, you will.'

'No, not yet,' said Robert. 'To inhibit you would be to wing the story, and send it flying through the province. But be cautious for the future ; the least trip will cause your fall.'

Madame Berthier tapped at the door, and the priest answered it.

'I want to speak with you,' she said, 'for one minute.'

'Privately ? '

'Yes.'

'Then walk this way.'

He conducted her to his sitting-room, and requested her to be seated. She did not remove her veil, but told him her name.

'You came to Château Malouve in search of Gabrielle André,' she said. 'Did they tell you she was there ? '

'Madame, I did go in quest of her. Pardon me for speaking plainly, but I knew she would be in great peril if she were there.'

'You were right, she would have been in great peril; I have protected her, however.'

'She is with you, then, madame ? '

'She is with me at present: she has been very ill. The shock of her father's death has been too great for her. She is recovering now.'

'Does the poor child remain with you?' asked the priest.

'At present; but I cannot say for how long. M. Berthier may be removing to Paris shortly, our time for returning to the capital approaches, and, if we go there—we—that is Gabriel, Gabrielle and I.'

'Who is Gabriel, madame?'

'An angel.'

'Pardon me, I do not understand.'

'He is my solace, my joy.'

'Madame!'

'He is my cat.'

'Proceed, I pray.'

'If we, that is, Gabriel, Gabrielle and I go to Paris, I cannot be sure that I shall be able to protect the girl. Here, in the country, servants are not what they are in Paris. There they are creatures of the beast!'

'Of whom, madame?'

'Of the beast—of my husband. What am I to do then? They will do what Berthier orders them; they will separate her from me; they will lock me up. They have done so before; they will even tear my angel from my shoulder.'

'Your angel, madame?'

'My Gabriel, my cat. I have great battles to keep him near me, how can I assure myself of being able to retain her?'

'What is to be done, then?'

'She cannot go home to her blue father; she cannot stay with yellow Gabriel. I ask you what is to be done.'

Lindet paused before he replied. The lady puzzled him, her way of speaking was so strange. He looked intently at her veil, as though he desired to penetrate it with his eyes. Madame Berthier saw the direction of his eyes, and drew the veil closer.

'Why do you stare?' she asked; 'my face is not beautiful: it is terrible. The beast calls me Madame Plomb, and I hate him for it; but,' she drew close to the priest and whispered into his ear, 'I know now how to make him blue, like me,—how to turn M. Berthier into M. Plomb. We shall see, we shall see one of these days!'

'Madame, what is your meaning?'

'Ah, ha! I tell no one that secret, but you shall discover my meaning some day. Now, go back to what we were saying about Gabrielle. What is to be done with her?'

'When you go to Paris?'

'Yes, I cannot protect her there. I am not safe there myself. Here I can do what I like, but not there.'

'I cannot tell you, madame, but I will make enquiries, and find out where she may be taken in and screened against pursuit.'

'You promise me that,' she said.

'Yes, madame, I will do my best. If you will communicate with me again in a day or two, I shall be more in a position to satisfy you.'

'Then I may trust in you as Gabrielle's protector when I am unable myself to execute that office?'

'Certainly. I will be her protector.'

Madame Plomb rose from her seat, and departed.

As she approached the château, she heard the furious barking of the two dogs, and on entering the gates she saw the cause. M. Berthier had wheeled an easy chair into the yard, and was seated in it at a safe distance from the hounds, armed with a long-lashed carriage whip, which he whirled above his head, and brought down now on Poulet and then on Pigeon, driving the beasts frantic with pain and rage. He had thrown a large piece of raw meat just within their reach, and he kept them from it by skilful strokes across the nose and paws. The dogs were ravenous, and they flew upon the piece of flesh, only to recoil with howls of pain. Pigeon had bounded to the top of his kennel, and was dancing with torture, having received a cutting stroke across his fore paws; then, seeing Poulet making towards the meat, and fearful lest he should be robbed of his share, he leaped down from his perch and flew after his brother, only to be nearly overthrown by Poulet, as he started back before a sweep of the lash.

Madame Berthier looked scornfully towards her husband.

'Ah, ha! my leaden lady!' cried he, as she 'drew near; 'you have been taking a walk; there is nothing to be compared with fresh air and exercise for heightening and refining the complexion. You are right, madame, to wear a veil; the sun freckles.'

He had recovered all that insolence which seemed to have left him on the day following her repulse of him.

'Sacré! you rascal! will you touch the meat? No, not yet,' and the whip caught Poulet across the face.

The blow was answered with a furious howl.

'Are you going, Madame Plomb? No, stand here and watch my sport. I do not like to have my sport interfered with, mind that. What I like to do, that I will do. Sacré! who will dare to stand between me and my game?'

'I will,' said his wife, walking towards the dogs.

'No, you shall not; you shall leave that meat alone.'

She stooped, picked up the piece of raw flesh, and threw it towards the dogs.

'You are a bold woman to go so near the infuriated hounds,' said Berthier, cracking his whip in the air; 'I daren't do it.'

'No, you are a bully; and bullies are always cowards.'

'Madame! you are uncivil. You bark like Pigeon and Poulet.'

'I shall bite, too.'

'Do you know what we do with barking, biting, snarling, angry, ungovernable beasts, eh? with those who show their teeth to their masters, who unsheath their claws to their lords? Do you know what we do with them, eh?'

He wiped his red eyes with the corner of his hand-kerchief, leaned back in his chair, and laughed. 'Shall I tell you what we do with dangerous animals, or with those who stand between us and our object? We chain them up.' He laughed again.

Madame gazed contemptuously at his fat quivering cheeks.

'We lock them up, we chain them up,' continued he; 'we make them so fast that they may bark as much as they like, but bite they cannot, for those whom they would bite keep out of their reach.'

CHAPTER XII.

MADAME BERTHIER had left Gabrielle in her yellow room, with strict directions to attend to the cat, and to take him a little stroll in the garden. The lady had descended to the court-yard with full intentions of visiting the church of Nôtre Dame, but the information given her by Adolphe had altered her intention. The walk to Bernay and back took longer than she had intended.

Shortly after madame had left the house, Gabrielle, carrying the dyed cat in her arms, descended the stairs and entered the garden. Her confinement to the house had removed the dark stain of the sun from her skin, which was now of a wheaten hue, delicate, and lighting up with every emotion that sent a flush to her cheek. The anxiety and terror which had overcome her, had left their traces on her face; the old child-like simplicity and joyousness were gone, and their place was occupied by an expression of timidity scarcely less engaging. She wore one of her own peasant dresses, so becoming to a peasant girl, and a pure white Normandy cap.

'Poor puss!' she said, caressing the yellow cat as she

M 2

entered the garden; 'do you love your mistress? I am sure you do, for already I love her, though I have not known her half so long as you have. How can that dreadful man treat her with so much cruelty? If he only knew how good she was——'

'You surely do not allude to me when you use the expression "dreadful man." No, I am convinced you could not have so named one who lives only to devote himself to you, and gratify your every whim.'

Berthier stood before her, having stepped from an arbour that had concealed him.

Gabrielle recoiled in speechless terror.

'Did I hear you say that you loved Madame Plomb?' he asked, advancing towards her. She shrank away.

'Did I hear you express affection for that leaden woman, with her blue complexion, her bird-like profile, her fierce black eyes, and her mad fancies?'

'Monsieur,' answered the girl, trembling violently, 'I do love her; she has been kind to me.'

'Then,' said the fat man, throwing up one hand and laying the other on his breast, 'I love her too.'

He looked at her from head to foot, feasting his eyes on her beauty and innocence. She attempted to look up, but before that bold glance her eyes fluttered to one side and then the other.

'Do not run away, I will not touch you,' he said, as she made a movement to escape; 'I want merely to have a word with you in confidence. If you will not listen to me here, I will speak to you in the house. Whither can you go to escape me? The house is mine. No door is locked or bolted which I cannot open.'

'Monsieur, pray do not speak to me!' exclaimed Gabrielle, joining her trembling hands as in prayer.

'I must speak to you, little woman,' said Berthier, 'for I have got a charming suggestion, strictly correct, you may be sure, which I want to make to you.'

'Let me go home!' she cried, covering her face with her hands.

'Home!' echoed Berthier. 'Where is your home? Not the Isle of Swallows. Your father is dead, you know that; and another farmer has taken the house. How stupid of the père André to put himself out of the world just when his daughter wanted a home!'

This brutal remark caused the girl's tears to burst forth.

'Home!' continued the Intendant, approaching her; 'this is henceforth your home. I offer you my wealth, my mansions, my servants, myself.' He put his hand on her shoulder.

She sprang from the touch, as though it had stung her.

'Foolish maiden, not to accept such offers at once. You are in my power; you have nowhere to flee to; you have no

relations to take your part against me. If I turn you out of
my doors, do you know whither to go? No; you have no
place to go to.'

' I have friends,' she sobbed.

' Name them.'

' I am sure Pauline Lebertre would give me shelter.'

' Who is Pauline Lebertre, may I ask?'

' The curé's sister.'

' At La Couture?'

' Yes.'

M. Berthier clapped his fleshy hands together and laughed.

' You are vastly mistaken,' he said, ' if you think that
every house is open to you now. I lament to say it, but your
presence in this château is likely somewhat to affect your credit
with some good people. It is with unfeigned regret that I
assure you that this charming mansion of mine is regarded
with suspicion. It is even asserted that you left your father
and home for the purpose of making your fortune here; that
the idea so weighed on the good Matthias, that he committed
suicide, and that therefore you are his murderer.'

Gabrielle leaned against a tree, with her face in her hands;
she could not speak; shame, anguish, and disgust overwhelmed
her.

' Do you think that the sister of a curé would invite you to
her house?'

'Monsieur, monsieur!' she cried; 'leave me, I pray.'

'Certainly, I will leave you to digest what I have told you,' he said, with great composure; 'but not just yet; I must place certain alternatives before you, and, if you are a discreet girl, you will make the choice I desire. If you leave my hospitable roof, you go forth branded as your father's murderer, with an ugly name that will ever cling to you. You will go forth to be pointed at and scorned, and to be shut out of the society of your friends. On the other hand, if you remain here, you may remain on honourable terms. There is a place, not the grave, which swallows up wives; and the husband is left not only to all intents and purposes a widower, but in the eye of the law wifeless, so that he may marry again. I am sorry to say it, but that place is about to swallow up Madame Plomb. I offer you her place. She will be dead,—dead to all the world, and dead by law. You may occupy the place of honour at my table, sit beside me in my carriage, dress as suits your taste, lavish money as you list. You shall be my second wife, and the curé's daughter will come bowing down to you and asking for subscriptions for the church and the poor, and you can give more than all the rest of the people in the village, and you can set up a magnificent tomb to your father, and have a thousand masses said for his soul.'

'Madame!' cried the girl, 'oh, dear madame, come to my rescue!'

'You trust to the leaden wife to protect you, do you?' asked Berthier, laughing. 'The leaden woman shall not be at hand to stand between us much longer. I have managed that she shall disappear.'

Gabrielle looked fixedly at him, and her heart stood still.

'Yes, I promise you that,' said Berthier; 'I will have no more knives drawn upon me, and presented at my throat. I have taken precautions against a recurrence of such a proceeding. Let me tell you, dearest, that she shall not be much longer in this house. In a very few hours I hope to see her removed to a place of security. Should you like to know whither?'—he sidled up to her, put his lips to her ear, and whispered a name. 'Now I leave you,' he said, drawing back; 'I leave you to make your choice. Think what it would be to be called Madame Berthier de Sauvigny, and to reign over the peasants of Malouve!'

With a snap of his fingers he withdrew. It was some time before Gabrielle had sufficiently recovered to escape into the house. She fled to Madame Berthier's room and threw herself into a chair; then, fearing lest her pursuer should intrude himself upon her again, she went to the door to lock or bolt it, but found that the bolt had been removed, and there was no key in the lock. Berthier had spoken the truth when he said that no place in the house was secure from his entrance. She reseated herself, and awaited Madame Berthier's return.

That lady arrived in good spirits. She had secured a protector for Gabrielle, and she had spoiled her husband's sport with the dogs.

'Well, my precious ones!' exclaimed she, as she entered. 'Gabriel! come to my shoulder. Where is my angel? I do not see him. Gabrielle, tell me where is the cat, or I perish.'

'Madame,' answered the girl, who had started to her feet on the entrance of the lady, 'I do not know; I left him in the garden.'

'Have you cherished him, and consoled him for my absence?'

'Madame, I have done what I could.'

'That is right. Oh! it is delightful, now I can leave the house without anxiety. Hitherto I have been torn with fears lest some mischief should befall my angel, whenever I have been absent from home; but now I leave him to you in all confidence. But—what is the matter with you? you have been crying.'

'Madame! you have been so good to me, but I cannot remain in this house. I cannot, indeed.'

'My dear child, I know that you cannot, and I have this afternoon been to find you a protector, and I have secured you one.'

'Who, madame?'

'The curé of Bernay.'

'Madame,' faltered the girl, ' does he know that I am here?'

'Yes, child.'

' And he will yet receive me?'

'I do not know that he will himself receive you, but he has promised to find you a refuge.'

'Madame, tell me, does he think evil of me?'

'Of you? No; why should he?'

'Because, madame, I am in this house.'

'Ah, to be sure; that is not to the credit of any young woman; but I have assured him that I stood between you and harm.'

Gabrielle flung herself before Madame Berthier, to clasp her feet; the lady caught her and held her to her heart.

'You are too good to me,' the girl sobbed. 'Oh, madame, how can I ever repay you?'

'You will pray for me.'

'Ever, ever!' fervently ejaculated Gabrielle.

'And for Gabriel, my cat.'

'Madame,' said the girl, clinging to the unfortunate lady, ' madame, how shall I say it?—but you are yourself in danger.'

'I am always in danger,' said the poor woman. 'Am not I married to a beast? But tell me, now, what has made you cry whilst I have been out? The beast has not been near you to insult you. If he has,'—she gnashed her teeth; all the softness which had stolen over her strange countenance altering suddenly to an expression of hardness,—'if he has, I shall draw my knife upon him again. And I should be sorry to do that, because I do not want to make him bleed; I have other designs in my head. Ah! they are secrets: we shall see! perhaps some day we shall be more alike than we are now. Well—' she seated herself and removed her bonnet and veil—'well, and how came you to part company with the yellow cat?'

'Madame! you are in danger.'

'I have told you that I am in danger every day. In danger of what? Of being grossly insulted; of being called Madame Plomb; of having my liberty taken from me. I have been locked up in my chamber before now, and the beast threatened me with something of the kind just now, as I passed him in the yard, teasing the dogs. That man is hated by all. The people of Paris hate him; his servants hate him; his dogs hate him; you hate him; and so do I,—I hate him. I am all hate.'

'Madame, let me tell you what he said to me.'

'I do not care to hear,—I can guess; he spoke of me and called me Madame Plomb,' she stamped, as she mentioned the name. 'He made his jokes about me. He always makes his jokes about me to the servants, to his guests, to any one—and, if I am listening and looking on, all the better.'

'Dear, dear madame, let me speak.'

'You do not know, however, how my father treats me. That is worst of all. But where is Gabriel? Where is the yellow angel? Come, we will make his cradle.'

In a moment she had the threads about her fingers.

The girl saw that her only chance of being attended to was to wait her opportunity.

'This is the cat's net,' said Madame Berthier. 'This is his basket.' She pursued the changes with her usual interest, till it came to that of her own invention. As Gabrielle put up her fingers for the construction of the castle, she said, nervously :

'Madame, what do you call this tower or prison?'

'I call it the cat's castle.'

'But you have another name for it. You told me about a dreadful prison in Paris——'

'Ah! the Bastille.'

'Yes, madame. Who are shut up in that place?'

'Political offenders, and mad people, and, indeed, all sorts of folk.'

'How are they put in there?'

'Why, those who have committed political offences——'

'No, dearest madame, the others.'

'What! the mad people?'

'Yes.'

'Their friends get an order from the king, and then they are incarcerated.'

'Are all mad people in Paris put there?'

'Oh dear no! they are sent to Bicêtre. But only those of very great families, or those whom it is not wise or prudent for their relatives to have sent to the general asylum, are imprisoned there.'

'Madame, have you ever feared?'

'Feared what, Gabrielle?'

'Feared lest——' the girl hesitated and shook like an aspen.

'I have often been much afraid of an accident befalling my darling Gabriel. Oh! child, the anguish and terror of one night when the dear cat was absent. He had not been in all day, and night drew on and no Gabriel came, so I sat up at the window and watched, and I cried ever and anon, but he did not answer.'

'Madame,' interrupted the girl, clasping the poor lady's hands, and utterly ruining the tower of threads; 'dear, dear Madame Berthier, have you never feared the Bastille for yourself?'

Those words struck the lady as though with an electric shock. She started back and gazed with distended horror-lighted eyes and rigid countenance at Gabrielle; her hands fell paralysed at her side; her mouth moved as though she would speak, but not a word escaped her lips.

At that moment the dogs began to bark furiously in the yard, and continued for some minutes.

Madame Berthier slowly recovered such self-possession as she ever had.

'Did he mean that?' she asked; 'he said that those who were dangerous were chained up. Gabrielle, tell me, did he threaten *that* to me?'

'Madame, he said as much.'

The unhappy woman was silent again. She seemed cowed at the very idea, her feet worked nervously on the floor, and her fingers twitched; every line of her face bore the impress of abject fear.

'Oh, Gabrielle! do not desert me!' she entreated piteously. 'I have no friends. My husband is against me, my father is indifferent. I fling myself on you. Do not desert me— Gabrielle, Gabrielle!' the cry of pain pierced the girl to the heart.

'My dearest madame,' said she; 'I will follow you.'

'Gabrielle, did you hear aright? Was it not the cat they were going to take to his castle? Hark!'

There was a sound, a tramp of feet in the corridor.

'Who are these, who are coming?' shrieked the poor woman.

The girl was too frightened to move from her place. She stood trembling, and the tread drew nearer.

'Fly to the door, shut it, lock it!' cried Madame Berthier, throwing herself from her chair on the ground and tearing her grey hair with her discoloured hands.

Gabrielle stood irresolute but one moment, then she fell on her knees beside her mistress, and raised her head and kissed her, as the tears flowed from her eyes over the frightened deathly countenance of the unfortunate woman, whose trembling was so violent and convulsive that the floor vibrated under her.

'Gabrielle!' gasped the poor lady, suddenly becoming calmer; 'if I be taken, remember M. Lindet is your protector. Do not remain here.' Then her mind rambled off to the horror which oppressed her.

The door was thrown open, and Berthier entered with his eyes twinkling, and his cheeks wagging with laughter. Behind him were some soldiers.

'In the king's name!' he exclaimed. 'Ha! get up!' He stood instantly before his wife, rubbing his hands. His eye lighted on Gabrielle, and he saluted her with a nod and leer. 'Now, dear! what did I say?'

Madame Berthier hid her face in the girl's bosom. All fierceness, all her courage, every atom of power seemed to have disappeared before the awful fear.

'I will raise her,' said Berthier.

'No,' exclaimed Gabrielle; 'she is in my care.'

'In your care!' laughed Berthier; 'much good your care will do her.'

The girl gently lifted the frightened woman to her feet, but she could not stand without support.

'She is dangerous,' said Berthier to the officers. 'Secure her. She attempted my life with a dagger. Take care, she may stab one of you.'

There seemed little danger of this from the quaking being before them, nevertheless they secured her with manacles.

Gabrielle clung to her. The soldiers thrust her aside.

'Let me accompany her! Oh, let me go with her!' she pleaded; 'I have no home but with her!'

'What!' exclaimed Berthier, 'no home! Why, this house is your home. You have none other.'

Gabrielle was separated from madame.

'Where are you going to take me?' asked the poor woman, faintly.

'To the Bastille,' answered her husband promptly, stepping in front of her and staring into her eyes dim with fear, 'where you will be secure, and knowing you to be there, I shall be safe.'

'Let her come with me,' she besought, turning her face towards Gabrielle.

'By no manner of means,' answered Berthier with a laugh;

'I intend to make her very comfortable here. Whilst you enjoy your cell, she shall have your room.'

'My cat!' gasped the wretched wife.

'Would you have me catch it for you?' he asked. 'No. You must go without. Soldiers! remove her.'

They obeyed. She offered no resistance. A carriage was in the yard, ready to receive her. As the men drew her along the corridor and down the stairs, her limbs refusing to support her, her eyes turned from side to side in a strained, uneasy manner, and moans escaped her lips.

Gabrielle, almost too stunned to think, stood and gazed after her, but when she saw that the soldiers were about to thrust her into the carriage, with her grey hair hanging loosely about her shoulders, and with no cover for her face, she rallied, and flying back to the room she had left, caught up the bonnet and veil Madame Berthier had so lately taken off, and hastened after her to the court. She sprang upon the step of the carriage, and with her own hands adjusted the straggling hair, put on the bonnet, and drew the veil over the face of her mistress.

'Gabrielle!' murmured the poor woman, and the girl flung herself into her arms.

'Come!' said Berthier; 'enough of this. Coachman, drive on.'

Reluctantly the mistress and the maiden parted. Gabrielle

stood looking after the carriage, as it rolled towards the gates amidst the furious barking of the hounds.

Just as it passed through the entrance and turned into the road, the head and arms of Madame Berthier appeared at the coach window, the latter extended, and her cry, shrill and full of agony, was echoed back from the front of the chateau:

'Gabrielle! save me, save me!'

'That,' said Berthier, rubbing his eyes, 'that is more than Gabrielle or any one else can do, excepting myself or the king.'

THOMAS LINDET stood at his window thinking. One by one the lights died out in the town. A candle had been shining through the curtain in Madame Leroux's bedroom for an hour, and now that was extinguished. The red glow of the forge at the corner had become fainter. For long it had shot a scarlet glare over the pavement, and had roared before the bellows. The clink on the anvil was hushed, the shutters were closed, and only a feeble glimmer shone through their chinks, and under the door. The watch had closed the tavern of the 'Golden Cross.' None traversed the square. Lindet saw a light still in Madame Aubin's windows. She had a child ill, and was sitting up with it. There was a glimmer also from the window of M. François Corbelin, and the strains of a violin issued from his room. There was no moon now. The stars shone in the black vault above, and the priest fixed his eyes upon them.

Save for the violin, all was hushed; the frogs indeed trilled as usual, but the curé was so accustomed to the sound that he did not hear them, or rather did not know that his ear

N 2

received their clamorous notes. Then suddenly he heard the
baying of some hounds, distant, but approaching.

A moment after, Lindet saw a figure dart across the
market-place, with extended arms, and rush to his door.
Looking fixedly at the form, he distinguished it to be that
of a woman. She struck at his door, and gasped, 'Let
me in ! they are after me.'

'Who are you, and what do you want ?' asked the curé from
his window.

'Oh ! quick, let me in,' she cried; 'the dogs ! the
dogs !'

'Who are you ?'

'I am Gabrielle——' she broke off with a scream, for
instantly from the street, out of which she had started, appeared the bloodhounds, baying and tracking her.

'For God's sake ! or they will tear me !' she cried.

Lindet flung himself down the stairs, tore the door open,
beat off the dogs with a staff he snatched up, as the girl sprang
in; then slammed and barred the door upon the brutes.

'Have they hurt you ?'

She could not answer ; her breath was nearly gone.

'Stay there,' he said; 'I will light a candle.' He groped
his way to the kitchen, felt for the tinder and steel, and
struck a light. Having kindled from it a little lamp, he returned to the girl. She had sunk upon the ground beside

the door, outside of which the hounds leaped and barked, and at which they attempted to burrow.

'How came you here?' asked the curé. He set down the lamp, and raised her from the floor in his arms.

'I have escaped,' she gasped. 'I ran. They are after me.'

Voices were now heard without, calling off the dogs.

'Bah! she has taken refuge with her dear friend the curé. I thought as much.' The voice was that of Foulon.

'Sacré!' exclaimed Berthier; 'I wish we had discovered her flight a little earlier. I wish the dogs had brought her down in the forest. Sacré! I wish——'

'My dear good Berthier,' said Foulon, 'what is the use of wishing things to be otherwise than they are? always accept facts, and make the most of them. Gustave! take the dogs away. They make a confounded noise.'

'Remain here,' said Lindet, in an agitated voice; 'I will go and summon Madame Pin, the old woman whose house this is. She is as deaf as a post.'

'Do not go!' pleaded Gabrielle, trembling; 'perhaps *they* may get in. Wait, wait, to defend me.'

Lindet stood and listened to the voices outside. The dogs were collared and withdrawn. Foulon tapped at the door.

'Do not open,' entreated Gabrielle.

'Well! Monsieur le Curé,' said the old gentleman through

the door; ' sly priest! so the little rogue is with you? What
will the bishop say? So late at night!'

The noise had attracted the musician to his window. The
mother of the sick child had opened her casement, and was
looking out. Madame Leroux started out of the dose into
which she had fallen, and appeared at her garret window.

' What is the matter?' asked the musician.

' Ah, M. Corbelin!' exclaimed Foulon, in a loud voice;
' what foxes these curés are! We have just seen one admit
a young and pretty girl to his house. Hark! it is striking
midnight. No wonder all the dogs in the town have been
giving them a charivari.' Then, in a low tone to Berthier,
he said: 'My good boy! I have served out our curé now,
for having repeated in the pulpit certain observations I made
in private. Those she-dragons yonder'—he pointed up at the
windows—' will have ruined Thomas Lindet for ever. Come,
let us go home.'

CHAPTER XIV.

IT was evident that the States-general must be convoked. All attempts on the part of the Court at evasion provoked so loud and so indignant a burst of feeling from every quarter of France, that Louis XVI finally resolved on conquering his repugnance and yielding to popular pressure.

When Brienne resigned the ministry, he engaged Louis to summon Necker, a banker of Geneva. Necker decided the king to convoke the States-general, and to determine the mode of convocation, the notables were summoned. Necker was now prime minister of France. He was adored by the people, who believed him to be liberal-minded and honest; and on his influence the Court relied to keep in check and subordination the third estate, and use its weight as a counter-poise to that of the nobility and clergy, who had acted so decided a part in resisting the crown in the equal distribution of taxation. As the object desired by the Court was to make the two privileged classes bear their share in the burden, and as the States-general consisted of three houses, of which two were composed of those enjoying immunities, it was evident that they would unite against the wishes of the king and Necker, and the Tiers État. To avoid this, Necker proposed that the number of those representing the third estate should equal the number of the noble and clerical delegates conjointly. The assembly of notables, perceiving the design of the prime minister, rejected the double representation demanded in favour of the communes, and the Parliament of Paris declared that the States-general must be composed in the same manner as in 1614, when they last met. An assembly of peers, held on the 20th November, expressed the same sentiment, and the notables were dismissed. The courtiers were so accustomed to consider their will the rule of government, that the opinion of the notables, the parliament, and the peers would have prevailed, had not the necessity of filling the deficit in the finances inclined the ministry towards the Tiers État. Necker procured a decree of council deciding the double representation, on the 27th December; as to the question of deliberations by orders or by the three houses united, that was remitted to the decision of the States-general, convoked for the end of April, 1789.

Although the hopes of the king rested on the third estate, he feared it. He desired that it should vote taxes; he resolved that it should do nothing more. Some persons advised him to assemble the States at Blois, at Orléans, or at Bourges, and to avoid Paris, which would exert an incalculable influence over the third house. Louis XVI, however, decided that the assembly should take place at Versailles, where the splendour of the Court was calculated to overawe the representatives of the people, and render them complaisant tools of the royal will.

When, in the autumn of 1788, it became apparent to the whole of France that a crisis would arrive in the following spring, and that there would be a struggle between the privileged and the unprivileged classes, which would end either in the country asserting its rights and liberties, or in its further and final subjugation, it became important to those whose representatives occupied the upper houses, that they should present a compact front to the common enemy—Justice.

The nobility were almost unanimous; but it became daily more apparent that the second privileged class was by no means so.· The Church was divided into two classes, the upper and the lower clergy, and the scission between them was almost as sharp as that between the noble and the roturier. The eyes of the Court were turned on the Church, which held the scales between the parties, anxious to know whether its bias would be cast on the side of the third, or of the higher estate. The bishops and high clergy were stirred into activity, and became political agents; they exerted their influence on all the clergy within their sway, to promote the election of candidates favourable to the *ancien régime.*

The opportunity of acting a part as a political agitator inspired the Bishop of Évreux, when recovered from his attack of apoplexy, to make the circuit of his diocese, and by flattery and promises extended to some, by pressure brought to bear on others, to secure the election of candidates recommended by himself as partizans of privilege and abuse. Indeed, his ambition was to be himself elected. His negotiations had not been as successful as he had anticipated; he discovered that his clergy were by no means so enthusiastic in their devotion to the existing state of affairs as were those who largely profited by them. Some listened to him and respectfully declined to promise their votes to him or his candidate, others would consider his lordship's recommendation, others again would give no answer one way or another. The bishop was personally unpopular; he had a domineering manner which offended his clergy, and a tenacity to his dignity, which rendered him disliked. If a living in his gift were vacant, he kept it open for six months, and then appointed to it a priest of another diocese; if he were written to on business by one of his clergy, he either gave him no answer, or did not reply for months. Towards the close of his circuit, he arrived at Bernay, not in the best humour at his ill success, and accepted Berthier's invitation to stay at Château Malouve. Thither Lindet was summoned.

Rumours had come to the bishop's ears that the liberal

party among his clergy, in casting about for a suitable delegate at the approaching convocation, had mentioned the name of the curé of S. Cross. No name could possibly have been suggested more calculated to irritate monseigneur; and the bishop had arrived at Bernay with a settled determination to crush Lindet. The means were simple : he had but to sign his name and Lindet was cast adrift; but he must have some excuse for inhibiting him; and to provide him with this, Ponce, the *officiel*, was summoned to Bernay. The excuse was, however, ready, and awaiting his arrival,—an excuse a great deal more plausible than he had ventured to expect. The bishop had not been an hour in the château before Foulon had made him acquainted with 'a scandal which had compromised Religion and the Church in that neighbourhood,' and had told him how that Lindet had received a young woman into his house at midnight, and had not dismissed her till next morning, when he had sent her to his brother, the lawyer, to be his servant.

Now it happened that the incident had caused no scandal in Bernay, as Foulon had predicted, for the musician had from his window witnessed what had taken place; Berthier's character was well known in Bernay, and the disappearance of Gabrielle had been widely commented upon. A few malicious persons, perhaps, alluded to the priest's part in recovering the girl, as indicating a very unaccountable interest in her, but the circumstance had roused a deep indignation against the Intendant in the breasts of the Bernay people, which was not allayed when it transpired through Lindet, that Madame Berthier, the protectress of the girl, had been carried off to Paris by soldiers, to be incarcerated in the Bastille.

When Thomas Lindet reached Château Malouve, he was shown into the yellow room, once occupied by the afflicted lady, and which Berthier had surrendered to the prelate as his office during his stay.

Lindet found the bishop seated near the window, at the head of a long table, beside which sat M. Ponce, acting as his secretary. Monseigneur de Narbonne bowed stiffly, without rising from his chair, or removing his biretta; his red face flushed purple as the priest entered, but gradually resumed its usual ruddy hue.

'I have received a paper, which M. Ponce will do us the favour of reading,' said the bishop in a pompous tone, without raising his eyes from the table, or for a moment looking the curé full in the face—'a paper which contains grave charges of a moral nature against you, Robert Thomas Lindet—your name is correctly stated, is it not?'

'Yes, my Lord.'

'But your brother, the lawyer, is also Robert.'

'Monseigneur, his name in full is Jean Baptiste Robert.'

'Then you are both Robert?'

'Both, my Lord; but I have always been called by my second name.'

'M. Ponce, will you kindly——' the bishop bent slightly towards his officer.

That gentleman rose, and taking up a paper, read in a voice devoid of expression:—

'We, the undersigned, did, on the night of September 3, 1788, see a young girl, Gabrielle André, secretly enter the parsonage of Robert Thomas Lindet, curé of S. Cross, at Bernay, between the hours of eleven and twelve at night, the said Robert Thomas Lindet himself admitting her, and closing and locking the door after her. And we, the undersigned, have ascertained that the said girl, Gabrielle André, did remain in the house of the priest that night till the hour of seven in the morning.'

This document was signed by Foulon, Berthier, Gustave, and Adolphe.

The bishop closed his fingers over his breast, leaned back in his chair, thrust his feet out under the table, settled his neck comfortably in his cravat, and looked at Lindet.

The priest grew pale, not with fear, but with indignation.

'Have you anything to say upon this?' asked the prelate, blandly. Lindet flashed a glance at him, and the bishop's eyes fell instantly.

'Is this true?' again asked the bishop, after a pause.

'Perfectly,' answered the priest in a hard voice.

'I ask you whether, or not, you have thereby brought scandal on the Church?'

'I do not care.'

'M. Lindet, please to remember in whose presence you stand.'

'I am not likely to forget, monseigneur.'

'Then answer in a becoming way.'

'My Lord! I ask to see my accusers.'

'This is no public trial.'

'I shall not answer till they are brought here face to face with me.'

'I am your bishop. I insist on your answering me what I ask. You are contumacious, sir. You forget where you are.'

'That also,' said Lindet, 'I do not forget. I remember but too distinctly that I am in the house of a man notorious for his crimes, and whose hospitality you accept. I ask you, my Lord, whether or not *you* have thereby brought scandal on the Church.'

The bishop half started out of his chair.

'This insolence is simply intolerable. To my face——'

'Better than behind your back. I tell you—the head of the Church in this diocese, the guardian of religion and morality—that you are outraging decency by lodging in this polluted den.'

'Leave my presence this instant,' said the bishop. 'Ponce! turn him out.'

'No,' said Lindet, taking a chair, and leaning his hands on the back to steady himself, for his limbs trembled with excitement; 'no, monseigneur; a charge has been brought against me, a slur has been cast on my character, and I ask to meet my accusers face to face.'

'Pardon me!' The door opened, and Foulon stepped in, bearing some peaches on a leaf. 'My dear Lord, I must positively offer you this fruit, the very last on the tree. I thought all were gone, but these are so luscious. Pray accept them.'

Lindet faced him instantly, with abruptness.

'Monsieur Foulon, I am glad you are here.'

'Ah, ha! my dear curé. Sly fellow! Do you remember the pretty little peasantess? Well, I allow she was pretty, bewitching enough to have captivated a saint, therefore quite excusable in a curé to have been ensnared.'

'Monsieur Foulon!' said the prelate with dignity, ruffling up, and throwing a tone of reprimand into his voice.

'I beg your lordship's pardon a thousand times, but he is too sly. He amuses me infinitely.'

Thomas Lindet had much difficulty in controlling his naturally quick temper. He gripped the back of the chair with nervous force, and his lips whitened and trembled.

'I know you will allow me,' said Foulon, withdrawing the chair; and bringing it to the table, he seated himself upon it.

Lindet, standing without support, shook like a leaf in the wind. He folded his arms on·his breast, and pressed them tightly against it, to keep down the bounding heart.

'Monseigneur,' he said, 'this person has charged me with having received a poor girl into my house.'

'I saw her slip in, and I heard you bolt the dôor after her,' said Foulon; 'you did not suppose that anyone would be about at midnight, eh?'

'Was she a relation?' asked the bishop.

'She was not, my Lord,' answered the curé.

'A relative of your housekeeper?'

'No.'

'Who was she?'

'She was a poor orphan girl, whom Madame Berthier, that person's daughter, had entrusted to my charge, to protect her from M. Berthier. The child was in danger here——'

'Excuse me,' said Foulon in a grave tone, addressing himself to the bishop, 'is this curé to bring charges of such a nature as this against my son-in-law, in his own house?'

'You are right,' answered Monseigneur de Narbonne; 'I insist on you, M. Lindet, exculpating yourself without slandering others.'

'M. Foulon,' said the priest, turning upon the old gentleman, then engrossed in snuffing; 'you know that what I say is true. You know that the child was decoyed into this house by your son-in-law; you know that your own daughter stood between her and her would-be destroyer.'

'He is mad,' said Foulon, calmly. 'Dear, dear me!'

Lindet could endure no more; his blood boiled up, and the suppressed passion blazed into action. He sprang upon the imperturbable old man, and caught him by the shoulders, and forced him round in his chair to face him.

'Take some snuff,' said Foulon, extending his box.

'Deny what I have said, if you dare!'

'Certainly not; I will deny nothing. Of course the girl was brought here; of course my Imogène stood between her and ruin; of course she besought you to stand protector to the child;—there, does that satisfy you? I grant all, you see, now be calm. Always say "yes, yes" to a maniac; it is safest,' he added, aside to the bishop.

'I think,' said Monseigneur de Narbonne, 'that I have heard quite enough of this,—enough to satisfy me that M. Lindet is not a fit person to minister in my diocese. I will trouble you,' he added, turning to M. Ponce, 'to give me that paper you have been so diligently and kindly drawing up for me. I must inform you,' he said, turning his face towards Lindet, 'that I withdraw your licence, and inhibit you from performing any ecclesiastical function within my jurisdiction till further notice.'

He took the paper from his secretary, and in a bold hand signed it—' F. Ebro.'

'You condemn and punish me, you destroy my character, and ruin me, without investigating the charge laid against me,' said the priest.

'You have acknowledged that the charge is substantially correct.'

'I have not acknowledged it, nor can you prove that my moral character is thereby affected.'

'I am quite satisfied that you are greatly to blame,' said the bishop. 'I will not hold a public investigation, because it would only increase the scandal, and I desire to spare you and the Church that shame. I am satisfied that you are to blame; that is enough.'

'I demand a thorough investigation,' said the curé, with great firmness.

'You may demand one,' answered the bishop, 'but you shall not get one.'

'What!' exclaimed Lindet; 'I am to be ruined, and to be deprived of the means of clearing myself!'

'*I* am satisfied,' said the bishop, drawing himself up.

'But I am not,' retorted the priest.

The bishop bowed stiffly, and then turning to M. Ponce,

said: 'I think we will proceed with other business. Good morning, M. Lindet. Here is your inhibition.'

The curé stood silent for a moment, looking first at the secretary, then at Foulon, who was engaged in pouring snuff into his palm; then at the bishop, who had taken up one of the peaches, and with a silver pocket-knife was pealing it.

'My lord bishop!' said Lindet, 'hear what I say. We, the priests of the Church of France, have groaned under an intolerable oppression: we have been subject, without redress, to the whims and caprices of the bishop; neither justice nor liberty has been accorded us. I shall resist this treatment. I shall not submit to be crushed without a struggle. I appeal to the law.'

'You have no appeal,' said the prelate, coldly; 'you are a mere curate,—a stipendiary curate, and not an incumbent; the incumbent is under the protection of the law, the curate is removable at the will of the bishop.'

Lindet paused again.

'These peaches are delicious,' said the bishop to Foulon.

'Then,' said the curé, 'I appeal to the country against ecclesiastical tyranny. You spiritual lords, with your cringing subserviency to the crown, with your utter worldliness, with your obstructiveness to all religious movement in your dioceses, with your tenacious adherence to abuses, and with your arbitrary despotic treatment of your clergy, have taught us to hate the name of Establishment; to cry to God and the people to destroy a monstrous, odious sham, and restore to the Church its primitive independence. I wait the assembly of the States-general, at which the clergy shall have a voice; and then, my Lord, then I shall speak, and you *shall* hear me.'

He turned abruptly on his heel, and left the room.

CHAPTER XV.

By an order dated January 24th, 1789, the king required that the desires and reclamations of all his subjects should be transmitted to him. Every parish was to draw up a statement of its grievances and its wishes, which was to be handed into the assembly of the secondary bailiwick, by it to be fused into one which was forwarded to the grand bailiwick. The secondary bailiwicks of Beaumont-le-Royer, Breteuil, Conches, Ezy-Nonancourt, Orbec, and Bernay, belonged to the grand bailiwick of Évreux. The nobility and the clergy drew up their papers separately.

Another operation, not less important than the composition of these *cahiers*, was to be simultaneously accomplished. This was the election of delegates.

According to the edict of the 24th January, the ancient distinction of electors and deputies into three orders, the clergy, the nobility, and the third estate, was maintained. These orders had a common electoral circumscription, the grand bailiwick. The mode of election in the two first orders was made the same, but it was different in the third.

The nomination of deputies for the clergy was to be made directly by the bishops, abbés, canons, and other beneficed clergy in the grand bailiwick. The curés, who subsisted on the *portion congrue*, in another word, nearly all the clergy in country parishes, could only vote in person if their parish were within two leagues of the town in which was held the assembly, unless they had a curate to take their place during their absence, and provide for the religious requirements of the people.

The election was equally direct for the deputies of the nobility. The nobles possessing fiefs within the jurisdiction of the grand bailiff, might appear by representatives, but all others were required to appear in person.

The third estate, on the contrary, in naming its representatives, had to traverse three stages. Eight days at latest after having received the notification, the inhabitants composing the tiers état in the towns and country parishes, above the age of twenty-five, were invited to unite in their usual place of assembly, before the justice, or, in his default, before their syndic, for the purpose of naming a number of delegates, the number being proportioned to the population—two for two hundred fires and under, three for more than two hundred, four for three hundred and over, and so on, in progression. These delegates were required to betake themselves to the seat of the secondary bailiwick of their arrondissement, and there elect one quarter of their number. Those who had passed this ordeal were next bound to transport themselves to the principal bailiwick, and there, united with the deputies of that particular arrondissement of the bailiwick, and with the delegates of the town corporations, to form, under the presidence of the lieutenant-general, a college to which was remitted the final election of deputies.

Such organization had this advantage,—it gave to the elections, at a period when the relations of men with each other were much more limited than they are at present, guarantees of sincerity which they could not have had by direct universal suffrage. At each stage the electors knew those who solicited their votes. A communication was established through an uninterrupted chain of confidential trusts, from the most humble member of the primary assemblies to the delegates sent to Versailles from the grand colleges.

On Monday, the 16th March, 1789, seven hundred and fifty ecclesiastics, four hundred and thirty nobles, and three hundred deputies of the third estate, assembled in Évreux for the final election of delegates.

At eight o'clock in the morning, the great bell of the Cathedral boomed over the city to announce the opening of the first session. From the summit of the central spire floated a white standard, powdered with golden lilies. Ropes had been flung across the streets, and from them were slung

banners and flags bearing patriotic inscriptions, 'Vive le Roy !'
and 'Vive les États Généraux.' The lilies of France fluttered
from the windows of the barracks, the hospital, and the Palais
de Justice.

The weather was cold. The winter had been of unpre-
cedented severity, and the snow was not gone. On the north
side of the Cathedral it was heaped between the buttresses in
dirty patches. It glittered on the leaden roof of the aisles.
In the streets it was kneaded into black mud; it lurked white
and glaring in corners. Women had been up at daybreak
sweeping the slush from their door-steps, and making the
causeway before their houses look as clean as the season permitted. The limes in the palace-garden had not disclosed
a leaf; the buds were only beginning to swell.

It was a bright morning, almost the first really sunny spring-
tide day that year, and it was accepted by all as a glad omen
of a bright era opening on France with the elections of that
day.

A stream of people poured into the Cathedral through the
west gate and northern portal. The nave was reserved for
the electors; the people of Evreux filled the transepts and
aisles. In the centre, under Cardinal Balue's tower, sat the
nobility, many of them dressed with studious splendour; the
clergy occupied the choir, and overflowed into the choir-aisles.
The third estate sat west of the central tower. This body of

men presented marked contrasts in the appearance of the members constituting it. Side by side with the lawyer and surgeon, in good black cloth suits, black satin breeches, and black silk stockings, sat the peasant delegate in coarse blue cloth jacket, brown cap,—that cap which has been mounted on the flag-staff of the Republic as the badge of liberty,—and shoes of brown leather without heels, laced in front. Next to him a miller, with a broad-brimmed hat, pinched to make it triangular, a velvet waistcoat, and a coat set with large mother-of-pearl buttons, and here and there also a curé in cassock turned green with age, and black bands, edged with white; for some of the country villages sent their priests to bear their complaints before the great assembly.

Never had that noble church looked more impressive than on that March morning. It is peculiarly narrow and lofty, and darkened by the immense amount of painted glass which fills the windows,—glass of the highest style of art, and great depth of colour, and thickness of material.

The bishop occupied his throne, and the Abbé de Cernay, dean of the chapter, sang the mass of the Holy Ghost, in crimson vestments.

Never, probably, has that grand church resounded with a finer choral burst of song than when, at the conclusion of the mass, those seven hundred and fifty priests, with the choir, and a number of the laity, joined with the thunder of the organ, in the *Veni Creator*, sung to the melody composed by good King Robert of France.

The assembly was then constituted in the nave of the Cathedral. The candles were extinguished, the fumes of incense faded away, the clergy who had assisted in robes retired to lay aside their vestments; seats and a table were placed in the nave at the intersection of the transepts, and M. de Courcy de Montmorin, grand bailiff of Evreux, took his seat as president. Beside him sat M. Girardin, lieutenant-general of the bailiwick, and on his left M. Gozan, procureur of the king. Adrian Buzot, chief secretary, sat pen in hand at the table. On the right, filling the northern transept, sat the clergy in a dense black body, with the bishops of Évreux and Lisieux at their head in purple velvet chairs, studded with gold-headed nails. The bishops wore their violet cassocks, lace rochets, and capes, over which hung their episcopal crosses. In the south transept were placed the nobles; and the third estate filled the first three bays of the nave below the cross.

As soon as the assembly was seated, and silence had been established, the grand bailiff rose. He was a venerable man, of noble appearance, with a fresh complexion, bright clear grey eyes, and a flowing beard whiter than the late snow without. Raising his *chapel* from his blanched head as he began his speech, he replaced it again. His voice, at first

trembling and scarcely audible in that vast building, gradually
acquired tone, and was, towards the close of the address, heard
by every one in that great concourse.

'I give thanks to Heaven,' said the old man, lifting his cap
and looking upwards, 'that my life has been prolonged to this
moment, which opens before us, under the auspices of a
beloved monarch, a perspective of happiness, which we should
hardly have ventured to hope for.

'What an epoch in our annals, and, indeed, in those of
humanity! A sovereign consults his people on the means
of assuring their felicity, and assembles around him all those
gifted with political knowledge, to strengthen, or rather, to relay
the bases of general prosperity.

'Already, from one end of France to the other, those social
ideas which establish the rights of man and citizenship on true
and solid foundations have been disseminated. Government,
far from attempting to hinder the spread of these ideas, has
allowed them a liberty in accordance with its own generous
purposes.

'It is for us, gentlemen, to show ourselves worthy of this
noble confidence reposed in us by our sovereign; it is for us
to second the views of a monarch who consecrates for ever
his power, by showing that he desires to endear it to his
subjects.

'Experience has taught kings, as it has their subjects, that this alone is the means of protecting and securing the royal prerogative from the seductions of their ministers, who too frequently have stamped the decrees of their selfish passions, their errors, and their caprice, with the seal of a cherished and sacred authority.

'In order that we may arrive at that patriotic aim, dear to our hearts, we have to endeavour to maintain concord and mutual consideration between the three orders. Let us then from this moment suppress our own petty, selfish interests, and subordinate them to that dominant interest which should engross and elevate every soul—the public weal.

'The clergy and the nobility will feel that the grandest of all privileges is that of seeing the person and property of each under national security, under the protection of public liberty, the only protective power which is durable and infallible.

'The third estate will remember the fraternal joy with which all orders have hailed the success of the third in obtaining its demands. Let it not envy its elder brethren those honorific prerogatives, rendered legitimate by their antiquity, and which, in every monarchy, accompany those who have rendered service to their country, and whose families are venerable through their age.

'Generous citizens of all orders, you whom patriotism animates, you know all the abuses, and you will demand their reform at the ensuing council of the nation.

'I do not agitate the question of the limit of the powers given to our deputies. Public opinion has decided that; in order that they may operate efficaciously, they must be, if not wholly unlimited, at least very extensive.

'Such are the ideas, gentlemen, which I submit to your consideration.

'I assure you solemnly of the sincerity with which I offer up my prayers for the public welfare. This hope—so sweet, yet so late in coming to me, now far advanced in years, is the consolation of my age, rejuvenated by the light of a new era which promises to dawn, inspiring with hope us who stand on the brink of eternity, and which will be the glory of our posterity. We shall lay the foundations, another generation will rejoice in the superstructure. I thank God that this feeble hand is called even to the preparatory work, and, gentlemen, I conclude with the words of the Psalmist: "*Respice in servos tuos, et in opera tua, et dirige filios eorum.*"'

The venerable bailiff sat down; a thrill of emotion ran through the assembly. In perfect silence, the roll-call and verification of powers was begun.

Amongst those names first proclaimed, in the order of the nobility, was that of Louis-Stanislas Xavier, son of France, Duke of Anjou, Alençon and Vendôme, Count of Perche, Maine and Senonches, Lord of the bailiwicks of Orbec and

Bernay. This prince, who was afterwards Louis XVIII, was represented by the Marquis of Chambray.

When the names of the clergy were read, Monseigneur de Narbonne turned his ear towards Adrian Buzot.

'Robert Thomas Lindet, curate of S. Cross, at Bernay.'

'I object,' said the bishop, raising his hand.

The secretary turned to him, and asked his reason.

'He is disqualified from appearing. He is under inhibition.'

Lindet sprang to his feet and worked his way to the front. 'I maintain,' said he, 'that an inhibition does not disqualify me from appearing.'

The bishop leaned back in his velvet chair, crossed his feet, folded his hands, and looked at the president.

'I have been inhibited without just cause, without having been given a hearing, or allowed to clear myself of imputations maliciously cast upon me.'

'M. Lindet,' said the grand bailiff, 'we cannot enter upon the question of the rights of the inhibition; we are solely concerned with the question, whether that said inhibition incapacitates you from voting.'

'Quite so,' the prelate interjected; then his cold grey eye rested upon Lindet, who returned the look with one of defiance.

M. de Courcy whispered with the Procureur du Roi.

' I think,' said the bishop, in a formal tone, ' that, whatever may be the decision on the legality of your appearing, M. Lindet, there can be but one opinion on its propriety. If you have not the decency to remain in retirement, when lying under rebuke for scandalous and immoral conduct, you will probably not be shamed by anything I may say.'

' My Lord,' began the curé, ' I protest—' but he was interrupted by the president, who, nodding to M. Gozan, the agent for the king, said:

' The objection raised by monseigneur appears to me not to invalidate the claim of M. Lindet to have a voice in the redaction of the cahiers and the election of the clerical delegates. The order of his Majesty makes no provision for the case of a clerk under censure, and silence on this point may fairly be construed in his favour. The sentence upon him was purely spiritual, his status as stipendiary curate remains unaltered. If he have a grievance, an opportunity is graciously afforded him by his Majesty of declaring it. The ends proposed would be frustrated, if all those who had grievances were precluded by an exercise of authority on the part of their lords, feudal or spiritual, from expressing them.'

The bishop coloured, bowed stiffly, and began to converse in a low tone with M. de la Ferronays, bishop of Lisieux.

The preliminary work of calling over the names of electors

and delegates occupied the session of that day. At four
o'clock in the afternoon it was dissolved, and the vast concourse began to flow out at the Cathedral doors.

But it was observed by the bishops, that the clergy showed
no signs of moving from their places.

M. de Narbonne rose from his violet velvet chair, and
with a smile at his brother prelate, and then at the dean,
suggested that they should retire through the private entrance
in the south transept to the palace garden.

He was about to cross before the table at which Adrian
Buzot was still engaged with his papers, when Thomas Lindet,
standing on his chair, addressed him.

'My Lord! you have this morning publicly attacked my
character, by asserting that my conduct has been "scandalous
and immoral." I demand of you, before these my brother
priests, to state the grounds upon which you base that
charge.'

The bishop, taking the arm of his suffragan, did not even
turn to look at the curé, but began to speak rapidly to his
brother prelate.

'My Lord! are you going to answer me, or are you not?'
again asked Lindet. 'I appeal to you as a Christian—not
as a bishop. You have damaged my character. State
frankly your reasons for doing so. Give me an opportunity
of clearing myself.' He had spoken calmly so far, but all

at once his natural impetuosity overpowered him, and he burst forth with the sentence: 'Stay! you have just genuflected towards the Host! you have bent the knee in homage to Him who is Mercy and Justice, whose minister you are. In His name I demand justice. Mercy I have long ago ceased to expect.'

'I had rather be keeper of a lunatic asylum,' said the Bishop of Lisieux, 'than be custos of a herd of wild curés.'

The Bishop of Évreux laughed aloud. The laugh echoed through the aisles, and was heard by the priests, as he laid his hand on the private door.

The dense black. mass of clerics rose, and the bishop darted through the door with purple cheek and blazing eye, as a hiss, long and fierce, broke from that body of priests he shepherded.

'Barbarians! blackguards!' said the bishop, shaking his fist at the Cathedral, as he shut the door behind him and quenched that terrible sound. 'Wait! I have chastised you hitherto with whips; when these States-General are over, I shall thrash you into subserviency with scorpions.'

CHAPTER XVI.

ON the following day, March 17, the three orders betook themselves to their several places of reunion, to draw up their memorials of grievances. The clergy assembled in the hall of the Seminary of S. Taurinus under the presidency of the bishop of the diocese, assisted by the Bishop of Lisieux, Féron de la Ferronnais. The nobility met in the Church of S. Nicholas, with the grand bailiff as their chairman, and the third estate occupied the audience chamber of the Viscount's court, and was presided over by M. Girardin.

The deliberations of the third estate presented no incident worthy of note. Unanimity reigned among the members, and its resolutions were in accordance with, and had indeed been prepared by, the discussions conducted in the earlier stages of election. What were the pressing grievances weighing on the people, have been already shown. The *cahiers* from the villages and towns which were read before it threw a clear light also on ecclesiastical abuses; the principal we shall extract from these documents for the edification of the reader.

Intolerable abuses had invaded the collation to benefices. The revenues which had been provided by the piety of the past for the maintenance of public worship, for the subsistence of the ministers of religion, and for the support of the poor, had accumulated in the hands of a few abbés about the Court and high dignitaries of the Church. M. de Marbeuf, archbishop of ·Lyons, was Abbot commendatory of Bec, the nursery of S. Anselm and Lanfranc; the celebrated Abbé Maury held in commendam the Abbey of Lyons-la-Forêt; Dom Guillaume-Louis Laforcade, a Benedictine resident at S. Denis, was Prior of Acquigny; De Raze, minister of the Prince-bishop of Bâle, was Prior of Saint-Lô, near Bourg-Achard; Loménie de Brienne, archbishop of Sens, who was minister of finance in 1788, and of whom M. Thiers well says, that 'if he did not make the fortune of France, he certainly made his own,' possessed 678,000 livres per annum, drawn from benefices all over France, and his brother, the Archbishop of Trajanopolis was non-resident Abbot of the wealthy Abbey of Jumiéges. This state of things drew from the redactors of the *cahiers* of the third estate many bitter recriminations. 'It is revolting,' said Villiers-en-Vexin, 'that the goods of the Church should only go to nourish the passions of titulars.' 'According to the canons,' said the parish of Thilliers, ' every beneficed clergyman is bound to give a quarter of his income to the poor. In our parish, with a revenue of twelve thousand livres flowing into the Church, nothing returns to the poor but the scanty alms of the ill-paid curate.' 'Is it not surprising,' said the people of Plessis-Hébert, 'to see so many bishops and abbés squander their revenues in Paris, instead of expending them on religious works, in those places whence they are derived?'

Fontenay wrote in stronger terms: 'The most revolting abuse is the miserable exspoliation of the commendatory abbeys. The people are indignant at it. They see the fruit of their toil pass into the covetous hands of a titular, deaf to the cries of misery, whose ears are filled with the clatter of political affairs and the rattle of pleasure. Let the king seize on the property of the Church and pay with it the debts of the State—this is what the country desires! The Church has no need of fiefs to govern souls.'

Whilst the high dignitaries rolled in riches, a large class of priests, and that the most deserving, vegetated in a wretched condition of poverty. These were the curés of parishes, who were deprived of the tithe which passed into the hands of some lay or high clerical impropriator, and who received only a small indemnity, called the *portion congrue*, scarcely sufficient to keep them from perishing with hunger.

The *cahiers* are full of commiseration for these poor disinherited sons of the Church. Villiers-sur-le-Roule and Tosny assert 'that the benefice of their curés, reduced to the *portion congrue*, is absolutely insufficient for their support, and for enabling them to render help to the poor. The Abbé of Conches absorbs half the tithe, and he does not give a sous to the relief of the parish.' At Muids, 'the collegiate church of Ecouis receives all the tithes. The chapter gives nothing to the poor, and seeks only to augment the revenue. The curé is reduced to misery.' The situation is the same at Saint-Aubin-sur-Gaillon: 'The extent of this parish makes the presence of a curate necessary, and as he receives from the Abbé de la Croix-Saint Leufroy, who holds the great tithes, only three hundred and fifty livres, and as the sum is quite insufficient, he is obliged to go round at harvest-time, like a begging friar, through the hamlets, asking for corn and wine and apples. Surely this is lowering the priest, and is adding an impost to the already taxed parish.' 'When the curés have hardly a bare subsistence,' says the memorial of Fontenay; 'when they are reduced to live on what is strictly necessary, what can they offer to the poor? They have only their tears. Let the curés have the tithe of the parishes in which they minister.'

Still more hardly treated were the town curés, for the *portion congrue* paid them was smaller in proportion than that given to the country priests, upon the excuse that the difference was made up by the increased number of fees. But it was forgotten that the charges and other expenses of a town, the calls on the priest's purse, were far greater in a populous city than in a country village.

The house of the clergy was the theatre of stormy scenes, which broke out between the high dignitaries and the curés living on the *portion congrue.* These latter had a numerical advantage; they formed a majority of thirty to one. On the evening of the 16th, instead of bearing to the episcopal palace the expression of their deference, they assembled, to the number of three hundred, in a chapel. There, disdaining all moderation of language, a curé of the diocese of Évreux boldly said that the inferior clergy had groaned too long under the oppression of the bishops, and that it was time to shake off a yoke which had become as odious as it was intolerable. A second orator, a curé of the diocese of Lisieux, no less energetically expressed the same opinion. A third priest, having risen to speak, began to defend the episcopate, whereupon he was silenced by the clamour of the throng of priests, and his cassock was torn off his back. When, on the 17th of March, the official deliberation of the clergy was opened at the Seminary of S. Taurinus, the Bishop of Évreux proposed to nominate a secretary, and mentioned his choice; but his nomination was rejected with a firmness which let him understand that the vast majority of his clergy were antagonistic to his wishes. Every proposition made by this prelate and his colleague met with a similar fate, and the memorial addressed to the Crown was drawn up without their participation, and in a spirit hostile to the high clergy.

On March 21, the Bishop of Évreux, smarting under the humiliations to which he was exposed, wrote a letter to M. Necker, Minister of Finances, filled with complaints. It contained the following passage:—' It is impossible for me, say what I will to them, to keep this assembly of wild, excited curates in control. I am cast, like a Christian of old, *ad leones.* These priests, calculating on their numbers, are inflated with pride, and bear down all remonstrance. And these are the men we are to send to the States-General, without a shadow of knowledge of our ecclesiastical affairs; without a trace of interest in the maintenance of our prerogatives; without a glimmer of - sympathy for our rights, jurisdictions, fiefs, and our territorial possessions. They are prepared to overturn everything; they are indifferent to the spoliation of the Church; they are even prepared to hail its disestablishment, if one were fool enough to suggest such a possibility.

' The high beneficed clergy are unrepresented; how can they be otherwise, when the great majority of the deputies are taken from amongst curés who have, as a general rule, no interest in defending our properties? You are too just not to be struck with the inconveniences which this general summons of our clergy to an assembly must drag down on us, and I venture to hope that in future I shall not be again subjected to the indignity of presiding over a tumultuous and disorderly rout, such as that at present assembled. My zeal for the public welfare, and my devotion to the Crown, have alone sustained me against the outrages I have endured, to the like of which I have never previously been subjected in my diocese.'

A few days after, the bishop received an answer from M. Necker, couched in these laconic terms :—

' Monseigneur, I grieve to hear of the schism in the assembly under your presidence. But who is to blame if the children revolt against their father? I have read somewhere the injunction, which you, my Lord, may also possibly have seen, "Fathers, provoke not your children to wrath." '

On the 23rd, the *cahiers*, or memorials of complaints and recommendations, were completed, and on the 24th the election of deputies took place. In the hall of the Seminary the election of clerical delegates was the scene of the final struggle between the upper and lower clergy, and it was fought with greatest violence. On the preceding evening the bishops had concerted with those clergy on whom they thought they could rely, and had resolved to bring forward M. Parizot de Durand, incumbent of Breteuil, and M. de la Lande, curé of Illiers-l'Evêque. The former was a worthy priest, greatly beloved for his piety, exceedingly obstinate in his adhesion to the existing state of affairs, and utterly averse to change in any form. He had a favourite maxim, 'quieta non movere,' which he produced on every possible occasion, and which was, in fact, the law of his life. It was in vain for those who saw the agitation of mind, and the effervescence of popular feeling, to assure him that nothing was quiet; the stolid old Conservative was not to be shaken from his position, and maintained that this excitement was due to the moving of things hitherto quiet, and that the only cure for it was to reduce them to their former condition of stagnation.

M. de la Lande was a man of family. He had been appointed in 1765 incumbent of the church of Nôtre-Dame in Illiers-l'Evêque ; he was a pluralist, enjoying, in addition, the incumbency of S. Martin, the second parish in the barony. The collation to these two rich benefices belonged to the Bishop of Évreux, who was lord of Illiers, the barony having been made over to the see by Philip de Cahors in the thirteenth century. M. de la Lande was a courtier, and was often at Versailles. In his parish he was liked as an amiable, easy-going parson, fond of his bottle, and passionately addicted to the chase.

It was arranged that the bishops and beneficed clergy should not appear prominently as supporting these candidates, but that they should be proposed and seconded by members of the assembly not suspected of being rigid partizans of the

ancien régime.   Monseigneur de Narbonne had given up
the hope of being himself elected, and deemed it prudent
not to allow his name to be proposed.

At nine o'clock the Bishop of Évreux took his seat in
the hall of the Seminary.   The large windows admitted
floods of light, and the casements were opened to allow
the spring air to enter.   The snow had wholly disappeared
during the last few days, and a breath of vernal air had
swept over the land, promising a return of warmth and beauty.
The swallows were busy about the tower of S. Taurin; from
the bishop's seat the belfry was visible, and the scream of
the excited birds that wheeled and darted to and fro was
audible.   Now and then a jackdaw dashed through the fluttering group with a dry stick in its beak, to add to the accu-
mulation of years which encumbered the turret stairs.   The
Cathedral bell summoned the electors, and they came to
their assembly-room in groups of two and three, and took
their seats in silence.   The bishop looked sullen and discontented; he sat rubbing his episcopal ring, breathing on
it, and polishing it on his cuff, and then looking out of the
window at the birds.   His large fleshy cheeks hung down,
and their usual beefy redness was changed to an unwhole-
some mottle of pink and purple.   His barber had not attended on him that morning, or the prelate had been too
busy to allow himself to be shaved, so that his chin and

upper lip presented a rough appearance, which helped to make him look. more ill at ease and out of condition than he had during the earlier part of the session. He took no notice of the clergy as they entered, and was regardless of Monsieur de la Ferronnais when he took his place near him. Every now and then he muttered to himself expressions of disgust at the situation in which he was placed, and aspirations for a speedy termination to the session.

'Good morning, my dear Lord,' said the Bishop of Lisieux, touching his arm. The Bishop of Evreux looked round sulkily, placed his hands on the arms of his chair, and raised himself slightly from the seat. Monseigneur de la Ferronnais was a bright old man, amiable, fond of fun, not particularly anxious about the turn matters took. He was sure that 'all would come right in the end.'

'This is your last day in purgatory,' he said to his colleague.

'I thank Heaven,' answered Monseigneur de Narbonne, without looking at him.

'You take these troubles too seriously, you lay them too much to heart,' continued the Bishop of Lisieux. 'Let the boys wrangle over their precious *cahiers* and *doléances ;* we know very well that they are sops—sops to Cerberus. The Government will never read them, and it pleases the poor fellows to be called to scribble their complaints. Possibly

the charming queen wants curl-papers for the ladies of the
Court, and has hit on this sweet expedient of obtaining paper
at no personal cost.'

'I cannot, and will not, stand this much longer,' said the
Bishop of Evreux. 'I am like the martyr who was stabbed
to death with the styles of his scholars. It is the indignity
which I am subjected to that galls me to the quick.'

'Put your pride in your pocket,' laughed M. de la Ferronnais. 'We have long ago learned to pocket our conscience
at the bidding of the Crown; perhaps our self-respect may
fill the other pocket, and so balance be preserved.'

The Bishop of Evreux did not answer. The Cathedral bell
had ceased, and, with an expression of impatience and disgust
visible to all in the room, he rang his hand-bell and opened
the sitting.

'Gentlemen,' he said, 'we have before us this day an important duty to fulfil. Let me ask of you to remember that
it is not to be undertaken lightly and in a spirit of private
pique. You have to elect delegates to the national council.
You are hardly aware how great are the issues in the hands
of that assembly. If you send men to utter there the wild
sentiments you have been pleased to express in your paper
to the king, you will revolutionise France and the Church.
That there have been, and still exist, abuses in the political
and ecclesiastical worlds, I am the last to deny. In times of

great excitement, extreme partizans of change may precipitate
the constitution into an abyss from which it would take cen-
turies of reconstruction to recover it.   You will be good
enough to remember that the Church in this land is established,
that it enjoys great privileges and possessions; that to wrest
from her those possessions would be to leave her suddenly in
a condition of destitution for which she is wholly unprovided,
and to rob her of her privileges will be to subject her to an
indignity from which it is your place to shield her, as your
spiritual mother and the bride of Christ.   Gentlemen, hitherto
you have exhibited yourselves as a compact and resolute body
of malcontents.   I do not use the word in an injurious sense.
I say you have exhibited yourselves as malcontents, as dis-
satisfied with the existing state of affairs in Church and State.
If you wish to have abuses rectified, it will not be by violent
men who endeavour to tear down every institution which by
its antiquity has become full of rents, but it will be by men of
calm judgment and reconstructive ability, who will carefully
and reverently restore and re-adapt what is decayed and an-
tiquated.   I ask of you, then, in the interest of your order,
to elect persons of matured judgment and practical experience.
It can be no secret to you that the fate of France depends on
the attitude assumed by your delegates.   The house of the
nobility is naturally attached to conservative principles, that
of the third estate is liberal and revolutionary.   It will be our

mission to arbitrate between these contending interests, on the one side to conciliate the people, and on the other to move the aristocracy to relinquish their most obnoxious privileges, and to lend their shoulders to ease the third estate of the yoke which, it is universally acknowledged, presses upon them unduly. Above all, let us avoid being divided in our own house. We touch both of the other estates. On one hand, we are allied with the noblesse; on the other hand, we are attached to the *tiers état*. Through our hierarchy we are in communication with the noble class, through our curates we pulsate with the heart of the unprivileged class. Let not that double union lead to a dissolution of our body, but rather to a harmonization of the other bodies. *Omne regnum in seipsum divisum desolabitur, et domus supra domum cadet.'*

This address, so full of good sense, was not without its effect upon the clergy. Some began to feel that they had been a little too hard on the privileged party in the assembly, and that an attempt at conciliation might now well be made.

Jean Lebertre, curé of La Couture, rose and said:

'Monseigneur, and you my fellow-electors,—At the coming assembly of the estates of this realm, it is well that all interests should be represented,—that which desires a redistribution of the funds of the Church, and that which desires that they should remain in the hands of a few as prizes to those who are most diligent and most deserving.'

A Voice : ' When are the prizes so given ? '

' Well,' continued Lebertre, ' suppose that they are given to the clergy who by birth or political influence have some claim to receive them, what then ? Is not the Church brought into intimate contact with both rich and noble, and poor and commoner ? If her clergy are to exert influence over those in the highest classes, they must be enabled to move in those classes, and to leaven them. To do so, they must receive an income proportionate to the requirements of such a life. God forbid that the Church should be only the Church of the poor and ignorant; and that she must become, if you rob her of prizes. Educated and intellectual men will not enter her orders unless they are provided with a competency. We country curés do not want wealth ; our lot is cast among the poor, and by being ourselves poor, we have a fellow-feeling for our flock, and our flock have an affection for us. The beneficed clergy, pluralists and commendatory abbots, are wealthy, and are thus enabled to enter into high society, and to infuse into it religious principles and a love of morality. Take away their means, and you withdraw all spiritual influence from the most powerful, because the highest, stratum of society. I propose as one candidate for the clergy of this assembly, M. Parizot de Durand, curé of Breteuil, a priest of unblemished character, and a man of solid common sense.'

M. de Durand was seconded.

But immediately after, the Abbé Lecerf started up and proposed Thomas Lindet, curé of Bernay.

Instantly an expression of anger,—a sudden dark cloud, obscured the countenance of the president.

'I take it as a deliberate insult to myself, that a man should be proposed to represent the clergy of the diocese who is under inhibition from me,' he said, in a passionate loud tone.

Monseigneur de la Ferronnais shrugged his shoulders, and tapping the Bishop of Évreux on the back of his hand with his middle finger, said: 'You have made as great a mistake now as you made a great hit by your first speech.'

That the Bishop of Lisieux was right became at once apparent. Lindet sprang up, on fire, in a blaze.

'There, there!' he said, stretching out his hands, that quivered with excitement and the vehemence of his utterance; 'see what he wants you to commit yourselves to—to support the absolute and irresponsible exercise of discipline. Why am I under inhibition? I will tell you all. A friend of the bishop's, then, is a man notorious for his immoralities, a man very great at Court, or be sure he would not be monseigneur's friend. Well, this man attempted to seduce a poor girl, a peasant's daughter. She fled from her seducer, and I protected her, and saved her, at the earnest entreaty of the man's own wife. He thereupon charges me with what he himself had failed to do, and the bishop, who is his guest, complaisantly, at his host's request, inhibits me without allowing me a fair hearing, and an open trial.'

'Are we going to be pestered with this nonsense here?' asked the bishop, angrily. 'I pronounce this not to be the place for such questions to be ventilated.'

'What place is?' suddenly asked Lindet, turning upon the prelate; 'I have asked for a trial, open and fair; I cannot get one. I have no wish to be your representative, gentlemen; but what I do wish is, that the whole body of clergy here should protest unanimously against these arbitrary judgments, and insist on impartiality in our judges.'

He sat down. A murmur of sympathy ran through the crowd. A curé of the town of Évreux sprang up.

'How shall we best declare our indignation at the exercise of authority which is unjust and arbitrary? Surely by electing the man who has thus signally been ill-treated. I second the nomination of M. Lindet.'

'I refuse to put his name to the meeting,' said the bishop.'

'My brother!' exclaimed Monseigneur de la Ferronnais, 'you are throwing everything into their hands. Be cool.'

'You are not competent to refuse,' said the Abbé Lecerf. 'If you abdicate your place as president, we shall elect another president. As long as you occupy the chair, monseigneur, you must propose whoever is named.'

'I contend,' spoke the dean, rising slowly, 'that this proposal is indecent. There are certain charges which it is not well should be given to the world, and discussed in public. If the bishop sees fit to exercise his prerogative, and to secretly punish a priest without publishing his reasons, he is perfectly justified in so doing. It is necessary to screen the Church from scandal.'

'It is never justice to condemn unheard,' said Lecerf.

'We have groaned too long under this arbitrary exercise of power. The bishop may suspend and inhibit any congruist in his diocese,' exclaimed another priest. 'If he chooses, he can at any future occasion, when his gracious Majesty summons us again,—he can, I say, hold the election in his own hands by suspending and inhibiting all those who are stipendiary curates, and thus throw all the power into the scale of the high clergy.'

'It is a question of liberty to elect or of servitude,' shouted another curé.

'Gentlemen,' said an old ecclesiastic of Évreux, 'I was present last autumn during a conversation between the bishop's *officiel*, M. Ponce, and an abbé, whom I see before me, but will not name,—an abbé, gentlemen, whom I have noticed to be exceedingly diligent in whipping up voters on the side of privilege. During the conversation at which I was present, the name of M. Lindet, curé of Bernay, was mentioned. The abbé here present stated that he had heard rumours of the intention of some of the clergy of the deanery of Bernay to make an attempt to nominate M. Lindet as a distinguished upholder of liberal opinions, and as a priest of much experience and of great influence. The officer of monseigneur, sitting yonder in the chair, replied to this that he had discussed the matter with the bishop, and that they had agreed to stop the nomination at all ventures. M. Ponce suggested an inhibition, and he said that the bishop had sent him to Bernay to find some excuse for serving one on the unfortunate curé of that parish. I address myself to his Lordship, our president. Let him deny this if he dares. If he does deny it, I shall at once mention the name of the abbé whom I heard in conversation with the *officiel.*'

A storm was instantly evoked: some clamoured for the name, others called on the bishop to answer, and others cried ' Shame, shame ! '

' Let the name of M. Lindet be put to the meeting ? ' asked the same old priest. ' His Lordship is sullen. Rise, all who vote for M. Lindet.'

Instantly five or six hundred electors sprang up and waved their hands above their heads.

' Those in favour of M. Durand, stand up.'

There was a clatter, as the voters for the inhibited priest sat down, and about fifty stood up.

'. Take the numbers,' rose in a shout from the others.

Monseigneur de la Ferronnais held his superior by the arm, or the Bishop of Évreux would have left the room in a fury.

'For Heaven's sake!' exclaimed he, 'do be calm. Accept this vote, and you will get your own man in as the second delegate.'

'I will have nothing more to say to this assembly of ruffians,' said the Bishop of Évreux, wrenching his hand away.

'I beseech you remain here.'

'Not another moment,' he said, rising.

There burst from the mass of priests a shout:

'He has vacated the chair!'

'Let the Bishop of Lisieux take it!' cried the Abbé Lecerf.

'The Bishop of Lisieux in the chair! Long live the new president!'

Monseigneur de la Ferronnais looked at the Bishop of Évreux.

'What is to be done?' he asked.

'Take the chair, in God's name,' answered the president, thrusting it towards him; 'I will not remain here another moment.'

'You must indeed remain,' said the Bishop of Lisieux, 'unless you are inclined to pass through all those infuriated priests to the door. There is no side entrance to be used as an easy mode of exit.'

Monseigneur de Narbonne scowled down the hall; his colleague was right, and he seated himself in the chair of his suffragan.

The Bishop of Lisieux rose to the occasion. As he took the place of the late president a smile illumined his face—a smile full of good humour, which was at once reflected from every face in the saloon.

'Be quiet, you babies!' he said, stretching his right hand towards the ranks of discontented priests; and then he laughed a bright, ringing laugh, full of freshness.

Instantly it was echoed from every part of the room.

'I was once in Spain,' began Monseigneur de la Ferronnais; —Monseigneur de Narbonne winced;—'I was once in Spain, at the city of Pampeluna. I found a crowd of people hurrying to the great square before the principal church. What did they rush there for? To see a bull baited. I returned to France. I stayed a day or two in the cathedral town of Bayonne. I found the city assembled on the quay of the Adour. Wherefore? To enjoy the sport of bear-baiting. Gentlemen! I have seen a bull baited, I have seen a bear baited, but never till this day have I witnessed the baiting of a bishop.'

He spoke with emphasis, and with that ease of gesture which a Frenchman knows so well how to make good use of. His words raised a storm of laughter and cheers. The Bishop of Évreux writhed in his chair. His suffragan turned towards him, extended his arms as though to embrace him, laid his head on one side, and in a tone full of commiseration said : 'He is down! shall we spare him? In the arena of ancient

Rome, the gladiator who fell elevated the index of his right hand to ask pity of the spectators——I see—' Monseigneur de Narbonne had his hand up to stop his colleague, but at the allusion, he instantly withdrew it with a frown. 'Now, my good spectators, who are also his assailants, do you stand *presso* or *verso pollice?* That is right! You are spared, my Lord Bishop of Evreux.'

He seated himself with rapid motion, and crossed his legs; then, composing his face, he said :

'I suppose I need not have voting-papers upon M. Lindet. It is hardly necessary for me to put his name before you again, but we must proceed formally. M. Lindet has been proposed by the Abbé Lecerf, and seconded by M. Rigaud. Those in favour of M. Lindet, hold up their hands.'

He counted the raised palms, collectedly, rank by rank, requesting each row when counted to lower their hands.

'Those opposed to M. Lindet, hold up their hands.'

In a minute, he declared Thomas Lindet elected delegate to the National Assembly.

'Now, gentlemen,' said the president, 'I wish in no way to influence your votes in other ways than that of sobriety and consideration. You must remember that the Church will not be fairly represented at the States-General, if those in the enjoyment of benefices be wholly excluded. Choose for your second delegate one as liberal, nay, as revolutionary in his views as you please, but pray choose one who may represent the moneyed interests of the Church. I leave it to your sense of justice and propriety.'

This little speech was received with hearty applause.

M. de la Lande was proposed, seconded, and carried almost unanimously.

The Bishop of Lisieux turned to his angry brother prelate, and whispered :

'Now we have got your own man in. You see what may be done with good-humour. If you had attempted to browbeat those curés any longer, they would have elected as their second representative a more furious democrat than even Lindet himself.'

'I have had humiliations enough to bear without being made the butt of your jokes before a rabble,' answered Monseigneur de Narbonne, sullenly.

CHAPTER XVII.

GABRIELLE had found a temporary asylum at the house of Robert Lindet, the lawyer. Robert lived in a small villa, with his brother Peter, on the side of the road to Brionne and Rouen. The house stood back from the dusty highway, with a long strip of garden before it, and a high wall completely shutting it off from the road. A row of trees occupied one side of the garden, ending in a green ivy-covered arbour, in which no one ever sat, as it occupied an angle in the high walls, and commanded no view, and was by its position excluded from air and light.

The garden was poor. Two little patches of flowers—larkspur and escholtzia and white lilies—were nearly the only ones that grew in it; the two former sowed themselves, and the latter remained where it had been planted in Robert's youth. The rest of the garden was turf. On it stood a hutch of white rabbits with black noses, which were constantly escaping over the garden and destroying the flowers. The house front consisted of two parts, the portion occupied by the lawyer and his brother, and that given over to the cook and kitchen, which latter portion was an incongruous adjunct to the trim little house. The kitchen was on the ground-floor, and a ladder staircase in the open air gave access to the bedroom above.

The house—little altered—is at present the abode of the Chaplain to the Convent of the Sisters of the Blessed Sacrament.

The lower rooms of the house being turned into offices, the brothers were wont, in cold weather, to sit over the fire in the kitchen, where Gabrielle presided.

Gabrielle was not happy. That last piercing cry of her protectress and friend, Madame Berthier, had entered her heart, and stuck there like a barbed arrow. As she lay awake at night, she thought of the huge prison, dark and cold, down whose passages no sunbeams streamed, and of the poor lady alone there, in solitude and despair. During the day she thought of her,—of the cold she must feel in her cell, of the deprivation of scenes of beauty and life. 'I ought to do something for her, but what can I do!' She asked those who knew anything about Paris whether there would be a possibility of her obtaining admission to the Bastille, to wait upon the prisoner, but they all replied with a shake of the head.

On March 25th, Étienne Percenez was sitting in the kitchen with the brothers Lindet, whilst Gabrielle washed dishes and forks and spoons at the sink in the window.

The conversation had run upon the political movements of the day, the abuses needing correction, the rights of the people which required acknowledgment. Gabrielle had listened without much interest, and the names of Necker, Artois, Sartines, De Brienne, &c., had entered her ear without attracting her attention, when all at once it was arrested by a remark of the colporteur :

'The Bastille and the lettres-de-cachet! Have they been protested against?'

'The time has not come,' said Robert Lindet; 'our cahiers mention grievances of which we are personally cognizant. When the States-general meet, then every nook and cranny of the old *régime* will be searched and swept out.'

'What can be more iniquitous than the lettre-de-cachet?' asked Percenez; 'the king gives blank forms for any one to fill in, and thus lives and liberties are sacrificed without trial. Saint-Florentin gave away fifty-thousand. What became of these blank orders of imprisonment? They were matters of traffic; fathers were shut up by their sons, husbands by their wives; Government clerks, their mistresses, and the friends of the mistresses,—any pretty woman of easy virtue inconvenienced by a strait-laced husband or father or mother, with a little civility, flattery, money, could get these terrible orders by which to bury those they desired to get rid of.'

'And sometimes,' said Robert, 'the Bastille was an easy

payment of a State debt. The Baron and Baroness Beausoleil spent their fortune and their time in opening valuable mines. When all their wealth was gone, they applied to Richelieu for payment, or at least a recognition of their services. The recognition was accorded them. They were shut up for life in the Bastille, apart from one another, and separated for ever from their children!'

'Ah!' exclaimed Peter; 'this is too bad. You know that the king had abolished these lettres-de-cachet. Why do you rake up old grievances which are long dead?'

'Dead grievances!' said Stephen Percenez; 'you forget, Monsieur Pierre, they are only asleep, not dead. It is true Louis XVI has forbidden the incarceration of any one at the request of their families, without a well-grounded reason. But who is to be judge of the soundness of the reason? And who forced him to decree that?—Madame Legros.'

'Madame Legros!' said Gabrielle, coming forward; 'tell me, who was she?'

'Did you never hear of Latude?' asked Percenez.

'Never,' answered Gabrielle. 'Was he a prisoner?'

'Yes, for thirty-four years in Bicêtre and the Bastille, thrown into the worst dungeons, by the spite of a woman—a harlot, Madame de Pompadour. He wrote his appeals for mercy, and pardon for crimes he had never committed, on rags, in his own blood; then they buried him in holes underground with-

out light, where he spent long years in domesticating rats.
Once a memorial addressed to some philanthropist or other—
one memorial out of a hundred, was lost by a drunken jailer—a
woman picked it up. That woman was a poor mercer, who
sat stitching in her shop door. She picked up the fluttering
sheet and read it, and resolved to liberate the miserable
sufferer.'

Gabrielle bent forward, with her eyes fixed on the
speaker.

'What did she do?' she asked, eagerly.

'What did she not do?' returned Etienne Percenez; 'she
worried every great man to whom she could obtain access
with her story of the wrongs of Latude, and his sufferings
in prison. She consecrated her life to his. All kinds of
misfortune beset her, but she held firmly to her cause. Her
husband remonstrated with her—he called her enthusiasm
folly, for her business failed, as well it might, when her time
was spent in seeking audiences with great Lords and high
Churchmen, and when her attention was fixed on something
other than caps and gowns. Her father died, then her mother.
Slanderous tales were raised about her: it was asserted that
she was the mistress of the prisoner, for whose liberation she
laboured, and sacrificed all. The police threatened her; but
she remained invincible. The story of Latude's sufferings
and of Madame Legros' self-devotion spread through France,

whispered from one to another. In the depths of winter, on foot, far advanced in pregnancy, the brave woman set out for Versailles, resolved to appeal at head-quarters. She found a femme de chambre inclined to take her memorial to the queen, but an abbé passing snatched it from her hand, and tore it up, bidding her not attempt to meddle. Cardinal de Rohan—he, you know, who was concerned in the affair of the necklace—was good-natured, and he endeavoured to move Louis XVI to pardon Latude—pardon him for what? for having in some way caused annoyance to his grandfather's mistress; in what way?—nobody knows. Three times the king refused to pardon and liberate this man whose life had been wasted in a prison. At last, in 1784, Madame Legros had so worked on public opinion, that the king was forced to release him. You see what woman can do!'

Gabrielle raised her eyes and hands to heaven.

'May God enable me to do the same for Madame Berthier!' she cried.

'There now, Étienne,' said Robert, with a curl of the lip; 'you have applied a match to a barrel of gunpowder.'

'Ah! if it were to blow down the walls of the Bastille!' said the pedlar, shaking his brown head.

'Dear friend,' said the girl, laying her hand on Percenez' arm; 'she who saved me in my hour of deepest need, she who stood between me and ruin, is now in that awful place.

Her last cry was to me to save her. Tell me, what can I do?'

'Nothing, absolutely nothing, except washing up dishes,' answered Robert Lindet.

She did not attend to him, but looked straight into Percenez' eyes. The girl was so beautiful, so earnest and enthusiastic, that the colporteur gazed on her with admiration, and did not answer.

'I must do something,' she proceeded to say; 'I hear her voice calling me, night and day. That cry of "Gabrielle, save me!" haunts me. I am tortured with inactivity.'

'My good girl,' Robert observed, 'there is not the slightest occasion for inactivity. There are the floors to be scoured, and the cobwebs to be brushed away, and the dishes to be washed.'

'Good, kind master!' cried the girl, turning to him; 'you have received me when I was homeless. But did I not tell you that I could not remain in your service? I warned you that I had something to do that must be done——'

'Fudge!' said the lawyer. 'You women are highflown, crazy creatures. You can do nothing for Madame Berthier; content yourself with the certainty of that, and stick to your kitchen-work, or, if you like it better, feed the rabbits.'

Percenez smiled. A smile on his rugged brown countenance was rare, and it had meaning whenever it appeared.

'Excuse me, M. Lindet,' he said; 'I have faith in enthusiasm. Before that every barrier goes down. It is absolutely unconquerable.'

'Enthusiasm is faith run to extravagance,' answered the lawyer. 'Enthusiasm is good for a dash, but it is not fit for continuous work. Enthusiasm would level a mountain, but it would never reconstruct it.'

'Hark!' exclaimed Peter, holding up his finger.

The others were silent and listened. They heard the bells of S. Cross pealing merrily.

'What can be the occasion?' asked Percenez.

Peter took his pipe out of his mouth, and walked slowly into the garden. Robert and Stephen followed him. From the high stone wall the clamour of the bells was echoed noisily.

'It is very odd,' said Robert; 'what can be the reason?'

At that moment the garden-door opened, and M. Lamy, one of the curates (*vicaires*) of Bernay, rushed in, his face beaming with pleasure.

'Well! what is the news?' asked Percenez.

'The best, the very best of news,' answered the priest. 'M. Thomas Lindet is elected delegate of the clergy to the Estates-general.'

'An enthusiast,' said Robert, with a smile aside to Percenez.

'Ah! M. Robert, and it is just his enthusiasm which has taken him ahead of all the rest of the class, and turned him into a delegate.'

Whilst Robert and Peter talked with M. Lamy, the little brown colporteur turned back to the kitchen, and said to Gabrielle: 'Well, what about your protectress?'

'My friend,' answered Gabrielle, earnestly and vehemently; 'I shall go to Paris, if I go on foot, and I shall see what can be done. I will implore the queen on my knees to use her influence to obtain the release of Madame Berthier.'

'You forget; that lady is not shut up as a political offender, but because she is insane.'

'I will do what I can,' answered the girl, simply. 'She has no one else to assist her—no one else to speak for her.'

'You are only a peasant-girl.'

'Well! what was Madame Legros?'

'Are you resolved?'

She put her hand on her heart.

'I must go,' she said. 'I have no rest here. I shall have no rest till I have done my utmost.'

'Paris is a dangerous place for a young and pretty maiden.'

'Ah! Monsieur Étienne, the good God, who raised up a protectress for me in my need before, will deliver me in any future peril.'

'What have you to live upon in Paris?'

'I do not know.'

'You must bear in mind that great distress exists there, that money is scarce and provisions are dear.'

'God will provide.'

'He will provide if He calls you there, not otherwise.'

'Is it not His call that I hear now?' asked the girl, her face brightening with enthusiasm. 'My friend, my father's friend, listen to me. There is a something within me, I cannot tell you what it is, which draws me from this place after my dear, unfortunate madame. Only yesterday I was walking in the wood above La Couture. I went to pray at a crucifix which I well know, for it was there that M. Lindet first stood my champion against him whom I will not name. I prayed there—I cannot tell you for how long, and I asked for a sign—a sign what I was to do.' She paused timidly, dropped her eyes, and continued in a whisper: 'Whilst I was on my knees, all on an instant I felt something leap upon my shoulder.'

. 'Well, child, what was it?' asked Percenez with a smile.

'It was Madame Berthier's yellow cat, it looked so lean and neglected, and its yellow dye was nearly worn off it. It knew me, for it rubbed its head against my cheek.'

'Nonsense, Gabrielle, do you call *that* a sign?'

'Yes, Monsieur Étienne, it was a sign to me. It would not have been so to anyone else, may be, but I know what that cat was to the poor lady, I know what she suffers now in being separated from it; and, if it were only to restore her cat to her, I would walk barefoot all the way to Paris.'

'I suspect the only success you will meet with will be that.'

'Well, and that will be something.'

'You are a resolute girl.'

'Monsieur Étienne, I *must* go.'

'Why so?'

'If I did not go, I should die.'

The little brown man looked fixedly at her, and then said:

'Gabrielle, I have known you from a little girl. I am going to Paris. Like you, I *must* go. I am fixed with a desire to see the working out of this great problem, the States-General. Gabrielle! the French people are like your Madame Berthier, chained and in prison. I do not know whether my feeble voice will avail to effect their release. You do not know whether yours will liberate one individual out of that great suffering family. Well! we go in hope, vague may be, but earnest, and resolved to do our best. We shall go together.'

'What do you say, monsieur?'

'I will go and visit my sister, Madame Deschwanden, and shall take you with me. We shall see what takes place.'

'You will help me to get to Paris?'

'Yes, I will.'

Miaw! The yellow cat, which had been asleep in a corner, was now wide awake, and at a bound had reached Gabrielle's shoulder.

How merrily in Gabrielle's ear sounded the bells of S. Cross!

CHAPTER XVIII.

OLD Paris is no more. Every day some feature of the ancient capital disappears. This is a commonplace remark. Everyone says it; but few realize how true it is. We, who revisit that queen of cities after an interval of—say, ten years, see mighty changes. Streets are open where were houses once; markets have altered their sites; squares occupy the place where we remember piles of decaying houses; churches appear, where we did not know that they stood, so buried were they in high, many-storied houses.

We can breathe in Paris now. Down the boulevards the breeze can now rustle and sweep away the stale odours which once hung all the year round ancient Paris.

But we have no conception of what that capital was in 1789. Paris had grown without system. None had drawn out a plan of what it was to be, where the streets were to run, and where squares were to open. The thoroughfares had come by chance, without order, without law, almost without object; the streets twisted and wound their way between walls black with smoke, and overhanging; the houses, with their feet in mud and garbage, and their heads in smoke, stood sideways to the road, as though they turned away to avoid a disagreeable sight and odour. Their narrow front to the street was topped with a high-pitched gable, unless some modern architect had squared it off. Here and there were cemeteries adjoining markets, a refuse heap on which lay dead animals in putrefaction, nooks, where beggars crouched in rags, blind alleys in which squalid children played, open sewers, and public cesspools.

The Seine, spanned by five bridges encumbered with low vessels moored head and stern, out of which the washer-women cleaned their dirty linen, resembled a wide stagnant ditch. The fall being slight, the river but leisurely carried off the filth from the sewers, the soap from the washing-boats, and the dye that flowed into it from the factories. Add to this the slops and sewage of the Hôtel Dieu, which contained six thousand patients suffering from all the loath-some disorders to which human nature is subject, and one can appreciate the *bon-mot* of Foote, when he was asked by a Parisian whether he had such a river in London, 'No, we had such an one, but we stopped it up (alluding to the Fleet Ditch); at present, we have only the Thames.'

Beneath the Pont Nôtre Dame, a net was every night let down to stop the bodies of drowned men, and of such as were murdered and thrown into the river.

At seven in the morning, twice a week, a bell was rung through the streets for the inhabitants to sweep before their houses; but for this, there would have been no possibility of walking, there being no foot-way.

Gabrielle and the little brown Percenez entered Paris on the 28th of April. The streets, crowded with people, astonished the girl. Her eyes turned with wonder from side to side. The height of the houses, the intricacy of the streets, the antiquity of the buildings, the number of crossings, shops, coffee-houses, stalls, were such as she had never seen before. Her ears were assailed by the cries of fruiterers and pedlars of all sorts with their carts, and by the rattle and rumble of wheels upon the stone pavement. As a coach drove by, the girl and her conductor stepped up against the wall, there being no footway; when a couple of carriages met, it was often difficult to avoid being run over. The hackney coaches, distinguished then, as they are now, by numbers in yellow painted on their backs, jolted past in shoals. Uneasy, dirty vehicles they were, with a board slung behind the coach-box, upon which the driver stood. Trim little sedan chairs on wheels some thirty inches high, dragged by a man between shafts like the handles of a wheelbarrow, dived in and out among the stalls and carriages, and rattled jauntily and expeditiously along. Sometimes a grand coach, behind which were suspended footmen in livery, with long white staves, rolled down solemnly and slowly, scattering the hucksters and sedan chairs, as a hawk disperses a flight of sparrows.

'Do you notice, Gabrielle,' said Percenez, 'the wheels of the private carriages are girt with tires made in small pieces, whilst the hired fiacres have their wheels girt with hoops of iron in one piece? You would be surprised, little girl, how much envy the jointed tires excite ; for only gentlemen of birth are entitled to use them.'

'Are we going the right way, Monsieur Étienne?' asked Gabrielle, timidly, for she was so bewildered by the novelty of her position, that she thought the streets of Paris a tangle in which none could fail to lose the way.

'Be not afraid, we are bound for the street S. Antoine. I know the road. I was here only five years ago, and Paris is not a place to change in a hurry.'

Just then they heard a body of voices shouting a song. Gabrielle looked round, and exclaimed :—

'Oh, Monsieur Étienne, here is a great mob advancing. What is to be done?'

'Do not be afraid,' answered the little man; 'listen, what is it they are chanting?'

The words were audible. As the band approached, every man, woman, and child joined in the song :—

'Vive le tiers état de France !
Il aura la prépondérance

Sur le prince, sur le prélat.
Ahi ! povera nobilita !
Le plébéien, puits de science,
En lumières, en expérience,
Surpasse le prêtre et magistrat,
Ahi ! povera nobilita !'

Percenez took off his hat, and waved it with a cheer.

On they came, a legion, a billow of human beings, bearing before them an effigy, raised aloft, of a large man with a white waistcoat, a snuff-coloured coat, a powdered wig, and wearing a decoration, the *cordon-noir*. The figure rocked upon the shoulders of the men who carried it, and the by-standers hooted and laughed. Away before the mob flew the hackney coaches and the wheeled chairs, like the 'povera nobilita' escaping from the rising people. Heads appeared at the windows; from some casements kerchiefs were flut-tered; from most, faces looked down without expressing special interest or enthusiasm.

The little brown colporteur caught the sleeve of a man who sold onions.

'What effigy is that ?' he asked.

'That is Réveillon,' was the answer.

'And who is he ?'

'A paper-maker.'

'Why are the mob incensed against him ?'

'He has made a great fortune, and is now bent on reducing the wages of his workmen.'

'Is that all?'

'And he has received, or is about to receive, a decoration.'

Percenez shrugged his shoulders; the onion-seller did the same.

'Monsieur Etienne!' said Gabrielle, timidly; 'do let us retire before this crowd. It will swallow us up.'

'You are right, child; we will get out of the way. I have no interest in this affair.'

He drew her back into a large doorway with a wicket gate in it. They stepped through this wicket into the carriage-way to the yard within. A violent barking saluted them. At the same moment, a gentleman emerged upon one of the galleries that surrounded the court, and, leaning on the balcony, called—

'Gustave!'

'Eh, monsieur?' exclaimed the porter, starting from his room.

'Shut and lock the door, before the mob come up.'

Percenez and Gabrielle recognised the voice and face of Berthier. Before Gustave could fasten the gate, the girl dragged her companion back into the street; in another moment they were caught in the advancing wave, and swept onwards towards the Faubourg S. Antoine:

What followed passed as a dream. Gabrielle saw rough
faces on all sides of her, wild eyes, bushy beards and moustaches. She heard the roar of hoarse voices chanting; she
felt the thrust and crush around her, and her feet moved
rapidly, otherwise she would have fallen and been trodden
down. She clung to Percenez, and the little man held her
hand tightly in his own. It was strange to Gabrielle afterwards to remember distinctly a host of objects, trivial in
themselves, which impressed themselves on her memory in
that march. There was a man before her with a blue hand-
kerchief tied over his hat and under his chin. The corner
of this kerchief hung down a little on the right, and Gabrielle
would have had it exactly in the middle. The green coat
of a fellow bearing a pole and an extemporized flag attached
to it, had been split up the back and mended with brown
thread. In one place only was the thread black. Gabrielle
remembered the exact spot in the coat where the brown
thread ended and the black thread began. The great man
who marched on her left had a bottle of leeches in his hand,
and he was filled with anxiety to preserve the glass from
being broken. How came he among the crowd? Gabrielle
wondered, and formed various conjectures. He was very
careful of his leeches, but also very determined to remain
in the midst of the throng. Above the heads and hats and
caps rocked the image of the paper manufacturer, and

Gabrielle saw the arms flap and swing, as it was jerked from side to side by the bearers. A dead cat whizzed through the air, and struck the effigy on the head, knocking the three-cornered hat sideways. The mob shouted and stood still. Then one of the men who preceded them with a banner laid his pole across the street, and shouted for the cat. It was tossed over the heads of the people, and he picked it up and attached it to the neck of the image of Réveillon. Then he reared his banner again, and the crowd flowed along as before.

Gabrielle took advantage of the halt to peep into a basket she carried on her arm. As she raised the lid, a paw was protruded, and a plaintive miaw announced to her that the yellow cat she had brought with her was tired of its imprisonment, and alarmed at the noise.

All at once the pressure on every side became less, the rioters had moved out of the narrow street into an open space. The girl looked up. Before her rose dark massive towers,—she could see five at a glance; one stood at an angle towards the street, drums of towers crenelated at top, and capped with pepper-boxes for the sentinels. The walls were pierced at rare intervals with narrow slits. One window only, of moderate dimensions, was visible, and that was high up in the angle-tower, oblong, narrow, cut across with a huge stone transom, and netted over with iron stanchions. The walls were black with age and smoke. The sunlight that fell upon them did not relieve their tint, but marked them with shadows black as night.

Adjoining the street was a high wall, against which were built shops and taverns. These, however, ceased to encumber the wall near the gate, which was in the Italian style, low pedimented, and adorned with the arms of France in a shield. Through slits on either side moved the great beams of the drawbridge.

As Gabrielle looked, awe-struck, at this formidable building, she heard the clank of chains and the creak of a windlass, and slowly the great arms rose and carried up with them a bridge that shut over the mouth of the gate, as though there were secrets within which might not be uttered in the presence of that crowd.

The mob fell into line before the gate and moat that protected it, facing it with threatening looks. All at once, with a roar like that of an advancing tidal wave, there burst from the mob, with one consent, the curse—'Down with the Bastille!'

Then they faced round again, and rushed upon the factory of Réveillon, situated under the towers of the terrible fortress.

'Up to the lanthorn!'

The cry was responded to by a general shout. In another moment a rope was flung over the chain stretched across

the street from which the lanthorn lighting the street was
suspended, and the effigy of Réveillon dangled in the air.
This execution was greeted with yells of applause; men and
women joined hands and danced under the figure. Some
threw sticks and stones at it; these falling on the heads of
the spectators, added to the confusion. At last, a young
man, catching the legs of the image, mounted it, and seated
himself astride on the shoulders. He removed the three-
cornered hat and wig and placed them on his own head,
amidst laughter and applause. The strain upon the lanthorn-
chain was, however, too great, and one of the links yielding
at the moment when the youth stood upon Réveillon's
shoulders and began a dance, he, the effigy, and the lanthorn were precipitated into the street. What became of
the man nobody knew, and nobody cared; the image was
danced upon and trodden into the dirt; the lanthorn was
shivered to pieces, and the glass cut the feet of those who
trampled on it.

The factory doors were shut and barred; the windows
were the same. The rioters hurled themselves against the
great gates, which were studded with iron, but they could not
burst them open. Some shouted for fire, others for a beam
which might be driven against them, and so force them open.
But the banner-bearer in the green coat stitched with black
and brown thread laid his pole against the side of the house,

swarmed up it, axe in hand, and smote lustily at the shutters of one of the windows. The splinters flew before his strokes, and soon one of the valves broke from its hinges, and slid down the wall. Next minute, the green man was inside, waving his hat to the people, who cheered in response.

They fell back from the door. Another man crept in at the broken window, and joined the fellow who had cut his way through the shutter. The two together unfastened the door, and the mob poured into Réveillon's factory. Adjoining was the house of Réveillon. Its doors were forced open at the same time as the paper-making establishment. The private entrance to an upper storey of the workshops from the house was burst by those in the factory, and the mob crowding in from the street met that breaking in from above. The besiegers having now taken complete possession, and meeting with no resistance (for Réveillon had taken refuge in the Bastille, and his servants had fled,) they spread themselves over the premises from attic to cellar. The workmen lately employed to make and dye the paper were foremost in breaking the machinery, and in tapping the large vats in which the white pulp lay, thus flooding the floors with what looked like curdled milk. Some descended to the cellars and drank the wine stored for Réveillon's table, others drank the dyes, mistaking them for wine, and rolled in agony in the whey-like fluid on the ground, spluttering out the crimson and green liquors they had imbibed. Those who had axes, and those who had armed themselves with fragments of the machinery, smashed mirrors, tables, pictures, broke open drawers and destroyed all the movables within reach, and then flung them through the windows among the crowd below. Among other objects discovered was a portrait in oils of Ré- veillon; this was literally minced up by the rioters, who waxed more furious as they found material on which to expend their rage. Two men, armed with a great saw, began to cut through the main rafters of the great room of the factory. When those who thronged this appartement saw what was taking place, they were filled with panic, and rushed to the door, or flung themselves out of the windows, to escape being trampled down by those behind. Some, entering the rag-store, rent open the bales, and strewed the tatters about in all directions. One man—it was he with the leeches—holding his bottle, still un- emptied and unbroken, in one hand, applied a torch to the rag-heaps, and set the store in a blaze; others fired the ware- house of paper. Flames issued from the cellars of Réveillon's house. It was apparent to all the rioters within, that, unless they made a speedy exit, they would perish in the fire. In- stantly a rush was made to the doors. As they poured through them, a horizontal flash of light darted into their eyes, followed by a rattling discharge, and several of the foremost rioters rolled on the pavement.

Late in the day, when all the mischief was done, a regiment

of Grenadiers had been ordered to the spot by the commandant of that quarter of the town, M. de Châtelet.

The mob replied to the volley by hurling paving-stones, broken pieces of Réveillon's furniture, iron fragments of the machinery; in short, anything ready at hand.

The man with the bottle of leeches ran out into the middle of the street, a torch in his right hand, flourished the firebrand over his head, and called on his companions to follow him against the soldiers. Two or three started forwards. The military fired again. The man leaped high into the air, hurled his firebrand into their midst, and fell his length, shot through the heart; his bottle broke, and the leeches wriggled over his prostrate form.

The Grenadiers did not fire again. A rumbling noise was heard, and along with it the tramp of advancing feet. In another moment the red uniforms of the Swiss soldiers gleamed out of the shadow of the street, and a battalion with fixed bayonets charged down the square in front of the Grenadiers, sweeping the mob before them. In their rear were a couple of cannon, drawn by horses, which were rapidly placed in position to clear the streets. But they were not discharged. The Grenadiers wheeled and charged in the direction opposite to that taken by the Swiss, and in a few minutes the scene of the riot was deserted by all save the dead and the dying, and the inhabitants looking anxiously from their windows.

Why had not the soldiers been sent earlier?

On the preceding day the mob had threatened this attack, but had been prevented from accomplishing their intention by the train of carriages that encumbered the road through the Faubourg S. Antoine, the 27th April being the day of the Charenton races. They had contented themselves with stopping all the carriages, and shouting through the windows, ' Long live the Third Estate!' The carriage of the Duke of Orleans had been alone excepted. The people had surrounded it, and cheered vociferously.

The reason why the destruction of Réveillon's factory was permitted by Berthier the Intendant, and Besenval the Commandant of the Forces in and around Paris, was that the Court had taken alarm at the threatening attitude of the third estate and the people of the metropolis, and it hoped to have an excuse for concentrating troops on Versailles and Paris.

The elections at Paris were not completed, the Estates-General had not met, but the crowd of nobles, headed by the Count d'Artois and the Princes of Condé and Conti, had seen that the King, by calling together the three estates, and by permitting Necker to double the representation of the Commons, had created a Frankenstein, which, if allowed to use its power, would strangle privilege. The Count d'Artois ruled the Queen, and the Queen ruled the weak, good-natured King. Marie Antoinette had imbibed fears from the Count, and had communicated them to the King, and he had begun to feel restless and anxious about the great assembly, which he had convoked. He could not prevent its meeting, but he could constrain its utterances, and he only wanted an excuse for massing around it the army, to force the third estate to vote money, and to keep silence on the subject of reform.

But where are Percenez and Gabrielle ? We have lost sight of them in the crowd. We must return to their side. We left them before the Bastille, as the mob rolled towards Réveillon's factory.

' Now, my child, hold fast to me,' said the colporteur ; ' my sister lives near this,—yonder, under the wall. She is married again; I always forget her new name,—it is not that of a Christian—at least, it is not a French name. She has married one of the Swiss guard, a widower, with a tall, hulking son, and she has got a daughter by her late husband, Madeleine. Ah ! you will like her,—a nice girl, but giddy.'

The little man worked his way through the crowd till he had brought Gabrielle before a small house that abutted upon the outer wall of the fortress. The door was shut and locked, and Percenez knocked at it in vain ; then he beat against the window-glass, but no one answered, the fact being that his sister, Madame Deschwanden—such was the name unpronouncable by French lips—and her daughter, Madeleine Chabry, were upstairs, looking out of the window at the mob and its doings, and were deaf to the clatter at their own door. Percenez soon discovered the faces of his sister and niece, and stepping back to where he could be seen by them, signalled to them, and shouted their names.

' Ah ! ' screamed Madame Deschwanden, clasping her hands, then throwing them round her daughter's neck, and kissing her, ' there is my brother Stephen ! Is it possible ? Stephen, is that really you ? What brought you here ? How are all the good people at Bernay ? I am charmed ! Madeleine, I shall die of joy.'

' Will you let us in, good sister ? '

' Who is that with you ? You must tell me. But wait ! I will open the door myself. Oh ecstasy ! oh raptures ! Praised be Heaven ! Come, delicious brother, to my bosom.'

CHAPTER XIX.

As soon as Madame Deschwanden had introduced her brother and Gabrielle to the inside of her house, she fell back, contemplated Percenez with outspread hands and head on one side, and then precipitated herself into his arms, exclaiming, ' Oh ecstasy ! oh raptures ! it is he.'

Having extricated herself from her brother's arms almost as rapidly as she had fallen into them, she said, ' Come along to the window, and see the rest of the fun.'

She caught Percenez in one hand and Gabrielle in the other, and drew them upstairs into the room in which she had been sitting before she descended to admit them.

' Étienne, you know my daughter Madeleine, do you not ? ' she asked abruptly ; then turning towards the new comer, and from her to her own daughter, she introduced them :

' Madeleine Chabry—Madame Percenez.'

' Pardon me,' said the colporteur, laughing ; ' little Gabrielle is not my wife.'

' Ah ! a sweetheart.'

' No, nor that either.'

'Well, never mind explanations,' said Madame Deschwanden ;
'they are often awkward, and always unnecessary. Of one
thing I can be certain, mademoiselle is charming, and she is
heartily welcome,' she curtsied towards the girl, and then viva-
ciously changed the subject. 'The sport! we must not miss it.
Oh! they have got into the factory, and into the house.
Oh! the exquisite, the enchanting things that are being destroyed. Perfidious heavens! I know there are angelic wall-
papers in that abandoned Réveillon's shop—I have seen them
with these eyes—and all going to ruin. Saints in Paradise !
such papers with roses and jessamines and Brazilian humming-
birds.' Then, rushing to the door of the room, she called
loudly, 'Klaus! Klaus!'

'What do you want, mother?' asked a young man, coming
to the door.

Percenez and Gabrielle turned to look at him. He was
a slender youth of nineteen, with very light hair and large
blue eyes. His face was somewhat broad, genial, and good-
natured. He was without his coat, his shirt-sleeves were
rolled up his muscular arms, and the collar was open at the
throat, exposing his breast and a little black riband, to which
was attached a medal resting on it.

'What do I want!' exclaimed Madame Deschwanden,
starting from the window into the middle of the room.

'How can you ask such a question, Klaus? Look at these walls. They are my answer.'

'My dear mother, what do you mean?'

'Klaus, you are little better than a fool. The people are sacking the factory, and there you stand. My faith! it is enough to make angels swear! And papers—wall-papers, to be had for nothing—for the mere taking. I saw one myself with roses and jessamine and humming-birds, and there was another—another for a large room. I saw it with these eyes—a paper to paper heaven! with a blue sky and an Indian forest of palms, and an elephant with a tower on its back, and a man holding a large red umbrella, and a tiger in the attitude of death, receiving a shot, and foaming with rage, and monkeys up a palm. Mon Dieu! you must get it me at once, or I shall expire. Klaus, I must and will have those papers.'

'You absurd little mother,' said Klaus, stepping into the room and laughing; 'do you think I am going to steal Réveillon's goods for you, and get myself and you and father and Madeleine into trouble? Be content.'

'Content!' exclaimed madame. 'Who ever heard such a word? *Content!* with papers—wall-papers, think of that, going a-begging. I know that those idiots yonder will burn the factory and save nothing. Klaus, you seraph, my own jewel!' she cast herself on his bosom; 'to please the mamma, though she be a stepmother in name but never one in sentiment, to please her who studies your fondest whims. You know very well,' said she, suddenly recovering herself, 'that I put myself out of the way only yesterday for you, that I sacrificed my own wishes to yours only yesterday. Did I not prepare veal *à l'oseille* for your dinner, and you know in your inmost heart that I preferred it *aux petits pois?*' Then instantly becoming indignant, she frowned, stiffened in every joint, became angular, and said, 'ingrate!'

'My dear, good mother——'

'Now look you here,' she interrupted; 'we will sit together on the sofa, in the corner, and whisper together. Come along.' She had him by the arm, and dragged him over to the seat she had indicated, and pinned him into the angle with her gown, which she spread out before her, as she subsided beside him.

'You know, you rogue, that my wishes are law to you. Do not deny it. Think of this. I wish, I furiously desire, I burst with impatience to possess at least one of those papers. Bring enough to cover all the walls. I see it in your eyes—you are going! it mantles on your cheek, it quivers on your tongue. Oh ecstasy! oh raptures!' she leaped from her sofa, and running to those at the window kissed them all, one after the other. 'He has promised. This room will speedily be a bower of roses and jessamine and Brazilian humming-birds. Quick, Klaus, mein sohn!'

'He will not go, mother,' said Madeleine, speaking for the first time; 'he is too conscientious.'

'Conscientious!' echoed Madame Deschwanden, covering her eyes; 'that I should have lived to hear the word. Madeleine! he is none of us. He has that nasty German blood in his veins, and it has made him conscientious. My aunt's sister's son married a Hungarian, and their child was always afflicted with erysipelas. I attributed it to his Hungarian blood, poor child! But, Klaus! conquer it, and, oh! get me the angelic paper—that with the humming-birds, never mind that with the tiger and the elephant; and so compromise the matter. I declare, I declare!' she cried, darting to the window; 'they are casting the furniture out of the house—tables, chairs, and breaking them! To think of the expense! Ah! there goes a mirror. Madeleine, oh! if we could have secured that glass. It would have filled the space above the sideboard to perfection. If I could have seen myself in that mirror, and called it my own, I could have died singing.'

Madeleine darted out of the room, and ran downstairs. Next moment her mother and Percenez saw her in the crowd, pushing her way up to the house with resolution and success.

'That is my own daughter!' cried the enraptured lady: 'she is in everything worthy of me; she is, indeed! She gave me much trouble as a child, I brought her up at my own breast, and see how she is ready to repay me. She will bring me a thousand pretty things. Oh, rapture! As for Klaus, I will not call him "mein sohn" any more. I will not frame my lips to utter his Swiss jargon. Go to your saints, boy; cut and carve away at them, and remember to your shame that you have refused the entreaty of your mother. No, thank goodness! I am not your mother. I should have overlaid you fifty times had you been mine; I might have guessed what a sort of conscientious creature you would have grown up.'

'What is Klaus's work?' asked Percenez, to turn the subject.

'Work!' repeated Madame Deschwanden, 'why, he is a wood-carver; he makes saints for churches, and crucifixes, and Blessed Virgins, and all that sort of thing, you know; but it don't pay now, there's no demand. Madeleine began that once, but gave it up. You can't swim against the tide.'

'Then what is Madeleine's work now?'

'Oh! she is flower-girl at Versailles.'

Gabrielle looked up. 'I am a flower-girl,' she said, timidly.

'Oh, indeed!' answered Madame Deschwanden, quickly

running her eye over her. 'You are good-looking, you will do, only fish in a different pool from Madeleine. But oh, ecstasy! here comes Madeleine. What has she got?'

Madeleine was indeed visible pushing her way back from the factory. She had something in her hands, but what, was not distinguishable. In another minute she was upstairs and had deposited a beautiful mother-of-pearl box on the table, a box of considerable size, and of beautiful work-manship.

'What is in it?' almost shrieked Madame Deschwanden.

'My mother, I cannot tell; it is locked, and I have not the key.'

Madeleine was nearly out of breath. She leaned against the table, put her hand against her side, and panted. She looked so pretty, so bewitching, that Percenez could hardly be angry with her, though he knew she had done wrong. Her cheeks were flushed, her dancing black eyes were bright with triumph, and her attitude was easy and full of grace. She wore her hair loose, curled and falling over her neck and shoulders. Her bodice was low, exposing throat and bosom, both exquisitely moulded; her skirt was short, and allowed her neat little feet and ankles to be seen in all their perfection. Gabrielle thought she had never seen so pretty a girl. She herself was a marked contrast to Madeleine. She was not so slender and trim in her proportions, nor so agile in her movements; but her face was full of simplicity, and that was the principal charm. Madeleine's features were not so regular as those of Gabrielle, but there was far more animation in her face. The deep hazel eyes of the peasant-girl were steady, the dark orbs of the Parisian flower-girl sparkled and danced, without a moment's constancy. A woman's character is written on her brow. That of Gabrielle was smooth, and spoke of purity; the forehead of Madeleine expressed boldness and assurance.

'You are the joy of my life, the loadstar of my existence!' exclaimed the mother, embracing her daughter, and then the box, which she covered with kisses. 'Oh ecstasy! oh raptures! this is beautiful. Klaus, lend me one of your tools to force the box open. . Perhaps it contains jewels! Klaus, quick!'

The lad placed his hand on the coffer, and said, gravely: 'I am sorry to spoil your pleasure, dear mother; but this mother-of-pearl box must be returned.'

'Returned!' echoed madame with scorn,—'returned to the mob, who are breaking everything. I never heard such nonsense.'

'Not to the mob, but to M. Réveillon.'

'To M. Réveillon! what rubbish you do talk! I shall keep the box and cherish it. Mon Dieu! would you tear it from me now that I love it, that I adore it?'

'We shall see, when my father comes,' said Nicholas Deschwanden. 'I have no doubt of his decision.'

'I shall kill myself,' said Madame Deschwanden, 'and go to heaven, where I shall be happy, and you will not be able to rob me of all my pretty things, and pester me with your conscientious scruples. See if I do not! or I shall run away with a gentleman who will love me and gratify all my little innocent whims. See if I do not! And so I shall leave you and your father to talk your rigmaroles about Alps and lakes and glaciers, and chant your litanies to Bruder Klaus and Heiliger Meinrad. See if I don't!'

The discharge of musketry interrupted the flow of her threats, and the vehement little woman was next moment again at the window.

'Oh, how lucky!' she exclaimed: 'Madeleine! if you had been ten minutes later you would have been shot. Count, Etienne; count, Madeleine; one, two, three, four, oh how many there are down—killed, poor things! Dear me! I would not have missed the sight for a thousand livres. Etienne, Madeleine, you Klaus! come, look, they will fire again. Glorious! Oh, what fun! Ecstasy! raptures!'

After the second discharge madame drew attention to the man who had been shot through the heart—he with the bottle of leeches.

'How he leaped! He would have made his fortune on

the tight-rope. Oh! what would I not have given to have danced with him. I am certain he was a superb dancer. Did any of you ever in your life see a male cut such a caper? Never; it was magnificent, it was prodigious. More the pity that he is dead. He will never dance again,' she said, in a low and sad voice; but brightened up instantly again with the remark, 'Ah well! we must all die sooner or later. Etienne, count the dead, now that the soldiers have cleared the street and square. My faith! what a pity it is that dead men are not made serviceable for the table; and meat is so dear!' Then suddenly it occurred to the volatile lady that her brother and his little companion had come to take up their abode with her—and meat so dear! She attacked Etienne at once on the point.

'My dearest brother, whom I love above everyone—yes, whom I adore,—I will not deny it, whom I idolize,—tell me, where are you lodging?'

'I thought you could give Gabrielle and me shelter for awhile,' answered Percenez. 'I am sure Madeleine will share her bed with Gabrielle, my little ward, and I can litter myself a mattress of straw anywhere.'

'And you have not dined yet?' asked Madame Deschwanden.

'No; we have not had time to think of dinner.'

'But you are hungry?'

'Certainly.'

'And thirsty?'

'Very thirsty, I can assure you.'

Madame Deschwanden caught both his hands in hers, and shook them enthusiastically.

'My own best-beloved brother! I talk of you all day long, do I not, Madeleine? You, too, Klaus, can bear me witness. I am rejoiced to hear that you are hungry and thirsty. And you like thoroughly good dinners?'

'Most assuredly, when I can get them.'

'And you too?' she looked at Gabrielle, who whispered an affirmative.

'And you enjoy a really good bottle of wine?'

'Trust me,' answered Stephen.

'Then,' said Madame Deschwanden, hugging her brother to her heart, 'the best of everything is yours, at the sign of the Boot, two doors off, on the right hand, and table-d'hôte is in half an hour. Terms very moderate.'

'But, my sister!' said the little colporteur, drawing out of her embrace, and regarding her with a sly look, 'I have come to take up my residence with you.'

'And dine at the Boot,' put in the lady. 'I can confidently recommend the table there. It is largely patronized by the most discerning palates'

'But, my sister, I am quite resolved to take my meals with you.'

'You cannot, indeed!' exclaimed madame; 'my cookery is vile, it is baser than dirt. I am an abject cook.'

'Oh, Josephine, neither Gabrielle André nor I are particular.'

'André!' exclaimed Madame Deschwanden. 'Do you tell me the name of this seraph is André? Is she the daughter of Matthias André of Les Hirondelles?'

'To be sure she is.'

Madame now cast herself on the neck of the peasant girl, sobbed loudly, and wept copiously.

'To think it is you! the daughter of Matthias, who adored me, when I was your age. Yes, child; your father when a young man was my most devoted admirer; but, ah, bah! every one admired me then, but he above them all. And if I had accepted him as my husband—to think *you* might then have been my daughter. Poor Matthias! how is he?'

Percenez checked her with a look and shake of the head.

'Well, well! we all die, more's the pity; and your mother— dead too! Ah well! every sentence ends in a full stop, and so does the long rigmarole of life. Then in pity's sake let life be a Jubilate and not a De Profundis.'

'About meals?' said Percenez. His sister's countenance fell at once, but she rapidly recovered.

'Exactly. You will hear all the news at the Boot. Superb place for gossip. Oh you men, you men! you charge us women with tittle-tattling, and when you get together—' she

wagged her finger at him and laughed. 'Now, be quick,
Étienne! my brother, and you, my angel, Mademoiselle
André, and get your dinners over quick, and come here and
tell us the news, and we shall have a charming evening.'

'My sister,' said Percenez, 'you must really listen to my
proposal. I may be in Paris for weeks—perhaps months.
I intend to pursue my business of selling newspapers and
pamphlets here in Paris for a while, that is, during the session
of the States-General, and I cannot think of troubling you
with my presence as a guest. Will you let us lodge with
you? I will pay you so much a week for my bed and board,
and Gabrielle shall do the same. She has a mission to per-
form in Paris, and though I am not sanguine of her success,
nevertheless she must make an attempt. She can join
Madeleine in selling flowers, and I will guarantee that you
are no loser.'

'My own most cherished brother!' exclaimed Madame
Deschwanden; 'do not think me so mercenary as all that.
Gladly do I urge you to stay here, and join us at our frugal
table. You are welcome to every scrap of food in the larder,
and to every bed in the house. Far be it from me to be
mercenary. I hate the word—I scorn to be thought it. *I*
care for money! No one has as yet hinted such a thing to
me! No; you are welcome—welcome to a sister's hospitality.
The terms, by the way, you did not mention,' she said, in a
lower voice; 'we have taken in boarders at——'

She was interrupted by the entrance of Corporal Deschwanden, her husband, a tall, grave soldier, with a face as corrugated and brown as that of Percenez; his moustaches and
the hair of the head were iron grey, his eyes large and blue,
like his son's, and lighted with the same expression of frank
simplicity.

The corporal saluted Percenez and Gabrielle, as his wife
introduced them with many flourishes of the arms and flowers
of eloquence.

'You are heartily welcome, sir,' said the soldier in broken
French; 'and you, fraulein, the same.'

Then seating himself at the table he rapped the board with
his knuckles and said, ' Dinner !'

Madame Deschwanden and her daughter speedily served a
cold repast in the lower room, the mother making many
apologies for having nothing hot to offer, as she had been
distracted by the Réveillon riot, and now her head was racked
with pain, and she prayed Heaven would speedily terminate her
sufferings with death.

The old soldier during the meal looked over several times
at Gabrielle in a kindly manner, and treated her with courtesy.
The girl raised her timid eyes to his, and saw them beaming
with benevolence. A frightened smile fluttered to her lips,
and he smiled back at her.

'You have come a long way,' he said; 'and you must be

tired, poor child! Ah! if you had oui mountains to climb'—
he looked at his son Nicholas—'they would tire your little feet.
Do you remember the scramble we had up the Rhigi, Klaus?
And the lake—the deep blue lake—Ach es war herrlich! And
the clouds brushing across the silver Roth and Engelberger
hörner.' The old man rose, brushed up his hair on either side
of his ears; his blue eyes flashed, and he sat down again.

'Now this is against all rule,' said Madame Deschwanden;
'here we are back at that pottering little Switzerland, and
the mountains, and the lake, before dinner is over; we shall
have the glaciers next, and the chamois, and the cowbells,
and the gentians, and of course wind up with the Bruder
Klaus.'

'Relaxation,' said the soldier, rapping the table with his
knuckles, after consulting his watch. 'Meal-time up; relaxation begins.'

'Then you are going to have the lakes and the cowbells and
the Bruder Klaus!' said Madame Deschwanden.

'It is their time,' answered the corporal.

'Then Madeleine and I are off.'

'I will rap for prayers,' said the corporal.

CHAPTER XX.

MADELEINE and her mother retired to the window, and beckoned Gabrielle to join them.

The corporal and the colporteur lit their pipes, and Klaus with his knife began to cut a head out of a bit of box-wood he extracted from his pocket.

' So, Master Percenez, you have come to witness the great struggle?' said the soldier, fixing his blue eyes on the little man.

' Yes, corporal, I have. I am interested in it,—but who is not? It seems to me that we must fight now, or give in for ever.'

' A fight there will be,' said the soldier; ' a fight of tongues and hard words. Tongues for swords, hard words for bullets. Did you ever hear how we managed to gain our liberty in my country? I tell you that was not with speeches, but with blows. I doubt if your States-General will do much. I do not think much of talking, I like action.'

' And are you free in Switzerland?' asked Percenez.

' Yes,' answered Deschwanden, ' we are free. We gained

our liberty by our swords. Our brave land was subject to the despotic rule of the Duke of Austria, and we were reduced to much the same condition as you French are now. We paid taxes which were exorbitant, we were crushed by the privileged classes, and robbed of the just reward of our toil. Then Arnold of Melchthal, Werner Stauffacher, and Walter Fürst formed the resolution to resist, and lead the people to revolt, and so they threw off the yoke and became free.'

'Father,' said Nicholas, 'do you remember the inn of the Confederates on the lake, with their figures painted on the white wall, five times the size of life?'

'Ah so!' exclaimed the corporal; 'have I not drunk on the balcony of that same inn over against Grütli? Have I not seen the three fountains that bubbled up where the Confederates stood and joined hands and swore to liberate their country from the oppression of their Austrian governors, to be faithful to each other, and to be righteous in executing their judgments on the tyrants?'

The old man brushed up the hair on either side of his head, rose to his feet, filled his tumbler with wine, and waving it above his head, exclaimed joyously:

'Here is to the memory of Arnold of Melchthal, Werner Stauffacher, and Walter Fürst!'

Percenez and young Nicholas drank, standing.

' Did you ever hear,' continued the soldier, reseating himself, 'how William Tell refused to bow to the ducal cap set up on a pole, the badge of servitude, and how the governor—his name was Gessler—bade the valiant archer shoot an apple off his son's head?'

' I have heard the story,' said the colporteur.

' And I have seen the place,' cried Nicholas; ' have I not, father?'

' We have both seen the very spot where the glorious William stood, and where grew the tree against which the lad was placed. The square is no more. Houses have invaded it, so that now Tell could not send an arrow from his standing-point to the site of the tree. Ah! he was a great liberator of his country, was Tell. Fill your glasses, friends! To William Tell!' He rubbed up his hair, rose to his feet, and drained his glass again.

' Have you ever heard how nearly Swiss freedom was lost, by treachery and gold? You must know that the Confederate States had vanquished Charles of Burgundy in three great battles, and had pillaged his camp, which was so full of booty that gold circulated among the people like copper. The cantons of Uri, of Schwytz, and Unterwalden—that latter is mine—desired peace, and those of Lucerne, and Berne, and Zurich desired to extend the Confederacy; so great quarrels arose, and soon that union which was the source of their strength

promised to be dissolved, and civil war to break out, and
ruin Swiss independence.   The Confederates were assembled
for consultation, for the last time, at Stanz.   The animosity of
party, however, was so great, that after three sessions of angry
debates, the members rose with agitated countenances, and
separated without taking leave of one another, to meet again,
perhaps, only in the conflict of civil war.   That which neither
the power of Austria, nor the audacious might of Charles of
Burgundy, had ever been able to accomplish, my people were
themselves in danger of bringing about by these internal dis-
sensions; and the liberty and happiness of their country stood
in the most imminent peril.'

'My faith!' cried Madame Deschwanden, shrugging her
shoulders, and throwing into her face, as she sat in the
window, an expression of disgust and contempt, 'they are
getting upon the Bruder Klaus.'

'Yes, wife,' said the soldier, turning to her, and brushing up
his hair, 'glorious Bruder Klaus!   Here's to his——but no,
you shall hear the story first.   So! up the face of a precipice
in the Melchthal lived a hermit, Nicholas von der Flue.   And
here I may add that our captain is called by the same name.
Well, then, this hermit, whom we call Brother Nicholas, or, for
short, Brother Klaus, left his cell at the moment of danger,
and sending a messenger before him to bid the deputies
await his arrival, he walked all the way to Stanz without

resting, and entered the town-hall, where the assembly sat. He wore his simple dark-coloured dress, which descended to his feet; he carried his chaplet in one hand, and grasped his staff in the other; he was, as usual, barefoot and bareheaded; and his long hair, a little touched by the snows of age, fell upon his shoulders. When the delegates saw him enter, they rose out of respect, and God gave him such grace that his words restored unanimity, and in an hour all difficulties were smoothed away; the land was preserved from civil war, and from falling again,—as in that case it must have fallen,—under the power of Burgundy or Austria.'

' I have seen the very coat Bruder Klaus wore,' said Nicholas, his large blue eyes full of pride and joy.

' Yes,' said the soldier, triumphantly; 'we have both seen his habit; we have seen his body, too, at Sachseln. Fill your glasses!' he rubbed up his hair, first over his ears and then above his forehead and at the back of the head, and starting to his feet, pledged Bruder Klaus of pious memory. Percenez and Nicholas joined enthusiastically.

' See!' said the latter, taking his black ribbon from his neck, and extending the medal to Percenez; 'on that coin is a representation of the blessed hermit; that piece has been laid on his shrine, and has been blessed by the priest of Sachseln.'

' Fetch him the statue of the glorious brother!' cried the

corporal to his son; 'let him see what blessed Nicholas really was like.'

The lad instantly dived out of the room, down a passage, and presently reappeared with a wooden figure of the hermit, carved by himself. The face was exquisitely wrought, and the hands delicately finished. The whole was painted, but not coarsely.

' He was very pale in the face, almost deadly white, and dark about the eyes,' said the soldier. ' We have his portrait, taken during his life, in the town-hall of Sarnen——' all at once the corporal's eyes rested on his watch.

'Herr Je !' he exclaimed; ' we have exceeded our time by three minutes.' He rapped with his knuckles on the table, and shouted the order :

' Music !'

Instantly his son Nicholas produced a flute, and warbled on it a well-known Swiss air. The corporal folded his hands on his breast, threw back his head, fixed his eyes on the scrap of blue sky visible above the roofs of the houses opposite, and began to sing, ' Herz, mein Herz warum so traurig '—of which we venture to give an English rendering :

> ' Heart, my heart ! why art thou weary,
>   Why to grief and tears a prey ?
> Foreign lands are bright and cheery ;
>   Heart, my heart, what ails thee, say ?

'That which ails me past appeasing !
  I am lost, a stranger here ;
What though foreign lands be pleasing,
  Home, sweet home, alone is dear.

'Were I now to home returning,
  Oh, how swiftly would I fly !
Home to father, home to mother,
  Home to native rocks and sky !

'Through the fragrant pine-boughs bending
  I should see the glacier shine,
See the nimble goats ascending
  Gentian-dappled slopes in line ;

'See the cattle, hear the tinkle
  Of the merry clashing bells,
See white sheep the pastures sprinkle
  In the verdant dewy dells.

'I should climb the rugged gorges
  To the azure Alpine lake,
Where the snowy peak discharges
  Torrents, that the silence break.

'I should see the old brown houses,
  At the doors, in every place,
Neighbours sitting, children playing,
  Greetings in each honest face.

'Oh my youth! to thee returning,
    Oft I ask, why did I roam?
Oh my heart! my heart is burning
    At the memory of Home.

'Heart, my heart! in weary sadness
    Breaking, far from fatherland,
Restless, yearning, void of gladness,
    Till once more at home I stand.'

As the old man sang, the tears filled his large eyes, and slowly
trickled down his weather-beaten cheeks. He sat for some
while in silence and motionless, absorbed in memory. Now
and then a smile played over his rugged features.

'I remember walking from Beckenreid to Seelisberg one
spring evening,' he said, speaking to himself; 'the rocks were
covered with wild pinks. We never see wild pinks here. And
the thyme was fragrant, multitudes of bees swarmed humming
about it. I remember, because, when tired, I sat on the
thyme, and listened to their buzz. Down below lay the deep
blue-green lake reflecting the mountains, still as glass. The
bell of Gersau was chiming. The red roofs were so pretty
under the brown rocks of the Scheideck and Hochflue. A
little farther on, upon a mass of fallen rock in the water, in
the midst of a feathery tuft of birch, stood the chapel of
Kindlismord.' He paused and smiled, and then a great tear
dropped from his cheek to his breast. 'I saw a foaming

torrent rush through the forest and dart over a ledge and disappear. The golden clouds overhead were reflected in the lake. I picked a bunch of blue salvias and a tiger-lily.' He drew a heavy sigh, brushed his hair down with his hands, shook his head, looked at his watch, and rapped the table with the order :

' Prayers ! '

Immediately all rose, and the old soldier led the way down the passage into Klaus's workshop.

Klaus, as has already been said, carved statues for churches. His room was full of figures, some finished and coloured, others half done ; some only sketched out of the block. On a shelf stood a row of little saints ; but the majority were from three to five feet high. In the corner was a huge S. Christopher, carrying the infant Saviour on his shoulder, and leaning on a rugged staff. His work-table was strewn with tools and shavings and chips of wood, and the floor was encumbered with blocks of oak and box, wood shavings and sawdust. In a niche in the side of the room, on a pedestal, stood a life-sized figure of the Swiss hermit, the patron saint of the Deschwandens, with a pendent lamp before it. A crucifix of ebony and boxwood stood before the little window which lighted the room, and was situated immediately above his work-table. The corporal knelt down, followed by his family and the guests, and recited the usual evening prayers in a firm voice, ending with the Litany of the Saints.

After the last response, the corporal made a pause, and rapped with his knuckles against the bench in front of him, whereupon Madame Deschwanden rose with a sniff and a great rustle of her garments, and sailed out of the room, leaning on Madeleine.

'You had better come, too,' she said to Percenez and Gabrielle; 'that father and son there have not done yet. They have their blessed Swiss saints to invoke in their barbarous jargon. But, as I do not approve either of their tongue or of their Klauses and Meinrads, Madeleine and I always leave them to themselves.'

The colporteur and his little ward rose, but not without hesitation, for the corporal and his son remained kneeling as stiff as any of the wooden figures surrounding them, with hands joined and eyes directed immediately in front of them.

'Oh my faith!' exclaimed Madame Deschwanden, as she reached the sitting-room; 'to think that I have been reduced to this,—to become the spouse of a clockwork-man made of wood. Heavens! Étienne, the corporal does everything to the minute; dresses, washes, eats, prays, dreams of his precious Schweizerland, all by the watch, and I—poor I—I am in despair. This does not suit me at all.'

Percenez attempted to console his sister, and she rattled on with her story of grievance, whilst Gabrielle, musing and not speaking, heard the solemn voice of the old soldier sounding from the workshop:

'Heiliger Meinrad!'

And Nicholas's response: ' Bitte für uns [1].'

'Heiliger Gallus!'

' Bitte für uns.'

' Heiliger Beatus !'

' Bitte für uns.'

' Heiliger Moritz und deine Gefährte!'

' Bittet für uns.'

' Heiliger Bonifacius !'

' Bitte für uns.'

' Heilige Verena!'

' Bitte für uns.'

' Heiliger Bruder Klaus !'

' Bitte für uns.'

Shortly after, the corporal and his son returned to the room. Gabrielle was sitting by herself in the dusk near the door— in fact, in that corner of the sofa into which Madame Deschwanden had driven Nicholas, when she wanted the paper with roses and jessamine and Brazilian humming-birds.

The young man walked towards her somewhat awkwardly,

---

[1] Holy Meinrad, &c. Pray for us.

and leaning on the arm of the sofa with his back to the window, said :

'You must be puzzled at our relationship in this house.'

'I do not quite understand the relationship, I own,' answered Gabrielle, shyly.

'I am not the son of madame,' said he, nodding his head in the direction of Percenez's sister, 'nor is Madeleine my own sister. My father married again, after my mother's death, and Madame Chabry was a widow with an only daughter. Do you understand now?'

'Yes, thank you.'

'I should like to hear your opinion about the box,' he continued. 'Do you think we have any right to keep it? Mamma is set upon it, so is Madeleine, but the question is, have they any right to it?'

Gabrielle looked at her shawl, and plucked at the fringe.

'You do not like to answer,' said Klaus.

'I think the box ought to be returned,' she-said, timidly, and in a low, faltering voice.

A smile beamed on the lad's broad face. He nodded at her in a friendly, approving manner, and said, 'So my father says. I consulted him in the other room. And now the difficulty is to get the box away. Observe my father.'

Gabrielle looked towards the corporal; he was standing near the window, with his back to the table on which the mother-

of-pearl coffer lay, and was engaged in animated conversation
with Percenez, Madame, and Madeleine. Gabrielle observed
that the old soldier made a point of addressing his wife and
daughter-in-law in turn, and then directing an observation to
Percenez. From sentences she caught, the girl ascertained
that the corporal was attacking the French character, and was
especially caustic on the subject of French women. His wife
was at once in a blaze, and Madeleine caught fire. Percenez
took up cudgels on behalf of his countrywomen, but the
soldier was not to be beaten by the three combined. As soon
as the conversation or argument gave symptoms of flagging,
he produced from his armoury some peculiarly pungent remark,
which he cast as a bomb-shell among them, and which at once
aroused a clatter of tongues.

'There's a story told in my country of a man who married
a Frenchwoman,' said the soldier, fixing his wife with his eye.

'I will not listen to your stories,' said Madame Deschwanden; 'they are bad, wicked tales. Stop your ears,
Percenez, as I stop mine. Madeleine, don't listen to him.
A Frenchman uses his tongue like a feather, but a German
or Swiss knocks you down with it like a club.'

'There is a story in my country,' pursued the corporal,
turning composedly towards the colporteur, 'of a Swiss farmer
who married a French mademoiselle.'

'Ah! I pity her, poor thing, I do,' said Madame Desch-

wanden, suddenly removing her hand from her ear and fluttering it in her husband's face; 'she doubtless thought him
flesh and blood, and only too late found him out to be a
Jacquemart—a wooden doll worked by springs.'

'So!' continued the soldier, calmly, 'the man died——'

'Of dry rot,' interpolated madame; 'there was a maggot
in his head.'

'He died,' the soldier pursued; 'and then, having left the
earth, he presented himself at the gates of Paradise.'

'Ah!' exclaimed madame; 'and he found that it was
peopled with Bruder Klauses—like the wooden saints your
boy carves.'

'Now you know, Percenez, my good friend, that there is a
preliminary stage souls have to pass through before they can
enter the realm of the blessed; that stage is called purgatory.
So! S. Peter opened the door to the Swiss Bauer and said,
"You cannot come in. You have not been in purgatory!"
"No," answered the farmer, "but I have spent ten years
married to a French wife." "Then step in," said the door-
keeper, "you have endured purgatory in life."'

'I will not listen to you,' screamed Madame Deschwanden,
resolutely facing the window and presenting her back to her
husband.

Madeleine followed suit, and was immediately engrossed in
what was taking place in the street.

'You Frenchwomen!' called the corporal, tauntingly, as he stepped backwards with his hands behind him. The mother and daughter turned abruptly, and facing him exclaimed together, 'We glory in the title;' then reverted to their contemplation of the street.

'Now,' said Nicholas, in a low voice, 'observe my father attentively; he is a skilful general.'

Corporal Deschwanden retreated leisurely backwards, as though retiring from the presence of royalty, till he reached the table, when his hands felt for the casket, and took it up; then, still fronting the window and the women at it, he sidled towards the door, keeping the mother-of-pearl box carefully out of sight.

Having reached the door, he asked Percenez if he would accompany him for a stroll. The colporteur gladly consented, and followed him out of the room.

The mother and daughter still maintained their position at the open window, till suddenly the former threw up her hands with a cry of dismay, sprang abruptly into the middle of the room, and shrieked out, 'I am betrayed! the thief! the rogue! the malicious one! He has carried off the mother-of-pearl box. I saw it under his arm. He showed it to Étienne, and laughed as he crossed the street. Madeleine! what shall we do? We will take poison, and die in one another's arms!' Then, after a volley of shrieks, she fell on her daughter's neck and deluged her with tears.

U

'I think that was a skilfully-executed manœuvre of my father's,' said Nicholas, aside.

Gabrielle smiled; but then, observing how distressed was her hostess, she said, in a low voice, 'I am afraid your mother is heart-broken over her loss.'

'Yes, for half an hour, and then she will have forgotten all about it. You will see, when my father returns, it will be with a locket, or a brooch, or a ribbon, and then she will be all "ecstasy and raptures," and will kiss him on both cheeks, and pronounce him the best of husbands.'

Gabrielle looked up into his face with an expression of delight in her eyes and on her lips.

The young man's eyes rested on her countenance with pleasure. After a moment's hesitation, he said:

'Mademoiselle Gabrielle, may I ask you one little favour? I know I have not deserved it by anything I have done, but you will confer a debt of gratitude on my father and on me if you will accede to my request.'

'What is it?' asked the girl, opening her eyes very wide, and wondering very greatly what he meant.

'Will you promise me not to take part with my mother and Madeleine against the Swiss? My father laughs, and I laugh, but what they say cuts us,—sometimes deeply. We are proud of our country;' he brushed his hair from his brow and straightened himself, his attitude and action a reproduction of his father. 'We have reason to be proud of it, and we do not like to be joked about it, and to hear slurs cast on it. Oh! Mademoiselle Gabrielle, I do not know why I ask this of you, but I should feel it dreadfully if you joined them against us, and so, too, would my father.'

'I promise with all my heart.'

'That is delightful!' exclaimed Nicholas, clapping his hands, whilst a joyous flush overspread his open countenance; 'and then, there is something more.' His face grew solemn at once. 'Do not speak against, or make a joke about, Bruder Klaus. You do not know what a man that was, what a saint he is, what he did for his country, what a miraculous life he led, what wonders are wrought yet at his tomb. You should have seen his portrait—the grave white face, and the eyes reddened with weeping, and the sunken cheeks! Oh, Mademoiselle Gabrielle, you may be sure that, among the greatest of saints, our Bruder Klaus——'

'What!' exclaimed Madame Deschwanden, looking up from her daughter's shoulder, as she caught the word; 'if that boy is not dinning Bruder Klaus into Mademoiselle André's ear already. Was ever a woman so overwhelmed, so haunted as I am with these ragged old Swiss hermits? I have the nightmare, and dream that Bruder Klaus is dancing on my breast. I look out of the window in the dark, and see Bruder Klaus jabbering in the gloom, and pointing at me with his stick. I wish to goodness the precious Bruder had committed a mortal sin, and his sanctity had gone to the dogs, I do !'

Nicholas drew nearer to Gabrielle, as though shrinking from his stepmother's expressions as impious, and willing to screen the girl from their pernicious influence. He stooped towards her, with his great blue eyes fastened on her with intensity of earnestness, as he whispered :

'You will promise me that ? Oh I please do, dear mademoiselle !'

'Certainly I will,' answered Gabrielle, frankly looking at him.

He caught her hand and kissed it, and then precipitately left the room.

END OF VOL. I.

www.ingramcontent.com/pod-product-compliance
Lightning Source LLC
Chambersburg PA
CBHW020810060726
47498CB00017B/1426